A Lord Apart

Jane Ashford

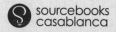
sourcebooks
casablanca

Published by Sourcebooks Casablanca, an imprint of Sourcebooks, Inc.
P.O. Box 4410, Naperville, Illinois 60567-4410
(630) 961-3900
Fax: (630) 961-2168
sourcebooks.com

Printed and bound in Canada.
MBP 10 9 8 7 6 5 4 3 2 1

Prologue

A STEEPLE CLOCK CHIMED AS DANIEL FRITH, VISCOUNT Whitfield, walked into St. James's Square in the heart of fashionable London. He was early, as he often tended to be, and that would not do for the odd dinner engagement that lay before him. So despite the filthy March weather, he slowed his brisk stride and took a turn about the square. Tendrils of icy fog beaded on his greatcoat and tried to work their way down his neck. He pulled his scarf up and his hat brim down. It was an unpleasant time to be in town, but he had business here.

The long list of tasks that thronged his mind these days came rushing back like a swarm of stinging insects. He'd been back and forth to the metropolis from his home in Derbyshire several times in recent months, as the responsibilities of his estates had descended upon him in a most unexpected way. With a thousand things to do, he'd been tempted to refuse this mysterious invitation. But the Earl of Macklin was a greatly respected figure. Not a friend or even, strictly speaking, an acquaintance, but a power in society and an age-mate of Daniel's father. Daniel's mind shied away from that subject as a sudden clatter of hooves brought his head around.

A high-perch phaeton careened into the square from the direction of Pall Mall, going far too fast for London streets, particularly in the growing dusk with the cobbles damp and slippery. One tall wheel came off the ground as the vehicle barely made the turn. The driver's exultant shout led Daniel to believe that the young sprig was drunk. When his companion laughed uproariously, Daniel concluded that he was, too.

The driver plied his whip, urging his team to an even more ridiculous speed. At the same time, his passenger pointed at Daniel and laughed again. The phaeton veered and raced toward him. For an incredulous moment, Daniel thought they meant to hit him. He leapt back as the equipage loomed, swerved, and swept through a large puddle at his feet. Daniel only just managed to throw up an arm in time to save his face from the sheet of icy water raised by the wheel. Like a frigid slap from a giant hand, it sluiced over the sleeve and shoulder of his greatcoat, splashed his torso, and ran down to drip from the hem. His immaculate top boots were spattered with mud.

Daniel's shouted curse was lost in the thunder of hooves. Drunken laughter floated back to him as the phaeton barely made it onto King Street and clattered out of the square.

Daniel shook his fist, in its sodden glove, as the sound faded. He hadn't seen their faces clearly enough to call them to account when he saw them again—sapskulls who ordered many-caped driving coats from their tailors and then fancied themselves absolute nonpareils. Idiots! Jug-bitten, bird-witted croakers.

Cold water soaked through his coat sleeve, and he shivered. He was flecked with mud from shoulder to toe, in no state to meet the illustrious earl. Daniel pulled out his handkerchief and tried to wipe his boots clean. There was nothing to be done about the spatter on his greatcoat. Rubbing at it would only smear the stains. He'd just have to shed the garment as soon as he reached the club. Which he could not delay any longer; he was dashed cold. Stuffing his soiled handkerchief into a pocket, he started walking.

Stepping into the warm brightness of White's was like entering a different world. The rich wood paneling and golden candlelight of the gentlemen's retreat replaced the icy fog. There was a buzz of conversation and a clink of glasses from both sides of the entryway. Savory smells rode the air, promising a first-rate meal. That was something to look forward to, Daniel thought, whatever else this occasion might bring.

Surrendering his wet coat, hat, and gloves to a servitor, and ignoring the fellow's raised brows at the state of them, Daniel followed a waiter to a private corner of the dining room, where he found Arthur Shelton, Earl of Macklin, awaiting him. Though the man was at least twenty years Daniel's senior, he hardly looked it. His dark hair showed no gray. His figure—inches taller than Daniel's medium height—remained muscular and upright. Daniel knew that his own snubbed-nosed face, dun-brown hair, and dark eyes might be judged commonplace beside his host's square-jawed, broad-browed visage, but a gallery full of family portraits back home assured Daniel that he more closely resembled the hardened warriors who'd followed William the Conqueror across the Channel. He offered his host a polite bow.

Lord Macklin's face showed few lines, and those seemed scored by good humor. "I'm delighted to welcome the first of my guests," the older man said.

Daniel was glad to learn that there was to be a party. He wished he wasn't the first to arrive. Did he dare ask what the deuce was going on?

"And here are another two approaching, I believe."

Wasn't Macklin certain? Didn't he know them either? Daniel turned to see who it might be. The newcomers appeared closer to his own age than his host's near half-century.

"Daniel Frith, Viscount Whitfield, may I present Roger Berwick, Marquess of Chatton," said the earl, nodding to the first man.

Chatton was thin, with reddish hair and choleric blue eyes. His greeting was clipped, and he looked even more puzzled than Daniel as to why he was here.

"And Peter Rathbone, Duke of Compton," said their host.

He didn't look much more than twenty, Daniel thought, and seemed a chancy sprig. Compton had black hair, hazel eyes, and long fingers that tapped uneasily on his flanks.

"And here is the last of us," said the earl after further mystified greetings had been exchanged. "Gentlemen, this is my nephew, Benjamin Romilly, Earl of Furness, the last of our group."

The new arrival resembled his uncle in coloring and frame. Anyone, seeing them, would have known them for relations. This earl looked glum rather than hospitable, however. Indeed, Daniel had rarely seen a glummer face. Furness looked as if he'd eaten something sour and was on the lookout for a place to spit it out.

"And now that the proprieties are satisfied, I hope we can be much less formal," their host added.

They stood gazing at each other. An ill-assorted group, Daniel thought. Chatton, with his red hair, looked like a dyspeptic fox, Compton a greyhound having an attack of nerves. Furness and his uncle were rather leonine, the skulking prowler and the benevolent king of the beasts. How did they see him? Daniel rather fancied himself as a badger—stocky and elusive and deceptively fierce. The idea amused him enough to divert his thoughts from his wet coat sleeve. Had it begun to steam a bit in the warmth of the club? Probably his imagination.

"Sit down," said their host, gesturing at the waiting table. As they obeyed, he signaled for wine to be poured. "They have a fine roast beef this evening. As when do they not at White's? We'll begin with soup though, on a raw night like this." The waiter returned his nod and went off to fetch it.

The hot broth was savory and warming. Daniel enjoyed it. The wine could be nothing but good, at White's. But Daniel was hard-pressed to make conversation when all he wanted to know was why they were here and how long this strange dinner was expected to last. "Vile weather," he said finally.

The rest of them agreed that it was a filthy night.

Compton praised the claret, and then looked uneasy, as if he'd been presumptuous, which was rather odd behavior for a duke. The rest merely nodded. After a bit, the ruddy marquess scowled, leaned forward, and opened his mouth. Daniel braced for an irritable remark, but the man grabbed his glass and downed more wine instead. All their glasses were being emptied and refilled more rapidly than usual.

Steaming plates were put before them, a relief in more ways than one. Eating reduced the necessity of talking, for one, and secondly, Daniel was dashed hungry by this time. His muscular frame required a good deal of stoking, and he liked to do it with fine food when he could. The beef was tender and perfectly cooked, with a piquant seasoning that added to its appeal. The roast potatoes had just the right combination of crunch and savor. Clearly, the kitchen had used goose fat in their preparation, as was proper. There was a pungent horseradish sauce that made his eyes water and a variety of tempting side dishes. He fell to with gusto. Compton might pick at it, and Furness mope, but Daniel knew how to enjoy a well-prepared meal.

He'd nearly finished when Macklin spoke again. "No doubt you're wondering why I've invited you—the four of you—this evening. When we aren't really acquainted."

Here it came at last then, the explanation. Daniel joined the others in turning to their host. Faces showed varying degrees of curiosity and relief. Was the earl going to ask them to contribute to some sort of charitable enterprise? Daniel wondered suddenly. Macklin had the look of a reformer. Having eaten the man's dinner, he supposed he'd have to cough up a reasonable sum.

"You have something in common," Macklin went on. "*We* do." He looked around the table. "Death."

Had the man actually said *death*? Daniel checked his companions and saw astonishment and impatience on their faces. Surely this was among the oddest social engagements he'd ever had.

The older man nodded across the table. "My nephew's wife died in childbirth several years ago. He mourns her still."

Furness looked more furious than grief-stricken as the table's attention shifted to him. He was clearly startled, and outraged, at having this information shared with strangers.

The earl turned to Daniel. "Whitfield's parents were killed in a shipwreck eight months ago on their way back from India," he continued.

Given the way things had been going, Daniel wasn't completely surprised by this unauthorized sharing of his private affairs. He called on the stoicism that had sustained him through this period and replied, "Quite so. A dreadful accident. Storm drove them onto a reef. All hands lost." He looked around the table and shrugged. "What can one do? These things happen." He met curious glances and deflected them. He didn't intend to discuss the sudden upending of his life with these strangers. Why would he? There was no point. Railing against fate changed nothing.

"Chatton lost his wife to a virulent fever a year ago," Lord Macklin said.

"I didn't *lose* her," the gentleman exclaimed, his

thin face reddening further. "She was dashed well *killed* by an incompetent physician and my neighbor who insisted they ride out into a downpour." He looked like a man who'd suffered an intolerable insult rather than a bereavement.

Daniel considered a hasty exit. He could legitimately plead a press of business and lack of time. It would be rude, but he could live it down. He braced to rise. The earl's blue-gray gaze shifted, caught him, and somehow kept him in his chair.

"And Compton's sister died while she was visiting a friend, just six months ago," their host finished.

The youngest man at the table flinched. "She was barely seventeen," he murmured. "My ward as well as my sister." He put his head in his hands. "I ought to have gone with her. I was invited. If only I'd gone. I wouldn't have allowed her to take that cliff path. I would have...done something."

"I've been widowed for ten years," interrupted Macklin gently. "I know what it's like to lose a beloved person quite suddenly. And I know there must be a period of adjustment afterward. People don't talk about the time it takes—different for everyone I imagine—and how one copes." He looked around the table. "I was aware of Benjamin's bereavement, naturally, since he is my nephew."

Furness gritted his teeth. Daniel thought he was going to jump up and stalk out, as he'd longed to do himself. But the earl spoke again before either of them could move.

"Then, seemingly at random, I heard of your cases, and it occurred to me that I might be able to help."

"What help is there for death?" said the marquess. "And which of us asked for your aid? *I* certainly didn't." He glared around the table as if searching for someone to blame.

Time to wrap this up and get on, Daniel thought. Pushing a little back from the table, he said, "Waste of time to dwell on such stuff. No point, eh?"

Compton sighed like a melancholy bellows.

"Grief is insidious, almost palpable, and as variable as humankind," said their host. "No one can understand who hasn't experienced a sudden loss. A black coat and a few platitudes are nothing."

"Are you accusing us of insincerity, sir?" demanded Chatton. His fists were clenched on either side of his plate, and his face was bright red. Choleric hardly covered it.

"Not at all," answered the earl. "I'm offering you the fruits of experience and years of contemplation."

"Thrusting them on us, whether we will or no," the other replied. "Tantamount to an ambush, this so-called dinner."

While true, this seemed unhelpful. Daniel disliked brangling, particularly at the dinner table. The thing was to get over rough ground as quickly and smoothly as possible, and escape. "Nothing wrong with the food," he said, ignoring the marquess's scowl. "Best claret I've had this year." He had only to offer thanks and depart, but their host spoke before he could.

"Well, well," said Macklin, clearly not affected by their responses. "Who knows? If I've made a mistake, I'll gladly apologize. Indeed, I beg your pardon for springing my idea on you with no preparation. Will you, nonetheless, allow me to tell the story of my grieving, as I had hoped to do?"

Such was the power of his personality that none of them refused. Even Chatton merely glared at his half-eaten meal. Lord Macklin ought to be running the government instead of arranging dinners for strangers, Daniel thought. He'd roll right over opposition.

"And afterward, should you wish to do the same, I'll gladly hear it," added the earl. He smiled—sage, reliable, a picture of paternal benevolence.

Inexplicably, a scene from years ago flashed through Daniel's memory. He stood, with his nanny and some other servants, watching a carriage drive away from his home in Derbyshire. He waved, but no hand showed at the vehicle's windows to return the gesture. The carriage merely grew smaller and smaller in his sight until finally it disappeared around a bend in the road. He hadn't realized he was crying until he was scolded for *unmanly* weakness.

A pang of regret shook Daniel. He shoved the memory aside. There was no reason to be thinking of this now. Lord Macklin didn't resemble either of his parents in the least. The oak paneling might be similar, but White's had nothing to do with his home. And wallowing accomplished precisely nothing. He dragged his attention back to Lord Macklin's words.

The earl said his piece, which Daniel found quite touching. And then the others spoke, briefly, with varying degrees of enthusiasm and candor. Compton came very near tears, while Furness was tight-lipped and laconic. The talk was surprisingly engrossing. Of course, when they were done, and the goodbyes had been said, none of it made the least difference. The important thing was to get on with life, Daniel thought as he headed back to his hotel. And he had a hundred things to do.

One

DANIEL SET HIS JAW AS HE SURVEYED THE PILES OF documents and ledgers before him and wondered if he'd ever see the bare surface of the desk again. The estate office in his ancestral home was a study in chaos. It seemed to him that records and correspondence had been flung through the door like stones skipped across water and left to molder where they landed. As with everything else, Papa and Mama had been more interested in visiting far-flung lands than in anything occurring in their own. And so the piles of paper on this desk had grown higher, the disorder had increased, and next to nothing had been done.

His father hadn't bothered to inform him that their estate agent had left some time ago. Whether the fellow had gone out of incompetence or frustration, Daniel didn't know. How could he? If he'd been told that Briggs was gone, he would have found a new agent, at least. Wouldn't he? But that was the point, wasn't it? His parents hadn't cared to tell him anything. He'd long ago stopped expecting them to. And so, when the weight of responsibility suddenly descended upon him with their deaths, it was compounded by this wretched mare's nest. There was so much information to absorb, so many decisions to make, while the information needed to do so could never be found.

Daniel gazed longingly at the green landscape spreading outside the windows. Of course he preferred riding and shooting and fishing and lively society to tenancy reports and dry columns of numbers. Didn't everyone?

Brushing aside the suspicion that he wasn't entirely blameless for his predicament, Daniel picked up another thick document. Regrets and resentments were a waste of time. Things were as they were. He should be working. He began to read.

A familiar irritation rose when he was scarcely three sentences in. Lawyers didn't want you to understand what they wrote, he'd concluded some time ago. They'd created their own twisty, impenetrable language expressly to confuse, so that you had to hire more lawyers to tell you what the devil the first ones had meant. He imagined gangs of them tittering in their fusty chambers, vying with each other to devise yet more obscure phrasing for some obvious point. *Tontine*, they'd cackle. *Partition of messuages lands.* Let's see what they make of *that*!

Well, they weren't going to defeat him; he was going to puzzle out this deed of conveyance without help or additional fees. But as he tried to push on, his brain jumped to the many other tasks awaiting his attention. Lists upon lists. The sheer volume made it difficult to focus on any one job. Particularly when the jobs were as dull as ditchwater and nearly as stagnant.

What the deuce was mortmain? Sounded like some sort of fungus. When he was interrupted a few minutes later by a brisk knock on the office door, Daniel felt only relief. "Yes?"

His stately butler came through. "You wanted to be told when anyone headed for Rose Cottage, my lord. A carriage has been observed approaching the place."

"Indeed." Daniel dropped the document back on its pile and rose. "Thank you, Grant."

Twenty minutes later, Daniel was riding down the avenue of trees at the front of his home and out into the countryside toward a dwelling at the far edge of his lands, once part of them but now separate under his father's will. Finally, a mystery that had been nagging at him for months would be solved.

❧

Dust kicked up by the horses' hooves drifted through the open window of the post chaise, and Penelope Pendleton felt the ominous tickle at the back of her throat that heralded a fit of coughing. She swallowed repeatedly to fight it off, but the cough would not be quelled. The spasms seized her, shaking her shoulders and vibrating through her chest, making her eyes water and her throat ache. There was nothing to do but hang on and ride it out.

Her younger companion shrank away from the paroxysm. "I'm feard you have the consumption, miss. What'll I do if you go and die?"

"Won't," croaked Penelope. She took a swallow of well water from a flask she'd taken care to bring. And then another. A cough tried to rise. She pushed it back. "It's nothing of the kind," she rasped when she could speak again. "This is just a lingering cold, Kitty. That's all." Which was undoubtedly true. She was certain. The smoky mills of Manchester had prolonged the irritation of her lungs. No more. And the coughing was over now, for a while at least. "I'll soon be well here in the country. See how pretty it is."

The Derbyshire countryside rolled away from them, lush and green under the June sun—hills crowned by clumps of trees, neat fields bounded by stone walls.

Her sixteen-year-old maid eyed it uneasily. "Are there bears?"

"Not for hundreds of years, Kitty."

"So there *used to be* bears?"

"Yes, I think so, but—"

"So some might be left, hiding in the woods. Or in a dark cave maybe. Just waiting to jump out and rip your insides." The girl clawed at the air with her hand.

"No." Penelope made her voice authoritative. "They were all hunted down long ago."

"Wolves? With red eyes and teeth as long as your thumb?"

Penelope shook her head. "No wolves." Small, skinny, and addicted to drama, Kitty was a challenging personal attendant. The girl had never been out of Manchester before, and she had a dim view of vegetation. She saw every forest tree as poised to fall and "crush the life out of you." In her mind, undergrowth teemed with monstrous *things* eager to sting and bite and tear. The lack of nearby shops was almost incomprehensible to her. Yet she'd wanted to come along in Penelope's employ. Kitty had an odd sense of adventure that seemed to savor the idea of impending disaster. Her enthusiasm counted for a good deal as Penelope salvaged what she could from the wreck of her family fortunes.

The carriage bounced in a rut. Penelope gripped a strap and held on. The journey from Manchester to Ashbourne, over fifty miles of bad roads, had been exhausting. She couldn't imagine what it would have been like without the indulgence of a post chaise. But all would be well when they reached Rose Cottage, the mysterious miracle that had descended upon her when she'd nearly lost hope. It simply had to be.

They had to stop twice for directions, but at last the chaise slowed, turned, and pulled up before their destination. Penelope pushed open the door and jumped down, her soul awash with gratitude and relief.

Rose Cottage might have been anything. On bad days she'd envisioned a broken-down hovel with gaping windows and rotting thatch surrounded by fever-ridden swamps. But in fact it was a real house, built of mellow stone with a slate roof. The central door promised decent rooms on either side, and a second story showed three windows. There were chimneys at either end. Carved stone lintels suggested age, but the structure looked sound. Yes, it was small compared to what she was—*had been*—used to. But that mattered not a whit these days. The source of the name was obvious. Climbing roses had gone wild in the neglected garden, engulfing one end of the building and filling the air with scent.

Penelope took the key she'd received from the solicitor out of her reticule and hurried up three steps to unlock the door. It opened on a small entry with stairs at the back and bare, dusty rooms on either side. No furniture graced the wooden floorboards. No draperies softened the windows. But Penelope had two wagons coming behind her, carrying all her worldly goods under the care of a crusty old manservant who had tended to her father and then her brother. She would soon have a bed and other necessities. Penelope smiled. Foyle would spit when he saw this place.

"Smells like old people," said Kitty, coming in on Penelope's heels.

There was also a dead sparrow in the fireplace on the left. But Rose Cottage was an actual house, and it really belonged to her. Penelope had the deeds in her trunk—miraculous evidence, in black and white, of her ownership. Though it was nothing like the spacious mansion where she'd grown up, the little stone building felt like sanctuary. "We will open the windows," replied Penelope. "And scrub it clean."

Kitty groaned theatrically.

Exploring further, Penelope discovered an extension on the back of the house, like the stem of a T, holding the kitchen. A door at one side led out to a small cobbled yard and privy. A neat little barn stood some yards away. Like the house, it seemed in good repair.

She returned to find the postilions setting down one of their trunks by the front door. "Upstairs, please," said Penelope. Looking grumpy but unsurprised, the two men hauled the luggage up the narrow stairs.

"That one goes back here," she said when they brought in the large hamper of food she'd packed. "In the kitchen."

When they'd set it down, she walked with them back to the chaise and paid them off. Five minutes later, the equipage was rattling away.

"You're letting them go?" said Kitty from the doorway. "Leaving us here all alone to starve?"

Penelope laughed. She couldn't help it. A wild freedom she hadn't felt in ages bubbled through her. "You saw me pack the hamper. I brought plenty to eat. And should Foyle be delayed for some reason, I believe I saw the remains of a kitchen garden beside the barn."

"What's a kitchen garden?" asked Kitty.

"A place where you grow vegetables. Perhaps herbs, too. We can see what we find."

"I won't eat stuff that comes out of the dirt!"

"But that's where vegetables come from, Kitty."

The girl shook her head. "They come from the greengrocer."

"Who gets them from farmers, who grow them in the dirt. We'll wash everything off." Reminded of something, Penelope went back to the kitchen and tried the hand pump beside the stone sink. A bit of pumping produced a stream of water, rusty at first and then clear and clean. She sniffed and then tasted it. "Good," she said. "We won't have to carry water." She removed her bonnet and shawl and set them on top of the food hamper on the floor.

Kitty gazed around the empty room. "Nothing to carry it in," she pointed out.

"Foyle will be here soon with my things. Perhaps by tomorrow. Let's make a fire. I saw some wood stacked by the barn." The day was warm, but there was something homey and reassuring about a fire.

"I'll get it, miss."

"I can help," Penelope said. She was going to have to learn a great many household skills that she'd never been taught. Carrying wood must be among the simplest.

Kitty held up a hand, palm outward. "It's for me to do, miss." Her features had taken on a stubborn cast. Penelope let her go. There would have to be a good many adjustments, some of which would offend Kitty's intermittent sense of correctness. But not today.

The thud of hooves sounded from the front of the house. Though it couldn't be Foyle yet, Penelope hurried out in hope.

She found a man dismounting a fine blood horse on her doorstep. Stocky, brown-haired, with blunt features and a square jaw, he wasn't classically handsome. But somehow he didn't need to be. He held one's attention by the sheer force of his presence. His expression suggested that he was accustomed to deference and obedience. Penelope took a step back. The last year had made her wary of such men.

The visitor looked her up and down. Was that disapproval? It couldn't be hostility. Unless he'd somehow received word… No. Not yet. Impossible. Penelope wondered if she'd rubbed dust on her face. Her gown was crushed and wrinkled from hours in the post chaise, but it had once been expensive.

"I'm Whitfield," he said.

The name was unfamiliar. Penelope relaxed a little. He must be a neighbor. She would have preferred not to receive anyone until she was settled, but good relations with the community were important. "Hello, Mr. Whitfield. I am—"

"Not mister."

"I beg your pardon?"

"Rose Cottage was part of my estate until my father willed it to you," he went on. "I'd like to know why."

"Your father?" Penelope forgot all else as she latched on to this piece of information. The solicitor who'd tracked her down and told her about the legacy had refused to give her benefactor's name. The bequest was anonymous, he'd insisted. If she wanted the cottage, she wouldn't ask. And really, wasn't gratitude rather more appropriate than questions? He'd been even more arrogant than this man. "Your father," she repeated. "Not Mr. Whitfield."

"My father, John Frith, Viscount Whitfield," he replied impatiently.

He was a viscount, and he was glaring at her.

Kitty appeared in the doorway. "There's spiders in the woodpile, miss," she said. "Big ones." She spread her hands four inches apart as she gazed at their visitor with open curiosity.

The tickle of a cough began in the back of Penelope's throat. Not now, not now, she thought, swallowing frantically. But she couldn't stop it. The spasm came. The hacking shook her.

Their visitor looked startled, then concerned. "For God's sake, get her some water," he said.

Kitty spread her hands. "We ain't got so much as a bucket, sir."

Penelope tried to say the word *flask*, but the coughing was too violent. She willed Kitty to remember the vessel, sitting upstairs with their baggage. Without success.

The truculent viscount put an arm around

Penelope's shoulders and urged her inside. By this time, she could think of nothing but her heaving chest and streaming eyes.

"Pump some water," the man said to Kitty when they reached the kitchen. "Hurry up!"

Kitty jumped to obey. The man examined the stream as it began to flow. Seemingly satisfied, he held cupped hands below the spout and let them fill, then brought the water to Penelope. "Here. Drink!"

Despite her plight, she hesitated.

"The water's good," he added. "It's a deep well."

It wasn't the water, Penelope thought; it was the curiously intimate service. But she was desperate. She bent and slurped liquid from his palms. Her lips brushed his skin as she drank. His fingertips touched her cheek, leaving a startling tingle behind. Finally, somewhat recovered, she croaked, "Flask."

Kitty struck her forehead with one hand and ran upstairs to fetch the item. When she returned, Penelope took a deeper drink.

"You take brandy for your cough?" asked their visitor. He sounded amused and a bit scandalized.

"It's water." Her brother had used this flask for brandy. Not so long ago, and yet it felt like forever. She drank again. At last the cough subsided. Penelope sagged, worn out by the paroxysm.

The unexpected viscount took her arm and led her out to the low stone wall that surrounded the front garden. "Sit. You're ill."

There was nowhere else to rest. Penelope sat. "I'm not. That is, I have a lingering cold, which will soon disappear."

"You can't stay here," he said, looking around as if he hadn't heard her.

"Yes, I can."

"I beg to differ—"

"Beg all you like. I'm not leaving." It was rude, but Penelope wouldn't be ordered about by this stranger. And no one would tear her away from her new home and sanctuary now that she had it.

"Who are you?"

"My name is Penelope Pendleton." She waited for a sign of recognition. He showed none.

"Why were you left a house by my father?"

"I don't know."

"How can you not know?"

"Well, apparently *you* don't know, and he was *your* father."

This made him stiffen. "Tell me about your family. Where do you come from? Who are your people?"

Penelope went still, hearing similar demands, in harsher voices, echoing in her memory. Freely offering information had not done her much good since the killings in Manchester. Truth was scorned and twisted by powerful men—like the one addressing her, perhaps. "Must you loom over me?" she said to gain time.

But that was a mistake because he sat down beside her on the wall, bringing those dark probing eyes much closer.

A cough threatened. This time, Penelope let it come, aware that her struggles made her unwanted visitor uncomfortable. By the time the spasm was over, she'd decided that she wasn't going to tell him anything. Not until she knew a great deal more. She sipped from her flask. "You really must excuse me," she rasped. "I'm not prepared to receive callers." This was her house. She had the right to refuse visitors, for the first time in endless months. A privilege she hadn't appreciated properly until she lost it.

The irritating young woman gazed at Daniel from watering eyes. Sylphlike, he thought. That's what she was. Damn sylphlike. He didn't care for sylphlike women—sylphlike people, actually. They seemed to think their fragile frames were a sign of virtue, in contrast to his naturally sturdy figure. All that willowy slenderness was more likely to be unhealthy. Well, just witness the horrific cough that kept overwhelming the chit.

Miss Penelope Pendleton was pale. Her oval face was undeniably pretty, surrounded by blades of blond hair. Her blue eyes were large and clear—and not the least doll-like, he noticed. Indeed, they had the steady, stubborn resolve of a woman with something to hide. Daniel was the local magistrate; he knew that look.

She coughed weakly into her hand. Now she was being piteous on purpose, to make him feel like a bully. There were twisty corners to this young lady. Daniel felt a brush of the astonishing sensation that had run through him when she had drunk from his hands. Her lips had been so delicate on his palms. He had to find out more about her, for a variety of reasons.

"I really think I must rest," she said.

He was betrayed into an exasperated laugh. "On what? The bare floorboards?"

"I have quilts—"

"You can't stay here alone," he interrupted. The thought of her curled up in a nest of bedding was all too vivid.

"I'm not alone. I have Kitty."

"And she is what, fifteen?"

"Sixteen," said the skinny young maid, who had not effaced herself but loitered in the open doorway of the house, watching them with frank curiosity.

"And a manservant." When he made a show of looking around the empty garden, Miss Pendleton added, "He's on the way with my furnishings."

"Furnishings. Really." She spoke as if her bits and pieces belonged in the Prince Regent's palace.

"Nothing worthy of a *viscount*, perhaps. But we shall be very comfortable." She rose and joined her servant at the top of the low steps, a clear signal that he was to depart. Daniel enjoyed ignoring it.

"I told you I can't cook, miss," said the maid.

Miss Pendleton's lips tightened. They were beautifully sculpted lips, Daniel noticed. Rather full and vivid for a sylph. "*I* can," she said.

Daniel suspected it was a lie. Or no, she didn't feel like a liar. Twisty but not deceptive. An exaggeration, rather. "What are you going to do here?" he asked. "This place isn't fit for habitation, and there's no room for a staff." He'd wager a significant sum that she'd grown up with a cook and butler and all the rest.

"There's no need for you to concern yourself," she said with the condescension of a duchess. She looked pointedly at his horse.

That's me put in my place, Daniel thought. He discovered he was more amused than offended. On top of being frustrated, he was so very tired of not knowing the things he needed to know.

"Do you think the gentleman might see about the spiders?" asked Kitty the maid.

Daniel was beginning to like this girl. "Happy to," he replied before Miss Pendleton could object. "I'll send over some fresh firewood, too. Uninfested."

"You needn't bother."

"Oh, I insist. It's only neighborly." Following Kitty around the house, Daniel vowed he was going to do far more than that, though he didn't intend to say so. But he couldn't let this mysterious newcomer get sicker. He had to find out first why his father had left her a house.

Two

PENELOPE WAS CHAGRINED WHEN THE WAGON FROM Frithgerd Hall showed up early the following morning, and three determined women equipped with brooms, mops, buckets, and rags marched into her house, informing her that "my lord" had sent them. She was to have no say in this plan, apparently. But when they spread out and began to clean the place from top to bottom, she had to admit she was overcome with gratitude.

The night had left her exhausted. The dust in Rose Cottage had exacerbated her cough. Her pile of quilts had done little to soften the hard floor, and she'd barely slept. Instead, she'd lain there going over and over the magnitude of the task before her. She knew how to *run* a household; personally performing the many tasks involved was another matter. Baking the bread, for example. She'd never acquired that skill. Milking a cow—should she acquire a cow? And chickens. Those who wanted roast chicken needed to dispatch the birds. Would Kitty find the idea repulsive or grimly fascinating?

Penelope could—and would—learn, of course. But in the empty night, the long list of things that needed to be done had seemed overwhelming. So, when her offers to help clean were set firmly aside, she'd let herself be herded out to the garden wall to sit for a while in the shade of an apple tree.

Kitty flitted in and out of the open front door, keeping Penelope apprised of their progress. The young maid was delighted with the company and worked harder with the helpers from Frithgerd than she would have on her own. It was clear that she'd soon have fast friends in the neighborhood. Penelope envied her.

Around eleven, the eldest of her benefactors brought Penelope a cup of tea and a ham sandwich. "I would have made that for you," Penelope said. She *had* packed the tea—with cups and a pot and a small saucepan—in her food hamper. As if she was going on a picnic, Penelope thought wryly. While she'd forgotten a broom.

"No need, miss," was the reply. The woman turned away.

"Won't you get a cup for yourself and sit a moment, Mrs. Darnell?" Penelope had been informed that this lady—clearly the supervisor of the expedition—was the gatekeeper's wife at Frithgerd.

Ruddy, round-faced Mrs. Darnell hesitated. "I should be getting back to work." But she couldn't hide her curiosity.

"I wanted to ask if you might know people who live nearby and are looking for work." Penelope smiled up at the older woman. "Not to live in. No room for that." She gestured at the small house. "But to come days. I'd like to find a gardener. And perhaps a part-time cook."

Mrs. Darnell thought about this. "I expect I might know of someone."

"And is there a farm where I could buy milk and eggs?" And the occasional chicken, Penelope thought. She'd decided against keeping chickens. Or a pig; she wouldn't have a pig.

"The Mattisons up the road there." Mrs. Darnell pointed at the lane. "Young Kitty could walk it easy."

"Oh, good. I suppose it's safe for her to do so?"

Her companion stared down at her as if the question was daft. This wasn't Manchester, Penelope thought. There were no rowdy apprentices roaming the lanes here, shouting their appraisals of lone females. Penelope wished Mrs. Darnell would sit down, but clearly she wasn't going to.

"And how far is it to the nearest village shop?" she asked. She'd included some staples with her furniture, but they'd soon need more flour and sugar and other supplies.

"A matter of four miles, miss."

Penelope was assailed by a sudden feeling of isolation. Eight miles was a very long walk, too far to be carrying any but the lightest of burdens. They would need some form of transportation, and she couldn't afford a carriage. Even a gig would stretch her means. Well, she'd leave this problem to Foyle. He'd have ideas.

"If there wasn't anything else, miss."

But there was much more Penelope wanted to

know. "Who lived here before I arrived? Do you know?"

"That'd be old Mistress Harner. Past seventy she was, which is why the place is knee deep in dust, I expect."

"Was?" Penelope quailed. Had the loss of her home killed the old woman?

"Is, I should say. She went to live with her daughter in Ashbourne, as Susan had been trying to get her to do for many a year."

"Oh, that's good then."

"His lordship sent her in a traveling coach," added Mrs. Darnell. "With a hot brick for her feet and all."

"Lord Whitfield, you mean?"

The older woman nodded. "The young lord. Who never thought to take the reins so soon, of course. But he's doing very well."

"His father died unexpectedly?"

"In a shipwreck. And her ladyship, too. Off on t'other side of the world. India, it was. A terrible thing." Mrs. Darnell grimaced. "You wouldn't get me out in the middle of the ocean with no land in sight. Not for any money."

"How dreadful." Penelope knew the shock of sudden death. But to lose both your parents in such a way must have been devastating.

One of the younger Frithgerd ladies came out with a question, and Mrs. Darnell went with her to consult. Penelope ate her sandwich, drank her tea, and allowed herself to enjoy the leafy shade over her head. After the trials of recent months, this seemed the height of luxury.

It was only after she'd seen off the cleaners with thanks that Penelope discovered the pile of items they'd smuggled in through the back door while she sat out front. They'd left a full oil lamp, a broom, a whole box of candles, and several bundles of food, as well as two folding cots upstairs. Walking around her now-spotless dwelling, she had to acknowledge the kindness behind this visit. Unless it was all calculation, to soften her up for another round of questions.

With a shiver, Penelope decided it was much more likely that Lord Whitfield had ulterior motives. But she couldn't really blame him for wanting to know why she'd been left this house. The gift was inexplicable. She'd planned to comb every inch of the place to try to solve the mystery. Penelope ran her fingers over one of the stone lintels. The wood floors and plain plaster walls offered no nooks and crannies to examine. There was no visible discrepancy between the inside and outside dimensions. Still, she would search, on a day when she was less tired out.

Downstairs, she found Kitty by the stone sink with a large slice of chocolate cake in her hand. "This is the best cake I ever et," the girl declared. She took another big bite, humming with pleasure as she chewed. "You should have some, miss."

The rich scent of chocolate wafting from the cake that sat on the side of the sink was irresistible. Penelope succumbed, cutting herself a slice. A symphony of flavors melted on her tongue. Was that cinnamon?

"This Frithgerd is the grand house hereabouts," said Kitty between bites. "Funny old name. They've got twenty bedrooms, Betty said. Can you imagine?"

Betty was the youngest of the Frithgerd cleaning party. Penelope had seen the two girls with their heads together as they scrubbed. She had no interest in the viscount's household, of course. She wouldn't be moving in his exalted circles.

"The young lord's only twenty-seven and not married," Kitty added. She licked crumbs from her lips.

Four years older than Penelope; she'd have put him at thirty at least.

"Betty thinks his lordship'll be bringing home a wife from London right soon," said Kitty. "With him being the new master and all. She figures the new vi-viscountess'll have a grand lady's maid who knows all the latest styles. Betty's learning to dress hair and hopes she'll teach her. She means to better herself."

A crumb of cake tickled Penelope's throat, and her cough caught. She fought the impulse, but it took hold of her like a terrier shaking a rat. She coughed and coughed to no purpose. There was nothing to cough *up*. When the spasm passed, she felt as if she'd been cudgeled from head to toe. "I'm going to lie down for a little while," she told Kitty.

"Good idea, miss. You look terrible."

Penelope was well aware of the dark circles under her eyes and looseness of her dresses. Let Kitty endure the trials she'd undergone these last months and see how she looked, she thought wryly. But she said nothing, merely climbed the stairs and lay down on the cot that had been set up in her bedchamber. Though small, it was vastly more comfortable than the floor. She would just rest here for a few minutes. She was so very tired.

Penelope woke to the sound of Kitty moving around in the small back bedroom over the kitchen. From the slant of light, it must be early evening. She'd slept for hours! She breathed carefully. No cough. Thank heaven for small favors. She should get up and…and what?

Penelope lay still, suddenly conscious of a crushing isolation. She'd lost her childhood home, her friends, her anticipated future. She had no occupation except learning the tasks of day-to-day living. Life stretched ahead of her, empty.

"Nonsense," she said aloud, sitting up. She was far better off than last autumn, when her brother's recklessness had brought everything down around their ears. And then in the midst of the hardest year of her life, word of this miraculous legacy had reached her. She had a small income from her mother's estate. No one had been able to touch that despite her brother's disgrace. It was enough to live comfortably in a house like this, and to have a few luxuries as well. She would find new friends; she would make a life. Penelope shook herself and rose to get on with it.

❦

Foyle arrived the following afternoon with the two large carters' wagons full of furniture. It was a relief to see the man, gnarled, laconic, and crotchety as he was. He'd been a part of the Pendleton household for as long as Penelope could remember, seeming old the whole time.

The drivers unharnessed the great draft horses, led them to a water trough by the barn, then loosed them in the grassy field behind the house. Foyle waited with a tapping foot until the drivers returned, then set about directing the unloading. The men seemed to find his growling commands funny, perhaps because Foyle was half their size. Kitty flitted around them like a butterfly among oxen, carrying small items into the house.

By the end of the day, Penelope had a proper bed in one upper chamber, with a wardrobe, dressing table, and washstand. Kitty had similar furnishings in the small room over the kitchen. One lower room held a settee and armchair before the fireplace, two small tables, and a bookshelf with the volumes Penelope had managed to bring. A larger table and chairs graced the other downstairs room, making it seem like a dining room, though she wondered whether she would ever need such a thing. There was a worktable for the kitchen, two straight chairs, and a tall cupboard for pans and dishes. The last upstairs room was nearly empty, a measure of how little she had left. But Penelope refused to think of that. She could unpack her clothes now. They could alter the draperies she'd brought to fit the new windows. It was a comfort to have familiar possessions around her, an overlay of home on this new location. She would keep her mind on that.

Foyle had discovered a room over the stalls in the barn with a small iron stove. He went off with one of the cots to install his things there, declaring he'd be snug as a bug. He would not be swayed from his determination not to live in the house, which was rather a relief considering the limited space. Penelope suspected that his decision was partly based on pro- priety and partly a wish for freedom. Foyle liked to roam. Tomorrow, she'd send him off to explore the neighborhood and make inquiries.

～∽～

Daniel knew he shouldn't welcome the knock on his estate office door. He'd vowed to work for at least three hours without interruption. But the columns of numbers in the yearly accounts had begun to blur. The arrival of his mysterious new neighbor had left him even more distracted than usual. He very much feared he was going to have to start at the top, again. How he hated numbers! "Come in!" he said.

His butler entered, expressionless but exuding disapproval. "A visitor has arrived," he said.

"A caller, you mean? So late in the day?"

"I believe the gentleman has come to stay, my lord. That was the impression I gained, at least."

"What? I didn't invite anyone."

"Indeed. I assumed you would have told me if you had, my lord."

"Of course I would, Grant." Daniel stood. "Let's see about this."

In the main reception room, Daniel found Lord Macklin awaiting him, as polished and impressive as he'd been in London three months ago. He greeted the older man with raised eyebrows.

"I was passing through Derbyshire," said the earl. "And I thought I'd stop by to see how you were getting on. Your letters were so interesting."

He *had* written Macklin several times after that March dinner. Why had he done so? Daniel didn't know, exactly. Some echoes of their conversation about grief? A feeling that Macklin embodied elements long missing from his life? The impulse had eventually faded among his piles of lists. "I'm still quite busy," he replied. Not very hospitable, but he hadn't invited the man, after all.

His coolness had no effect. "I'm delighted at the opportunity to see Frithgerd," said Macklin. "I've heard a good deal about it. Your father and I entered society in the same season, you know."

"I didn't." Daniel felt a flash of resentment. Could anyone know *less* about their parents than he did? He pushed the thought aside.

"We thought ourselves top of the trees, complete to a shade." The tall, dark-haired guest smiled as he looked around the room. "This can't be the oldest part of the house."

"No, that's the east wing."

"Ah. Have you records of its construction? I wonder how the original building fits with your name."

"My name?" Daniel had never heard that Lord Macklin specialized in odd conversations. On the contrary, the earl was renowned for social finesse. But this was the second strange encounter they'd had.

"'Frith' is an Old English word. It means something like peace or protection, I understand. Or security perhaps."

"Old English. Like Saxon, you mean?" Daniel had known that his bloodline went back before the Conquest, but no one had mentioned this.

"Or Angle," said the earl.

"What?"

"As in Anglo-Saxon?"

Perhaps the older man had gone quietly mad, Daniel thought, and no one had noticed yet because he was too much revered.

"I remember being told that 'Frithgerd' meant sanctuary or sacred place," added Macklin. "Any enclosed area given over to the worship of the gods, really."

"Gods? What gods?"

The older man shrugged. "Well, Odin? Thor? I'm no expert."

"Papa told you all this?" Daniel simply didn't believe it. His father had never shown the least interest in history, or any knowledge of it, for that matter. They may not have had many significant conversations, but Daniel was certain of that much.

"Now I come to think of it, it wasn't John. Your grandfather buttonholed me at some banquet or other and gave me a lecture on the ancients."

That sounded more likely. Daniel remembered his grandfather as an inveterate talker. Of course, the old fellow had been losing his wits by the time Daniel met him.

"I didn't appreciate it at the time, but bits stuck with me, obviously," Lord Macklin continued. "A fascinating tale. I wonder I never talked with John about it. Too much else going on, I suppose. And I didn't see as much of your father as I would have wished in recent years."

Daniel felt an unwelcome pang, an unsettling mixture of pain and resentment that was all too familiar. He suppressed it.

"He was always on the move," added the earl, his tone gentle.

With no time for family connections, Daniel thought. Scarcely even a letter. But he didn't wish to be reminded of that. Or of anything else, really. If the earl had come to talk more about grief, he'd be disappointed. "We're in mourning here. I haven't been entertaining guests."

The earl waved this aside. "Oh, you needn't bother entertaining me. I can look after myself. Perhaps I can even be of use to you." Before Daniel could think of another excuse, he added, "Have you learned any more about the mysterious legacy you wrote me about? It did make me curious."

"A woman has arrived and moved into Rose Cottage."

"A woman?"

"A young lady." When Lord Macklin raised his eyebrows, Daniel added, "Not like that."

"Like?"

"I had thought…as one would, perhaps a mistress or some such thing. Though Papa never…and how would he have had the time when he was scarcely ever home? Anyway, she isn't. Not that sort at all. She claims she doesn't know why the house was left to her."

"Really? And you believe her?"

"I do." Miss Pendleton's bewilderment on that subject had been unmistakable.

"How very strange."

"Indeed."

"We must go over and see her tomorrow and look into this matter further."

"What? No!" It was out of the question. Even if

Daniel hadn't had a thousand other things to do, he didn't intend to call on Miss Penelope Pendleton again. She'd made it clear he wasn't welcome. And he would soon forget the touch of her lips brushing across his palms. Of course he would. A man could accomplish anything with decisive action and mental fortitude.

Three

But his fortitude proved insufficient. Somehow, Daniel found himself riding out with Lord Macklin the following afternoon to call on Miss Pendleton. There'd been no dispute about the expedition, which he'd been resolved *not* to make. The earl was invariably cordial and kind. He suggested rather than demanded. And yet his plan for the day had prevailed.

Equally puzzling, they were attended on the ride by a gangly lad named Tom, who apparently had no last name. Perhaps fifteen years old and said to be from Bristol, Tom had a homely, round face, bright blue eyes, and prominent front teeth. His smile, a near constant, was carefree and friendly. Though he wore a fine new coat, his appearance and manner suggested that he was a servant—more than a groom or footman and certainly less than a private secretary—yet he seemed to have no particular duties. He spoke of being on an adventure. Daniel wasn't clear who or what he was, but it seemed churlish to object to such a sunny presence.

Today, Rose Cottage looked prettily peaceful in

the June sunshine. Ruddy blossoms hung from the twining briars that engulfed one end of the house, filling the air with a sweet scent. They dismounted by the front garden wall, and Tom took all three horses' reins. Daniel strode up to the front door to knock. A moment later, it was opened by the young maid Kitty. The girl turned toward the stairs and called, "It's his lordship come back." She stepped aside to let them enter, indicating the room on the left of the entry.

Daniel hesitated. "The horses." It hadn't been a long or strenuous ride, but their mounts could use watering.

"Mr. Foyle'll take them," said the maid.

As if conjured, an elderly man in an old-fashioned tricorn hat, dun coat, and buckskin breeches came around the side of the house and muttered, "Barn's this way." The fellow had the wind-roughened face of a countryman and hands twisted by years of hard work. This must be the manservant Miss Pendleton had mentioned, Daniel thought. He and Tom went off with the horses. Daniel led Lord Macklin inside.

He found the interior of the house transformed. The dust and echoing emptiness was gone, replaced by cozy elegance. Obviously, Miss Pendleton's furniture had arrived, and it included a number of fine pieces that had certainly come from a far grander dwelling. The brocade of the draperies looked quite expensive as well.

"Good afternoon."

Daniel turned to find the young lady he'd met in this place a few days ago. She also looked much better, more rested and less pale. Or perhaps that was just a reflection of the crisp, pink cambric gown she wore. Her blue eyes met his evenly. "Miss Pendleton," he said with a bow. "May I introduce Lord Macklin, who is visiting me? We came over to see how you are getting on."

"Quite well, thank you." Miss Pendleton sat down in an upholstered armchair and gestured toward the settee like a grand lady perfectly accustomed to calls from noblemen. Daniel was more than ever convinced that she had grown up in far different circumstances. They sat. "It was kind of you to send over the cleaners," she added.

Daniel had been poised to fend off effusive gratitude, but she offered no more than that. For some reason, it irritated him.

Murmurs from the kitchen, which was after all only a few feet away, suggested that Tom had come in through the back door. And indeed when the maid returned with refreshment, he was carrying the tray.

"This is Tom," said Daniel. He left it at that. Let Macklin offer more information, if he had any.

He said nothing. Tom went out with the maid, a giggle drifting back in their wake.

Miss Pendleton poured tea into cups of fine china and served them slices of chocolate cake that was as good as any Daniel's cook could produce. He acknowledged that he was surprised at all she'd accomplished in such a short time.

"Miss Penelope," said the earl. "Was your father fond of Homer?"

"No, I was named after a great-aunt."

She sipped her tea and didn't ask who Homer

might be—another sign that she came from a cultured household. It was maddening to know so little about this woman who had intruded into his life. Indeed, Daniel was suddenly sick to death of the muddles and mysteries his heedless parents had left behind. "Where are you from?" he asked. "Where did you grow up?"

Macklin shot him a sidelong glance. Daniel silently admitted ineptitude. His question had been abrupt, rude. But he was impatient. He wanted to know who she was and why she'd inherited a house that should by rights have been his. Not that he needed Rose Cottage. It was just the principle of the thing. Once he knew, he could forget the whole matter and get on with his many duties.

"North of Manchester," Miss Pendleton replied.

Daniel hadn't realized that a tone of voice could be aggressively vague. Her eyes were as steely as a gauntlet thrown down. Why must she be so prickly? he wondered. What did she have to hide?

"Why is your man staring at us?" asked the earl.

Daniel followed Macklin's gaze and saw the old fellow who'd taken their horses. He was stationed outside the window by the fireplace glaring in at them. Did he see himself as a chaperone? There was no sign of any other, unless one counted the gormless young maid.

Their hostess leaned over to look. "Oh, that's Foyle. He fancies himself as a kind of household guardian."

"Rather like a gargoyle," said Macklin.

They both turned to look at him, startled, and the usually imperturbable earl grimaced. "I beg your pardon. That was impolite. It's just that his face is so... full of character."

A short laugh escaped Miss Pendleton. "Foyle wouldn't even mind the comparison. He always said he was craggy as a mountain. He used to make faces to amuse us when I was small."

So she had a family retainer, on top of everything else, Daniel thought. He was formulating more searching questions when Foyle turned to look at something behind the house. The man scowled, raised a fist, shook it as he shouted something inaudible, and ran off.

The sound of more running feet and raised voices followed. It sounded like a riot.

"What in the world?" said Miss Pendleton.

They rose and went out to discover the source of the uproar.

The back of her property was full of goats, Penelope saw when they rounded the side of the house. White goats, brown goats, multicolored goats. Several clattered over the cobbles of the yard. One stood on the roof of the privy, staring down at them with bright-yellow eyes. How had it gotten up there? A small black goat capered before the open doors of the barn, hopping as if it had springs in its legs, to the obvious consternation of the horses tied up there. More goats were in the kitchen garden plot, eating the vegetables. Penelope saw one take a careful mouthful of a carrot top, pull the root from the ground, and eat it with gusto. Foyle was down there, looming over a small boy and yelling. Kitty and the lad Tom stood on the kitchen stoop observing the show.

Penelope wove her way across the yard, avoiding goats, conscious of two noblemen on her heels.

"Nobody's been living here," the goatherd was saying. "So it seemed a shame to waste the turnips, y'see."

"Well, somebody lives here now," Foyle answered. "So take your animals away and keep them off."

"I'll try, mister," the boy whined. "But they're used to coming here now, y'see. And I can't always make them mind me. You'd best get a fence."

"I'll get a shotgun," growled Foyle. "It's up to you to keep the creatures away from our property."

"You can't be shooting master's goats!" the boy wailed. "They ain't like sheep. I can't make 'em do what I want."

"Is that Sam Jensen?" said Lord Whitfield.

Penelope started. She hadn't realized he was so close behind her.

The boy spotted him and ran over. "My lord! It ain't my fault, sir. There was nobody here, and the goats found the garden all on their own."

A shriek from Kitty indicated that a goat had run into the kitchen. Tom dashed in and returned with the small animal in his arms. He grinned, not looking at all apprehensive. "Did you see their eyes?" he asked. "Right odd, they are." He showed the animal to Kitty. She backed up a step.

A sound made Penelope turn. There was a goat teetering on top of the woodpile and seeming to leer at her. The pupils of its yellow eyes were dark horizontal slashes rather than circles. They were rather odd.

"Perhaps it will eat the spiders," said Lord Whitfield.

She turned to look at him. His dark eyes were gleaming with humor. His face had lost all trace of pomposity. "Goats are vegetarian," she said. "I think."

"They are," said the stately Lord Macklin. "Although they will taste all sorts of rubbish to see if it's palatable."

Lord Whitfield smiled. Penelope was shaken, and then overtaken, by laughter, and he joined in. Her neighbor seemed a different person, laughing. His blunt features were transformed, as if a curtain had been drawn back to expose a lively, engaging personality. She got the notion that, like her, he hadn't laughed so heartily in a while. She felt intimations of an old lightness and freedom that had been absent from her life for such a long time.

And then Penelope realized that her older visitor was watching them with more interest than their brief acquaintance warranted. Her laughter faltered, and degenerated into a cough. Struggling to control the spasm, she wondered who Lord Macklin was. Why would such an obviously superior person call at Rose Cottage? Had he come here looking for her? The Manchester matter had been declared closed. She had no more to say; that had been made perfectly clear. She'd been left to gather the tatters of her life around her and move on. Her new circles would not include noblemen who were clearly powers in the land. Coughing, she turned her back on him. Penelope had been visited by too many authorities over the last year to welcome any sort of inquiries.

Lord Whitfield had walked away. Now he returned with a cup of water. "Here."

Penelope took it, drank, and assuaged her cough. Fatigue, only partly physical, descended on her.

"We must gather up these goats and take them… somewhere," Lord Whitfield added.

"How do you propose to do that?" asked Lord Macklin. He sounded amused and interested rather than toplofty.

"They are herd animals. We will herd them." He turned to the boy in the garden. "How do you move your goats about, Sam?"

"It's more like I follow them, my lord. They go where they like."

"But you have to get them home at the end of the day."

"Oh." Sam wiped his nose on his sleeve. "I try to catch hold of Nanny. They'll follow her. Mostly. Usually."

"Which one is Nanny?" Penelope asked. She moved toward the garden.

"No," said Lord Whitfield. "You go and sit down. We'll gather them up."

Penelope stiffened. She didn't like being ordered about, and she couldn't allow a viscount and whatever exalted rank Lord Macklin held to chase goats around her cottage.

"Tom," said Lord Whitfield, beckoning.

The lad hurried to his side.

"And, er, Foyle." He crooked a finger at her manservant. "We will execute an encircling maneuver. Sam, you will capture Nanny."

"What about me?" asked Lord Macklin. He was definitely amused.

"Rear guard," replied the younger visitor. "Head off stragglers."

The campaign began, and Penelope's property descended into chaos.

Goats were in fact nothing like sheep. They didn't clump up and stare apprehensively when people ran in a circle around them. They scattered, hopped like rabbits, and took the opportunity to butt if anyone turned his back. Young Tom was knocked into a heap by the largest goat, which he appeared to find hilarious. The goats also seemed to be enjoying themselves.

Penelope recruited Kitty, and they set themselves to block the way to the front of the house. Kitty shrank back when a trio of the animals ran at them, but Penelope flapped her skirts, shouted, and turned them away. She had nearly despaired, however, when Sam pounced on a large white goat and threw his arms around her neck. She turned to bite him, but he evaded her teeth.

"Nanny?" called Lord Whitfield.

Sam gave a muffled affirmative. Penelope saw that his captive wore a collar with a small bell.

Lord Whitfield pulled a handful of turnips from the earth, strode over, and held them under Nanny's nose. She sniffed, interested. He took a step. She followed. He took another. She came along. "Form a perimeter," he told his troops. "Offer this sort of lure if you can find it."

The others snatched up more turnips or carrots and held them out. Most of the goats seemed to appreciate the help with excavation. With Nanny in the lead, they moved in the same direction. Slowly, the men led the herd away. Penelope heard Lord Whitfield ask the goatherd about the nearest corral, and then the cavalcade disappeared behind the barn.

"Gor," said Kitty. "I had no notion the country was such a terrible place."

"No one was hurt," said Penelope. "It was just a few goats."

"But they have devil eyes!"

"Different eyes."

Kitty shuddered. "I'm going to dream about demons with yellow eyes coming after me." She made clawing motions with both hands.

"Oh come, Kitty. Look at cats. Their eyes aren't like ours."

"Yes they are."

"They have vertical pupils. And some of their eyes are yellow."

Kitty frowned at her. "Cats are on our side."

"Our—"

"They sit in laps and catch mice and purr. Goats rampage about and trample gardens. Didn't you see that big one sneak up behind Tom and knock him down?"

"She tried it on Foyle, too," Penelope replied.

Kitty nodded as if this clinched her argument. "I'll heat the big kettle of water, miss, in case the gentlemen want to wash up after those goats drag them through the mud."

There'd been no sign of dragging. Or of mud, for that matter. But hot water was a good idea. She should have thought of it.

It was more than an hour before the men returned—disheveled and laughing. The sudden influx of masculine energy was like a rush of wind through the house. They ought to have mugs of ale to toast their victory, Penelope thought, but she had none to offer.

A household included so many items that she'd taken for granted in the past. Would a local inn sell her a keg of beer? Foyle would be happy to ask about that. Not that she would be entertaining parties such as this in future. A viscount wasn't going to be a frequent caller at humble Rose Cottage. Penelope sat in the armchair with folded hands and told herself this was all to the good.

The impromptu goatherds made noisy use of the hot water. Lord Whitfield was the first back in the front room. "Thank you for repelling the invasion," she said, standing.

"It was actually rather fun." He grinned. "If anyone had told me that Macklin could sweep the legs from under a goat and chuck it over a fence… Well, I wouldn't have believed them."

Penelope saw the boy he'd been in that grin—carefree, adventurous, full of laughter.

"I don't mean he threw the creature," Whitfield added. "He snatched it up and…*placed* it. But Macklin! The arbiter of polite society and model of elegance. With his arms full of goat." His smile urged Penelope to enjoy his amazement.

She was conscious of a deep yearning to join him in simple laughter. She suspected, imagined, that they would find the same things amusing, and it would be pure joy to share them. But that was ridiculous. She had no basis for such an idea. And more importantly, her life was no longer simple. Spare, secluded, yes, but not simple. She fell back on commonplaces. "Lord Macklin is a relative of yours?"

Whitfield's laughter died. Penelope felt its departure

like a new bereavement. "He was a friend of my father. More than I realized."

Her visitor's father was a sore subject. Talking of him would lead to questions about her legacy, and then on to arguments. She didn't want to fight with him. What else to say? "I don't suppose you know where I could get a dog?"

"A dog?"

"Or perhaps two. Watchdogs. To bark at the goats if they come back and chase them off. I can't always count on a troop of irregulars to wade in." He looked bemused. She didn't blame him. "I supposed you had dogs at Frithgerd."

"Yes."

"Not that I would take your dogs away, of course. But someone must know where you got them. Or perhaps there's a litter…not that puppies would be of much use against the goats."

"The combination would be pure chaos, I imagine."

A picture rose in her mind, puppies romping among the hooves, the resulting havoc. "It would, wouldn't it?"

"You might be better off with geese," he mused. "They can be quite—"

"No!"

Whitfield blinked.

"I hate geese," Penelope admitted. "I was mobbed by a…a gaggle when I was four years old. They nipped at my hands and my hair and terrified me. Philip had to beat them off with a stick."

"Philip?"

Penelope swallowed a wave of sadness and resentment and deep chagrin. Now she'd done it. Why had she mentioned his name? And how could she expect to avoid it? "My brother," she said. "He's dead," she added before he could ask where Philip was and why she wasn't living with him.

"I'm sorry."

She had to change the subject before he moved on to the awkward questions. But her mind had gone blank. Or rather, it had filled with memories of interrogation. Her hands were shaking. Lord Whitfield would notice that weakness and wonder what it meant. He would insist on knowing.

But he didn't.

When Penelope glanced up, she found surprising sympathy on her neighbor's blunt features. He seemed puzzled, yes. But he also looked as if he knew it could be horridly painful to speak of a family member. How had *he* learned this? She was moved by the oddest impulse. She wanted to take his hand.

Emotion trembled in the air between them. His brown eyes didn't drill into hers as others had tried to do, she noted. He was sturdy and muscular, but he didn't *loom*. She suspected him of more kindness than he would admit. Tears stung at the idea.

Then Lord Macklin came in, trailed by Tom and Kitty with a fresh pot of tea. Everyone sat down. The gentlemen began to recount the highlights of the chase. Kitty lingered to listen. Macklin made joking comparisons to a military campaign, while Tom acted out some incidents with broad gestures. There was a good deal of laughter.

Penelope joined in gladly. She welcomed the light mood and, even more, the interruption. It gave her time to remember that these were not her friends and safe confidants. She'd made that mistake before, and suffered for it. Lord Whitfield had been quite sharp about the Rose Cottage legacy, and he probably would be again. He was the major landholder in this part of the country and could make things difficult for her. Lord Macklin had practiced charm, but she knew nothing else about him.

And so Penelope donned her social armor and smiled and chatted about nothing for twenty minutes more. When she bid her callers goodbye, she was cordial and distant. And if Lord Whitfield looked dissatisfied, she simply couldn't help it.

"An interesting young lady," said Macklin as the men rode back toward Frithgerd together. Tom trailed a discreet distance behind them.

"Yes," said Daniel. He was aware of feeling disgruntled, and that he had no justification for such a state.

"Quite a conundrum," the earl went on. "When was the legacy to her added to your father's will?"

"It was part of the original document, made ten years ago."

"Was it indeed? And yet you knew nothing of it?"

"My father didn't share such details with me. Not enough time between his various journeys." Daniel heard the bitterness in his tone. He spoke again to dispel it. "Of course, I was told the main terms. The disposition of the estate and so on."

His older companion nodded. "So still a mystery.

One might profitably make inquiries about a landowner named Pendleton who lived north of Manchester, I suppose."

"A landowner?"

"I would say that Miss Pendleton comes from the gentry. Do you disagree?"

Daniel shook his head. The signs of her upbringing were unmistakable.

"And she said she grew up north of Manchester."

"She had a brother named Philip, now dead." Immediately, Daniel felt as if he'd betrayed a friend. She'd looked so stricken when she'd mentioned her brother. But for God's sake, all he wanted was to understand why she was here.

"That should help. Inquiries will take a little while, of course."

They would take less time for Macklin. He knew everybody. "I suppose it will do no harm to investigate," Daniel replied.

The earl raised an interrogative eyebrow.

"I don't intend to make any change," Daniel continued. "She can have the house. I just want to know why Papa left it to her, not take it away."

"Even if the reason is disreputable?"

"It isn't!"

Macklin turned to look at him.

He'd spat the words as if his own honor was being questioned, Daniel realized, and he felt unaccountably angry. "I can't believe that it is," he amended. "Or, if there is some irregularity, it won't involve Miss Pendleton. She isn't that sort of person."

"Of course not."

Daniel resented the amusement in the older man's voice. He kicked his heels and urged his mount into a gallop.

Four

Penelope's cough improved markedly over the next week, confirming her hopes that it would soon be gone altogether. During the warm June days, she made arrangements with the neighboring farm to purchase milk and eggs and found the daily help she'd planned to hire. The young man who took charge of the garden had to chase off the goats a second time, and he recommended a fence. Foyle argued that this was giving in to the marauding animals, but Bob said it would help keep off rabbits and other intruders as well.

A widow who lived nearby agreed to come in half days to cook. Mrs. Hart was glad of the addition to her income and the company. She enjoyed teaching her skills to Kitty and Penelope, and Penelope soon discovered that baking was a pleasure. She produced a good loaf of bread on her third try.

She told herself she was resigned to her small new life. She couldn't help missing the social round that had been part of her girlhood, but if she needed a topic to occupy her mind, there was always her unexpected inheritance. She examined every inch of

Rose Cottage, from the small space under the roof to the earthen cellar to the nooks and crannies of the barn. She found no secret compartments or hidden documents or clues that led to some other location. Through her gratitude, the mystery nagged at her. Why had a man she'd never met, indeed never even heard of, left her a house?

She was considering the larger crevices in the front garden wall and wondering whether any of them might hold secrets when a curricle swooped up the lane and stopped before her. Lord Whitfield held the reins, with just a groom up behind him. "Good afternoon," he said as the groom jumped down to go to the horses' heads.

Penelope was concerned to realize how glad she was to see him—not just as someone to talk to, but for his own sake. That was not a good idea.

He stepped down, turned, and reached back into his vehicle. "I've brought you the dogs you wanted," he said, lifting two young hounds down from the curricle and placing them at Penelope's feet. "Walk the horses," he told the groom.

"Staying for a bit, are you?" Penelope couldn't help saying. He might be the lord of all the land hereabouts, but he wasn't in charge of Rose Cottage.

Her noble visitor looked startled. "I thought I'd introduce the dogs."

"See that I can handle them, you mean?"

His expression gave him away, but he wasn't foolish enough to agree out loud.

One of the dogs nosed Penelope's skirts. Both were white with brown and black patches and ears that hung below their jaws. Though they had long legs and large paws that promised further growth, they weren't puppies. They surveyed their new surroundings with bright eyes, sniffing at the bottom of the wall and the flowers in the front garden. "Foxhounds?" asked Penelope, recognizing the breed.

Lord Whitfield nodded. "They are. But some dogs don't want to hunt. The farmer who bred these two said they just don't have the urge. He thought they'd be happy as family watchdogs. He…umm…altered them."

Penelope bent and extended a hand. The dogs came over to greet her, interested.

"I thought I'd get them accustomed to—" Daniel began, but she'd snapped her fingers at the hounds and led them away. He followed the three of them around the cottage to the kitchen door.

There he waited with the dogs. Almost as if he was a dog himself, Daniel thought, amused and a bit irked.

Miss Pendleton emerged from the house with a small dish of chopped meat. "What are the dogs' names?" she asked.

"The farmer called them Jum and Jip. He names his litters by letter. You can choose other names if you wish."

"I see no reason, particularly if they are accustomed to those. Jip!"

One of the dogs cocked an ear. Penelope held out a morsel of meat. The hounds crowded up to her, and she gave the treat to Jip. "And Jum." She fed the other. Then she headed across the yard, holding the dish well up. When one dog started to leap for it, she said "No," in a tone that brought instant obedience and roused Daniel's admiration. She didn't require his help, he realized. Yet he had no wish to leave. Watching her take charge of her new acquisitions was a positive pleasure.

Miss Pendleton led the dogs into the small barn. "Sit," she said.

Daniel knew the command was an experiment. She had no way of predicting what the hounds had been taught. But she sounded absolutely certain they'd do as she asked. Jip and Jum sat.

"Good," she said, giving each dog a tiny bit of meat. "Good dogs." She led them around the barn. "You will live here," she added, showing them the front stall.

The tramp of footsteps on a narrow stair in the corner heralded the entry of her manservant. Foyle was his name, Daniel remembered. The old fellow glowered at him.

"These are Jip and Jum," said Miss Pendleton. "Our new watchdogs and chasers of goats."

Foyle came over and crouched with more agility than his craggy face predicted. He held out his hands. The dogs sniffed and licked them, wriggling with delight when he ran his fingers over their sides. The man couldn't be as grim as he liked to appear, Daniel thought, if dogs liked him so readily.

"Good bones," said Foyle.

"Do we have a bit of rope?" asked Miss Pendleton.

Foyle found some, and she made improvised leashes for the two dogs. Then she led them out of the barn. Impressed and increasingly fascinated, Daniel went with her. She didn't dismiss him.

She walked the hounds down the lane to the side of the Rose Cottage property and then along the northern edge. She knew the boundaries to an inch, Daniel noticed. He admired the precision and resented it just a little, reminded of the enigma of his father's legacy. When either dog showed an impulse to mark a tree or stone, she stopped and allowed it. "I'm encouraging them to learn their territory," she said after a while.

"I know." Did she think he hadn't noticed or didn't understand? "You're good with them."

"We always had dogs," Miss Pendleton replied. Her tone had gone nostalgic.

"Which is the first you remember?"

"My mother's lapdog, I suppose. Though it's more what I've been told than a real memory. They say Pug stood guard over my cradle and scarcely let the nursemaid near me." She blinked and looked self-conscious, as if sorry she'd revealed any detail of her past.

Daniel spoke before she could withdraw further. "My earliest friend was an outsized dog named Stranger."

"Stranger?"

"Because he was one. No one knows, to this day, where he came from. I found him when I was out walking with Nanny and dragged him up to the nursery. Even though he was twice my weight. And covered in mud." Daniel smiled, remembering. "I was positively foul to everybody until they agreed I could keep him."

"Your parents didn't want you to?"

"Oh, they weren't around. My parents were great travelers. They were always off on some trip or other." He pushed quickly past this admission. "I had to convince Nanny and the housekeeper, which was not easy, I must tell you. Stranger had teeth as long as my hand. The cook thought he was a wolf."

"You were how old?"

"Four or five. Somewhere in between."

"He doesn't sound like a pet for a child."

Daniel shook his head. "Stranger had the sweetest temper in the world. He'd hold my fingers in his mouth and never think of biting down. He pulled me out of a slough once." They reached the back boundary of the property and turned, pausing for the dogs to examine and mark a tall oak. "Best friend I ever had," Daniel added.

"The best?"

He supposed it sounded odd. "There weren't many other children about the place."

"You must have made friends at school."

He shrugged and nodded. "Stranger never understood about school. Always thought he should come with me. In his last days, he hung on till I came home for the holidays before he…went." Daniel's throat thickened. Why had he told her that? This story had been meant as a diversion, not exposure. He gave his companion a sidelong glance. Miss Pendleton drew confidences like no one he'd ever met before. How did she do that?

"It's so hard when a beloved animal dies," she replied. "And they seem to feel the same. My father's old spaniel pined for months after he died, and then just lay down one day and never got up again. Philip said—" She broke off, biting her lower lip.

Her brother was definitely a sore subject. The way

she avoided speaking of him didn't seem like simple mourning. Daniel couldn't puzzle out her tone. He wanted to ask. He wanted to know more about her. But he knew she didn't wish to tell him. A familiar sting of annoyance made Daniel pull back. He'd had more than enough of people who insisted upon remaining distant, in every sense of the word.

"How many dogs do you have at Frithgerd now?" asked Miss Pendleton in a more reserved tone.

Daniel matched it. "Just four. Two who are good for hunting rabbits. And two who hang about the stables." He hadn't had a really close bond with a dog since Stranger, Daniel realized. They turned up the other side of the Rose Cottage land, heading back toward the lane.

"You don't keep a foxhunting pack?"

They would chat now, Daniel thought, as acquaintances did. And neither would be any wiser at the end. He'd learned that lesson long ago. "No, though I sometimes go out with the local hunt. We have an interesting stone-wall and grass country. Do you hunt?"

"I? Oh, no."

She tried to make it sound as if the mere idea was ridiculous, but he thought she was familiar with the sport. The sharp desire for more information about her surfaced again, not only because of his father's legacy to her. He couldn't resist. "Did your brother?"

Miss Pendleton stiffened. She turned away from him. "What have you got there?" she said to the dogs. They'd found a dead hedgehog and were nosing the remains. "Leave it!" She pulled them along and walked faster. She did not answer his question.

Daniel burned with silent humiliation. His parents had been just the same, on the rare occasions they'd spent time together. As if a query was an embarrassing solecism, better off ignored. He didn't need this. Rose Cottage lay ahead. It was past time for him to go. And not come back. Even if Miss Pendleton encouraged him to do so. Which she clearly wouldn't. He searched for bland phrases. "Ralston, the farmer who bred the dogs, will probably be by to see their new home."

"He's welcome to."

She sounded like a different person—grander, colder—letting him know he'd overstepped. Deuce take her and her reticence, Daniel thought. Yet another part of him continued to wonder what had happened to bring her here.

Back at the barn, Foyle had arranged an ancient blanket over some straw as a dog bed and set out bowls of water. Miss Pendleton removed the ropes. The dogs drank noisily.

"You need a gig or a dogcart," said Daniel, looking around the empty building.

"Foyle is handling it." The words came out sharper than Penelope would have liked, but Daniel's question had roused her fears again. Exposure might be inevitable, but she wouldn't make the mistake of offering too much. She could still hope that the recent past would remain buried.

She turned and strode toward the house, feeling him at her back. Their entire conversation had been more intimate than was wise. She couldn't go walking about the neighborhood with Lord Whitfield, alone.

Country people gossiped. She knew this from the loss of many people she'd thought real friends. She couldn't get into the habit of expecting him to visit, or of needing his help. Loss was far more painful than solitude, Penelope thought, and he belonged back at his great house, not here.

❧

At Frithgerd, at that moment, an informal conference was taking place in one of the bedchambers. Arthur Shelton, Earl of Macklin, handed a letter he had just sealed to his valet and glanced over at young Tom, who sat by the window waiting to join him on a tramp about the estate. "Our host has gone out?" Arthur asked.

"He took some dogs to the young lady at Rose Cottage," said Tom.

"Purchased especially for her," added Clayton, the valet. "And the household is wondering why."

"I 'spect it's to chase off the goats," said Tom. He smiled. He'd enjoyed the goats' spirited resistance to being herded.

"But why is his lordship supplying them?" Clayton replied. "That is their question."

Arthur considered it a hopeful sign. He'd come to Frithgerd on a mission, and his recent experience suggested that a lively young lady could be just what was needed.

"Everybody's making up stories about why she's inherited Rose Cottage," said Tom.

"What sort of stories?" Arthur asked.

"The usual drivel," answered Clayton, his round

face disapproving. The valet had been with Arthur for more than twenty years, and the earl valued his canny insights as much as his personal services. "She's somebody's mistress, or discarded mistress, or the old lord's love child, or a disgraced cousin waiting for a baby to show. People have such common minds."

"One of the grooms reckoned she was a hindoo who used her foreign magic to wreck the old lord's ship on his journey home," said Tom. When the other two turned to stare, he added, "The first sight of her put an end to that tale."

"You can't fault *his* imagination," said Arthur.

"It's not going to be easy for Miss Pendleton to settle into the neighborhood with gossip like that flying about," said Clayton.

Arthur nodded. Clayton looked unassuming, with his wide cheeks and snub nose. Many failed to notice that his brown eyes were exceedingly sharp. "That's one reason I'd like to find out more about this legacy," he said. "Let's get that letter off."

With a bow, the valet departed. Arthur led Tom downstairs and out into the gardens. They walked a while in the mild June air, silently companionable. On the surface, they had little in common, the earl thought. And some people were bewildered by his friendship with a boy born into the slums of Bristol who didn't even know his own last name. But when he'd encountered Tom on a visit to Somerset a few weeks ago, Arthur had been impressed by his sunny temper and active curiosity.

The lad was so eager to learn and experience. He was inspiring, and Arthur enjoyed his candid opinions and manner. Other noblemen might have called it effrontery, but there were many dry sticks in the House of Lords. Arthur hoped to help the lad to a bright future, whenever it became clear what sort of help Tom really wanted.

"Perhaps you can include Rose Cottage in your rambles," he said. Tom spent a good part of each day outdoors. He was a natural rover and didn't like to sit still.

"Spy on them, like?" The lad sounded unhappy with the idea.

"No. More keeping a watchful eye, and perhaps becoming a friend." Arthur had no doubt he would; friendship was one of Tom's gifts. "Isn't the maid Kitty about your age?"

Tom snorted. "Don't go matchmaking for me, my lord."

Arthur raised his eyebrows.

"It's all very well to look sideways, but I've watched you at work, haven't I? Getting your nephew leg-shackled."

"That was all his idea."

"Was it now?"

Arthur laughed. "Mostly. But I had no such idea about you and Kitty. Why, you're barely fifteen."

Tom nodded. "Long as we're clear on that, I don't mind. It's odd, this legacy, ain't it? Folks usually know why they're left things."

"They do."

"I might go on over there now."

"A splendid idea."

Tom veered off, and Arthur continued his stroll.

When he saw a curricle pull into the stable yard, he walked in that direction and observed the return of his host. Whitfield looked disgruntled.

Daniel made no remark when his houseguest fell into step with him as he headed for the house. "So you took Miss Pendleton some dogs?" Macklin said. His tone was bland.

"How did you know that?"

"Someone in the household told my valet," the earl replied.

"Have they no better things to talk about?"

"Our dependents are interested in everything we do. For the goats, was it? Tom thought so."

"The goats, yes," Daniel said.

"And general protection, I suppose. For an unmarried young lady, living alone."

He might as well have said that Daniel should take care about visiting her. Daniel fought down a spurt of anger. He'd heard bits of the gossip about Miss Pendleton. One neighbor had asked him smiling questions that had verged on the offensive. For her sake, he shouldn't go walking alone with her. So he was to be deprived of that pleasure, as well as all else. Daniel frowned, wondering where that thought had come from.

"Have you found any earlier records about Rose Cottage?" the earl asked. "You were going to look."

"I tried, but Frithgerd's records are a jumble, to put it charitably. We appear to have no filing system beyond shoving estate documents into whatever cubbyhole is nearest to hand at the time." Daniel's anger, finding a convenient target, expanded to fill his chest. "I can't answer half the questions I'm asked, because I can't find the information I need. So, no, nothing about Rose Cottage." Not to mention the fact that his father had never told him anything or lifted a finger to keep the place in order. "There are only so many hours in the day when I can be reading and sorting." Without going stark mad from frustration and boredom, he thought. As they entered the house, Daniel turned toward the estate office. The weight of the task descended on him. "I should get back to it."

"It sounds as if you need help."

Did Macklin intend to offer his services? Daniel couldn't imagine the earl delving into Frithgerd's papers. It would be like having the Chancellor of the Exchequer overseeing his efforts. "I need a new estate agent. No one informed me when the last one left."

"I could ask among my friends, if you like, see if anyone might be able to recommend a good agent."

"Yes, all right." He needed to get hold of himself, Daniel thought. "Thank you."

"I'm happy to help."

The earl's benign tone and expression roused echoes of the dinner he'd arranged in London in the spring and the sympathetic talk that had unexpectedly followed. The occasion stood out in Daniel's memory as one of the exceedingly rare times when people had spoken to each other with naked sincerity. He still didn't understand how Macklin had managed that.

"It's so very pleasant here," Macklin went on. "I do wonder that your parents were forever leaving home."

Those last three words shook Daniel like a sudden loss of footing. He found himself asking, "Do you have any idea why they traveled all the time?"

"Not specifically."

Of course he didn't. Disappointment welled up, along with an odd kind of relief. It would be worse to discover that they'd confided in others and not him, Daniel realized.

"But I'd wager a good deal that it was due to your mother," Macklin added.

"Why do you say that?" He'd just assumed his father made all their decisions.

"A theory only," said the older man. "But your father never showed any interest in leaving England before he married. Of course I only knew John from the age of eighteen. But we spent a good deal of time together during several seasons in London and some country visits, and we talked as young men do." He smiled. "In our cups and out of them. Grandiose plans and impractical dreams."

Intrigued by this glimpse into his father's youth, Daniel immediately wanted to hear more. What plans and dreams? He knew so little about the two people who had created him. For the first time, he was glad that Macklin had come to Frithgerd.

"John didn't speak of travel," the earl went on. "Not even the grand tour of Europe, which was popular then. He was more interested in horse racing and boxing matches, if I recall correctly. Then he met your mother."

"At the Duchess of Rutland's masked ball." Daniel had heard this story, at least. "Papa was dressed as

Mark Antony, and she was Cleopatra. They took it as an omen."

Macklin nodded. "They didn't seem to mind how that story ended."

"What?"

"Assassination? Flight? Eventual disaster?"

"They'd thought of the same era," replied Daniel, confused. "Their minds ran in a similar way." This was one of the few family legends he possessed.

The earl shrugged. "John was certainly smitten with Miss Walsden, as your mother was then. A beautiful girl. And John's father's opposition was oil on the flames, of course."

"He objected?" No one had told Daniel this. "Why? I thought Mama was born into some ancient line." His mother's parents had been dead by the time he came along. She mentioned second cousins a time or two, but Daniel had never met them.

Macklin nodded. "Like John's own. And like John's a small family, with few representatives. John told me his father would have preferred a prolific clan. He was worried that the Friths were dwindling and wanted to repopulate their ranks."

"That sounds positively medieval." Was this the reason he had no siblings, Daniel wondered. Was his singular status some sort of rebellion?

"He was a rather archaic figure. I remember one evening when he hunted John down at an evening party and lectured him—in front of a group of young friends—about the weight of history and responsibility his name carried. He felt John *must* see how much more important this was than the latest odds at Newmarket. Calling it a weight was a mistake, I always thought."

He smiled as if to share a joke, but Daniel was too absorbed by this glimpse into the past to laugh. "So my grandfather's objections to the match made no difference?"

"No. John wanted Serena Walsden. He offered for her, and she accepted."

"Good for him!"

"Perhaps she was. She certainly broadened his interests. Most girls talk chiefly about themselves, don't you find? But Miss Walsden was full of information she'd read. Much of it was about faraway spots and politics, if I recall correctly. I never knew her well."

Daniel remembered his mother enumerating the sights she'd seen in Jamaica or New York or some other far-flung destination. She always had a ready list, though he'd never gotten much sense of the feelings these places had evoked in her. She could go on and on, however, in a continuous, unvarying flow. When Daniel dropped a few details about his own life and interests into the conversation, she'd received them in the same manner, as if he was listing points in a school essay. She made him feel like some tedious acquaintance rather than family. As for his father, he'd clearly been more interested in pleasing his wife than in listening to his son. Together, they'd formed an outwardly cordial but ultimately impenetrable front.

He'd resented it, Daniel acknowledged, even more than he resented their constant travels. And so he'd begun avoiding Frithgerd and everything to do with it. Which had hurt only himself, in the end, he thought wryly. It had left him ignorant about his responsibilities when they fell upon him.

"I never spent much time around her," the earl went on.

It took Daniel a moment to remember that Macklin was speaking of his mother.

"They were married and came down here. After you were born the following year, they started traveling. It was difficult to catch a glimpse of John after that."

Daniel knew that problem all too well. He'd thought of himself as a boy at the mercy of a father with wanderlust. But was he instead the product of a woman who had produced an heir as required and then set off to do as she liked for the rest of her life? Regardless of what anyone else might have wanted?

He felt slightly dizzy, as if his brain was shifting inside his skull. In the confusion, something struggled to well up. It felt like danger.

He grew aware of his position, standing in the corridor outside the estate office, engaged in a conversation that ought to be private. He pushed his bewilderment aside. There was no point in repining. And there was so much to do. "If you'll pardon me, I should get back to work."

"Of course," said Macklin, stepping away.

Did he look smug? But why should he? Daniel went into the office and shut the door behind him. Immediately, he felt oppressed by the litter of documents. His grandfather had chosen precisely the right word, he thought. His heritage was undoubtedly a weight.

Five

FOYLE MANAGED TO FIND A SERVICEABLE, WELL-USED gig and a horse to pull it at a price that Penelope could afford. Driving up the lane from Rose Cottage some days later, she felt a mixture of elation and sadness. She always enjoyed handling the reins of a vehicle, even a humble one such as this. Yet she'd learned her driving skills from her brother, and now they reminded her of a bond and a life that were gone forever.

"We turn there." Kitty, who sat beside her, pointed left. They were headed for the village to stock up the larder.

"I thought it was straight ahead."

"Both of 'em lead there. This way's more interesting. Mr. Foyle told me."

Penelope shrugged and made the turn. Foyle had been tramping all around the neighborhood. He would know.

They tooled along between fields lush with summer. The wind of their passage ruffled the strings of Penelope's bonnet and cooled her cheeks. She realized that she hadn't coughed even once in two days. She felt better than she had in months.

They passed the corner of a high stone wall on the right. "It looks like there's an estate along here," Penelope observed.

Kitty nodded. "It's that Frithgerd place."

Penelope's hands jerked on the reins. The horse shied, puzzled. Penelope corrected.

"Frith." Kitty said it with a small spitting noise. "Funny old name. Betty claims the place is so grand. Better than anything in Manchester, she says. When she's never even been there. Or seen a town bigger than Derby." The young maid sniffed. "I'll see that for myself before I believe it, I told her."

"I don't want to go near Frithgerd." This wasn't strictly true. Penelope was curious about Lord Whitfield's seat, as she was about the man. She caught herself thinking of him all too often and wondering what he was doing. Which was why she should *not* lurk about his house as if hoping to see him. Could she turn the gig around in this narrow lane? Not easily.

"Not to go in, miss. Just driving by, like."

"We won't be able to see—" The gatehouse came into view. She couldn't turn now. Backing and edging would be far more obvious than moving quickly past.

"Slow down," Kitty urged. "We can look through the gates."

They were open. Curiosity warred with caution in Penelope, and as a result she neither slowed nor hastened. They rolled past the opening at a sedate pace.

"Heigh-ho!" called a male voice. A youth rose

from the sunny bench outside the gatehouse, where he'd been talking to an older woman. It was Tom, and his companion was Mrs. Darnell, who'd helped clean Penelope's house. Gatekeeper's wife, Penelope remembered. A compelling reason *not* to drive by Frithgerd like a stupid gawker.

Mrs. Darnell put aside the peas she'd been shelling and rose.

Penelope recognized that she had to stop. It would be the height of rudeness to drive by without a greeting. This woman had been kind to her, even if it was under orders.

"Got a gig, eh?" said Tom as he strode out to meet them. "Nice-looking animal." He patted the horse's neck.

Mrs. Darnell came out into the lane behind him. "Good day, miss."

"Hello, Mrs. Darnell. We're heading for the village shop you recommended. Just passing by."

Kitty craned her neck, trying to see the house through the gates.

"You'd have been better off taking Cob Lane," said Mrs. Darnell. "It's a mile farther this way."

It would be churlish to put the blame on Kitty. "I'm still learning my way about," answered Penelope. She gathered the reins. "It was good to see you, Mrs.—"

Her young companion jumped down and scurried over to the gates. "I'll just go to where I can see around those bushes," she said.

"Kitty!"

Tom went after her. When he reached her side, he pointed to some sight beyond Penelope's view.

Hoofbeats approached from behind the gig. Penelope prayed for strangers, but she wasn't surprised to find that it was Lord Whitfield and his distinguished houseguest. Her luck was running that way. They trotted up on a pair of glossy mounts that made her horse look shabby and stopped beside her equipage.

"You took my advice," said Whitfield, examining the gig as if its condition had anything to do with him.

"I followed my own plan," Penelope replied.

"You must come in and have some refreshment." Whitfield moved on as if she would of course follow.

For the first time, Penelope felt utterly humiliated by her new position in life. She'd taken much in stride, but to be discovered in front of his grand house, in her thirdhand gig, as if she'd been angling for an invitation, was mortifying. Lord Macklin's interested glance was not helpful. He gave an impression of sharp intelligence. It was all too likely he saw her chagrin. "No time, I'm afraid." She spoke briskly. "We're on the way...on an errand. Kitty!" She saw that Kitty and Tom had disappeared around a turn in the drive. Of course they had.

Whitfield looked back over his shoulder. "Surely you have a few minutes."

Drive on, abandoning her maid; sit here like a sulky child until Kitty returned; or give in? There was only one choice. Penelope turned her horse and maneuvered through the gates.

The first curve in the drive revealed the house. Frithgerd was a long, low building of gray stone, its roofline somewhat jumbled by additions over centuries, its walls mellowed by ivy. Mullioned windows gleamed in one wing.

Whitfield dismounted to hand Penelope down from the gig. The vehicle was taken to the stables, and he ushered her into a lofty hall with great, dark beams above and a flagstone floor. "This part is Tudor," he said. "On a cold day, you can burn a sizable tree in that fireplace and still not warm the room."

That had sounded disparaging, Daniel realized. He hadn't meant to be. The sight of Miss Pendleton at his gates had flustered him. He thought of her so often. He'd forced himself not to call at Rose Cottage. And then there she was. "There's a Van Dyck in the gallery," he heard himself add. What had become of his savoir faire?

"Miss Pendleton might be interested in your estate records," said Macklin.

Daniel frowned at him. He didn't want to show her that jumble. She'd think it a shambles. And she would be right.

"Oh, do you have anything about Rose Cottage?" she replied.

"Whitfield's been searching, but he hasn't found anything yet," said the earl.

"Perhaps I could help. I used to manage——" She stopped abruptly, her cheeks reddening.

"Ah" came to the tip of Daniel's tongue. But he managed not to say it. She used to manage what? He couldn't resist trying to find out. "Come and see," he said. With a bow, he escorted her along a corridor to the estate office. Only when they reached it did he notice that Macklin hadn't followed.

Fleetingly, he wondered if the older man was up to something. But Miss Pendleton's exclamation of "Oh my" chased the idea from his mind.

Inside the office, his visitor was standing still, surveying the masses of papers. "I'm not sure I understand your method of organization," she said.

Because there wasn't any, Daniel thought. As anyone could see. She didn't need to make a point of it. "Our agent left some months ago," he said.

Miss Pendleton walked over to the desk. She eyed the stacks of documents with an odd expression. She looked…avid? At once, Daniel dismissed this inadequate word. She looked like a drunkard gazing at a foaming pint. She looked like a sheepdog vibrating with the need to herd. Her fingers flexed. She wanted to plunge her hands into his papers, he realized. She wanted to wrest information from their pages like a falcon tearing into a mouse. Why had he ever thought her wan and sylphlike? "Perhaps you could help me look through things," he said.

She turned to him. Daniel was shaken by the flare of excitement in her blue eyes. How had he missed the fierce spirit inhabiting that slender body? And what might a man do to have that look directed at him? "There must be information about Rose Cottage here somewhere," she said. Her fingers twitched again.

It took him a moment to find his voice. "We might look for it together." From the way her gaze raked him, Daniel felt as if he'd suggested a far more intimate activity. Suddenly, his piles of papers seemed less of a burden. "I would appreciate your assistance," he added. "You seem as if you might know your way about a records room."

"I do." Two murmured words, yet full of longing and melancholy.

The quick rise and fall of her breath under the bodice of her gown was very distracting. Had she agreed or not? Her eyes burned. Daniel wanted to know what lay behind them. Would joy bloom there as fiercely as this present emotion? She stood very still, her fists closed at her sides. The work of sorting would be an altogether different matter with her at his side. "Our two families must have some connection," he said. "Or communication between them, at least. How else to explain the legacy?"

Miss Pendleton looked away, and he cursed himself for mentioning families. She'd made it clear she didn't want to talk about them.

She muttered something. It might have been "They'll find out anyway." If that made any sense.

"I beg your pardon?" said Daniel.

When she turned back to him, the fire had disappeared from her blue eyes. They'd gone bleak. "Haven't you made inquiries about me?"

He could see she hated the idea, and he wished he could deny it. Excuses crowded his mind, but none seemed persuasive in this moment, when his chief desire was to lure that fierce, vivid woman back into the light. He started to say that they'd heard nothing as yet. But she spoke again before he could.

"Lord Macklin looks like the sort of man who can find out whatever he wants. And do whatever he

wants. So do you, for that matter. Peers of the realm."
She spoke the last phrase with great bitterness.

Daniel felt as if he was feeling his way through a
pitch-black landscape. "Macklin knows a great many
people," he admitted.

"I'm sure he does. I suppose he's a great friend of
Lord Sidmouth."

"The Home Secretary?" Where had that venom
come from? And what did a government minister have
to do with anything? Daniel groped for something to
say, anything that might end the struggle racking her.
But nothing occurred to him. Perhaps because her
cheeks had flushed, and her chest continued to rise and
fall in a way that compelled his attention. He had to
keep tearing his gaze away.

Miss Pendleton's breath sighed out. Her shoulders
slumped. "Oh, what difference does it make?" Her
tone was angry and impatient. "It's only a matter of
time until you find out. I don't know why I thought
I could keep secrets." She raised her chin and stared at
him. "My father was Sir Jared Pendleton, baronet. He
had a place in Lancashire, where I grew up."

The last two sentences seemed at once jerked out of
her and practiced. As if she'd recited them many times
before in just that defiant manner.

"Papa died three years ago, and my brother, Philip,
came into his title."

The mysterious brother, who always caused her to
look resentful and desolate.

"But Philip…" Her brief silence seemed full
of heartache. She took a breath and gathered her
thoughts. "From the beginning then. Some years

ago, my father opened a small coal-mining operation on our land, as others had been doing. Philip was curious about the workings. He followed every step in the process. He used to visit the new factories in Manchester too, to see how they worked. Mechanical things always fascinated him."

She paused. Daniel nodded to show that he was listening. In fact, he was riveted. Not by the tale she was telling, which seemed mundane so far, but by her willingness to share it.

Miss Pendleton sighed again. "When Philip looked at these innovations, he didn't see ingenuity or financial opportunity, as some do. He saw a vast future of oppression. That was one of his pet phrases. He predicted a wave of ugliness about to break over our heads. People viewed as cogs and gears instead of individuals. An ocean of soot and smoke. He could be so eloquent, describing that scene. He gave one chills." She wrapped her arms around her ribs. "And he was determined to *do* something about it. Change is inevitable, he used to say, but the *direction* of change can be shifted. That was his obsession." She fell silent, as if she couldn't bear to go on.

Daniel waited. When she didn't speak, he said, "But then he died." She'd mentioned that her brother was dead. Bereavement didn't quite explain her silence, however. There was more to this.

"Before he was *murdered* last August at the Peterloo Massacre." Her eyes burned again, with a harsher light than before.

Daniel nearly took a step back under that glare. "Peterloo? The Luddite riot in Manchester?"

"It was a gathering to hear speeches about parliamentary reform."

"Sixty thousand men, didn't they say? That seems more like an insurrection."

"Unarmed men," she responded, though her face showed ambivalence. "And the government called in mounted cavalry to cut them down, as if Manchester was a battlefield and they were the enemy instead of English citizens."

"You were there?" Daniel was shocked at the idea.

"Of course not."

"But you're a radical."

"No." Miss Pendleton sank into the desk chair, suddenly looking very tired. "No, I'm not. Wasn't. Ever."

She leaned back, looking more like the exhausted young lady who'd first arrived at Rose Cottage than the vibrant creature who'd lusted after his documents.

"I wasn't like Philip," she continued. "I helped our local people without thinking too hard about the cause. Families starve, you know, when they lose their livelihood to the new machines."

"I have seen it," said Daniel. "So your brother was a Luddite?"

Miss Pendleton gave a toneless laugh. "If you knew how often I've heard that question. Did he join the frame-breakers, when did he, who are his associates? I don't think a baronet was the sort of man accepted into their secret circles, but I'm not sure. Philip didn't tell me anything."

"So you wouldn't be endangered," Daniel guessed.

"I'd like to believe he thought of me in that way. But I don't." The last word was clipped. She rubbed her forehead. "There was a long inquiry after Peterloo. Lord Sidmouth's agents are extremely... thorough. I was questioned at great length about my brother's activities. They found it difficult to believe that I knew nothing of them."

"Even though you gave your word?" Daniel hadn't expected anything like this. He didn't like to imagine her being accused. His feelings about the Manchester marchers were more complicated.

Miss Pendleton was staring at him as if he'd spoken in a foreign language. "My word?"

"That should have been enough."

"Should it?"

"Of course."

She blinked. "Well, it wasn't. Lord Sidmouth's people found my ignorance impossible to fathom. I had to assure them of it some hundreds of times before they were convinced." She shrugged. "Or gave up. They let me go anyway."

"Let you—"

"You may as well know everything," she interrupted. "I can have no more secrets. Philip was posthumously convicted of treason and stripped of his title and estates. Our home went to the government. I expect they've sold it by now." She gazed at the desktop. "Philip's home, really," she murmured. "I knew that. But I'd lived nowhere else." She raised her chin again. "So you asked about my family. That was it. I have none now."

They had this in common.

"It's a relief to have said it out loud," she went on, sounding surprised. "Rather than dodging people's questions, waiting for the story to come out." She sat straighter.

How could he ever have thought her a waif, Daniel wondered. She was as fiercely alert as the falcon he'd pictured earlier, unhooded now and poised to hunt. Her unveiled presence, her confidences, felt like a priceless gift.

"So does that give you your hoped-for connection between our families?" Her tone had gone satirical.

"I don't see how, no."

"Your father was not a Luddite?" She smiled.

Daniel was bowled over, rendered breathless by the first real smile she'd ever shown him. Previous stretches of her winsome lips had been polite fictions, he realized. Social masks to deflect questions. There was nothing insipid or vague in her pretty face now. It was a moment before he could say, "Papa was mostly out of the country. I don't think he was aware of developments in England." Daniel glanced at the masses of papers. "Even on his own estates. He certainly never spoke of politics. Neither did my mother."

Miss Pendleton gave him a look that said she appreciated this addition.

"I can ask Macklin. He might know more about my father's political views."

Some of her brightness dimmed. "I suppose you must tell other people what happened to me."

The fatalism in her voice bothered him.

"Of course you will do as you like," she added. "I'm in no position to impose conditions."

"You didn't do anything wrong."

"I didn't, but you will find that hardly matters. Once one is tainted with suspicion, even by association, people edge away. They assure each other that there's no smoke without fire, and other such idiotic analogies."

"Your friends didn't stand by you?" He felt a protective contempt.

She made a throwaway gesture. "Some were sympathetic, up to a point. But what was there to stand by? They were in Lancashire, and I…wasn't."

He saw her surrounded by suspicious officials, having lost the only home she'd ever known. Was she penniless? "They might have offered material help."

"I have ample funds." She snapped out the words.

Daniel had no doubt that *ample* was an exaggeration. But her face had closed. She wasn't going to discuss this topic. He left it, for now. "I won't tell anyone but Macklin," he said. "He'll need to withdraw his inquiries. But he won't spread the story."

She didn't look as if she believed him. The shields that had made him think her bland were snapping back into place. Daniel was surprised at how intensely he wanted the stooping falcon back. "So will you help me with this mare's nest of documents?"

He got his wish. Emotion flamed in her face. "You'd let me?" Her fingers moved as if to grasp the pages, then pulled back. "Even after what I've told you?"

"Of course. That makes no difference." The look of naked gratitude he received in return for these words rendered him mute.

"I helped my father manage his estate," Miss

Pendleton said. "He trained me, and I loved it. Philip was away at school and university and then off... wherever he went. Papa and I—" She closed her lips and blinked back tears. "You'd really trust me?"

The raw emotion in her face was too much all at once. Daniel waved at the various caches of papers. "I'm in dire need of aid." He went over to open a groaning wardrobe against the far wall. It released a cascade of pages that nearly knocked him down, and it wouldn't be closed again.

"Great heavens, this is years of stuff," said Miss Pendleton.

"You have no idea. More than twenty." Or fifty? Had his grandfather done better? Did he come from a long line of failed hoarders?

"But why didn't you... That is—"

She'd confided in him. She deserved some return for her openness. "My parents and I were...somewhat estranged."

"Oh."

"They told me nothing about Frithgerd, or anything else, really. As I mentioned, they were rarely in England."

She nodded. She was listening. She looked interested. There was no sign that she meant to cut him off with bored commonplaces. That ought to have made it easy to speak. Yet somehow it didn't.

"I responded in kind." He gazed at the mess surrounding him. "Cutting off my nose to spite my face, it seems now."

Miss Pendleton raised her eyebrows. Was she bewildered or disapproving? He couldn't tell. He was suddenly afraid to try. Instead, he gestured at the drift of paper that had fallen from the wardrobe. "You could come over whenever you like. The deluge is always here." That had sounded daft.

"Perhaps tomorrow."

His heart leapt. "Of course. Anytime you like."

"You'll be here?"

"I thought we would work together." Daniel pictured the two of them sitting side by side, heads bent together over...over desperately boring records and accounts. That part was too bad.

"Of course." She folded her hands like a child resisting a pile of sweets. "I wouldn't want to overstep. I understand that your information is confidential."

Had she wanted to be alone with his documents? The idea made Daniel weirdly jealous.

"Two o'clock then?"

He nodded as she stood.

"I should find Kitty now and finish my errands."

She turned to go, and he could only follow. That last bit hadn't gone well. Miss Pendleton seemed to have a different vision of their collaboration. But she'd be back tomorrow. That was the important thing. She'd be here, and he'd find a way to say some of the things that had refused to emerge.

Her gig was fetched, along with her wandering maid. Macklin reappeared for the farewells, and their charming visitor departed. Daniel watched until her carriage was no longer visible and then turned to his houseguest. "Come into the library," he said. "I have something to tell you."

The earl's expression grew more and more amazed

as Daniel told him what he'd learned about Miss Pendleton. "So there's no need to make further inquiries," he finished.

"If she was telling the truth," replied Macklin.

"Miss Pendleton is no liar!" The accusation incensed Daniel more than was reasonable.

"She seems sincere," the older man agreed, his thoughtful expression unaffected by Daniel's vehemence. "However, the government action against her brother that you describe is unusually harsh, particularly since he was dead. It suggests complications. Or enemies."

"Enemies," Daniel repeated.

"If he'd offended powerful people, she might shade the truth, out of fear."

Daniel remembered Miss Pendleton's bitter tone when she'd spoken of her questioners.

"The political situation is quite unsettled just now." Macklin looked grave. "Every radical reformer the government could put their hands on is in jail or transported. A few were hanged. His Majesty's ministers have not forgotten France and the guillotine. Workers in the new factories are particularly suspect. There are watchers all over the country."

"Lord Sidmouth's agents," replied Daniel, echoing the phrase she'd used during their conversation. It was true that he barely knew Miss Pendleton, but he hated the idea of doubting her.

"Public order is important," said Macklin.

"It is. But I never liked the idea of sending British troops against our own citizens."

Macklin shook his head. He pursed his lips, then

said, "I can't withdraw the inquiries I've sent out without rousing even more attention."

"I suppose not." Daniel moved restlessly.

"The replies might shed light on her brother's case. Perhaps for her as well, if he told her nothing."

"She said he didn't!"

"And I get no sense of deception from her," Macklin agreed. "She has no reason to trust us, however."

Daniel didn't like that idea either. "She will once she gets to know me. Us. She's going to help me organize the family papers."

"Really?" Macklin raised his eyebrows.

"We both want information about Rose Cottage." He refused to give up his plan. "There's nothing in Frithgerd's records to threaten the government. Rent rolls and deeds pose no danger."

"No. But she may bring trouble with her."

"Then we must help!" Daniel interrupted, swept by a fierce, protective anger. "My father—your old friend—left her a home. He would have wanted that."

"Mystery upon mystery," replied Macklin. "It's all very odd. We must feel our way."

Should they need a way into the government, there was no better man than Macklin, Daniel thought. They wouldn't, of course. Penelope Pendleton was an innocent. But once again, he was glad of Macklin's unexpected presence in his house.

Six

When Penelope entered Frithgerd the following afternoon, she was buzzing with anticipation. For as long as she could remember, she'd loved putting things to rights, bringing order to unproductive chaos, and ideally learning things as she worked. She'd discovered her talents alongside her father in his estate office. Fed by his praise for her efforts, her knack for organization had grown into a true skill. She knew how to do this, and she was good at it. One of the many strains of the last year had been having nothing to do. All the tasks that had brought her satisfaction had been taken away. But now she was being called into action again. And more. At Frithgerd, at any moment, she might turn over a page and solve the puzzle of her legacy.

The fact that Lord Whitfield would be working at her side had nothing to do with her excitement, she told herself. Well, next to nothing. Or nothing to the point. He *had* trusted her, as no one had done for a long time. She paused briefly to savor that fact. The look on his face when he'd assured her that she was needed had nearly made her cry.

The footman who was escorting her looked back over his shoulder.

Penelope started walking again. Thankfully, she'd resisted tears. What would Lord Whitfield have thought? And she expected he'd be more of a hindrance than a help in the actual task. The state of his records showed that he had no gift for organization. Yet her pulse sped up when she was admitted to the estate office and found him waiting there.

His smile lit his blunt-featured face. He looked wholeheartedly glad to see her. When had she last received such a welcome?

"Good day, Miss Pendleton. I've ordered tea and a plate of muffins to ease our labors." He indicated a tray, set atop a stack of papers as there was no clear spot for it. "Are you fond of muffins?"

Penelope felt her own smile spread over her face. She could sit down with him and drink tea and learn more about his history and opinions. She could laugh perhaps, or make him laugh. She could even flirt a little, as she'd done as a girl. Even though she was a girl no longer, irrespective of age. "Is there jam?"

"Assuredly there is jam." Whitfield glanced at the footman as the servant went out. "Leave the door open, Ned," he added.

The viscount was treating her as if she had a social position to lose. And with that courtesy, Penelope was reminded that she didn't. She had no family, no true friends, no standing. And she mustn't imagine that Lord Whitfield's politeness and curiosity about Rose Cottage changed anything fundamental in her life. Far better to concentrate on the task at hand

and find her pleasure there. "We should get started," she said.

"Drudgery first, muffins later?" he replied wryly.

She wouldn't have predicted it after their first meeting, but he had a beguiling charm—the sort you might not discover until you were waltzing with him, his dark eyes inches away, his hand warm on your back. Which she would never get to do, Penelope told herself severely. Why was she thinking of such a thing? What had become of her fabled concentration? "It's best to take a systematic approach," she said. "As a first step, we should be certain that all the records in the house are here."

Lord Whitfield looked around the cluttered office. "You want more than this?"

"It isn't a case of wanting." Penelope felt a curious catch in her chest on that last word. How long had it been since she had been allowed to want? She turned to the wardrobe with its cascade of documents. "It's so we can do a thorough job. There's nothing worse than putting things into perfect order, and then coming upon a pile that was left out."

"I can think of a few worse things," he replied, smiling again to show it was a joke.

Ignoring the yearning of her heart, Penelope said, "From what I've seen, I suspect your records may have been scattered about the house."

"We found an old deed in the epergne on the dining room table."

Penelope laughed. "So you should have the house gone over and all the papers brought here."

"We'll be buried in fusty old documents!" Whitfield

shook his head. "And I'm not going to be popular with my housekeeper."

"You may be surprised. If you tell her you're going to put it all in order and be rid of the clutter, I expect she'll be delighted."

"It's true she's wanted to clear out some bits. I couldn't let her throw anything away until I looked at it."

"You see."

"But *you're* going to put it in order," he said. "You promised."

"I thought you meant to help." Yesterday, she'd wanted to be left alone with the job. Now the idea that he might go filled her with dismay.

"Well, yes." He surveyed the papers as if they had a foul odor. "We'd better use the parlor next door for the rest."

"A splendid idea. In fact, we should set it up as our filing space. We can divide documents into chronological piles."

"Chronological," he repeated.

"By year," Penelope explained.

"I know what it means." He turned in a circle. "Boredom and dust, that's what it means."

"How can it be boring when you might discover just the fact you need at any moment? Or some fantastic nugget of your family history?" Penelope turned to the small bag she'd brought. "As for dust…" She took out two lengths of cloth.

"What are those?"

"Sleeve stockings."

"I beg your pardon?"

She pulled tubes of dark material over the sleeves of her dress. They reached well above the elbow and buttoned at the wrists.

"What the deuce?" said Daniel.

"They keep my gown clean when I work with old documents. Or other dusty things. My father's man of business told me about them. His clerks keep ink off their coats this way."

"Do they indeed?" He was smiling in a way that made her lips curve up in response.

"I know they look a bit odd, but they're much easier to clean than my gown. And if the laundress can't get out every speck, well, it doesn't matter, does it?" She held up her arms for his inspection.

She looked silly and adorable and supremely competent all at the same time, Daniel thought. It was a potent combination.

She sat down at the desk, picked up a sheaf of papers, scanned the top one, and then leafed through the rest. "Are these your lists?"

"Right," said Daniel, bringing his mind back to the tedious task at hand. He only got to sit with her if he went through the wretched records. "Things to do. I check off items as soon as they're accomplished."

She looked down and flipped through the pages again.

"Date at the top, you see, all right and tight," Daniel added. And remembered, for some reason, the Latin master at school who'd looked over his translations with sad compassion.

"These lists go back months, and the things to be done are the same. Except that there are more and more of them." Miss Pendleton gazed at him. "They all begin with *revise task list.*"

Daniel nodded. "Takes a deuced amount of time." Often it used the whole morning, and left him so irritated that he had to get out of the house.

"But do you actually *do* any of them?"

"Loads. Those lists are gone, because they're all checked off."

"I see."

She seemed to doubt him. Daniel started to defend himself, and then realized that his case was weak. "Sometimes I feel like that king—what was his name?—who tried to fight off the sea with his sword."

"Canute?" said Miss Pendleton. "I believe he was making a point about the impossibility of doing so. But my father was just the same. About papers, I mean, not the sea."

She gave him a look that warmed Daniel right down to his toes.

"That's why I started helping him," she went on. "The accounts in particular made him frantic. And Mama—who'd been managing a great deal of them— grew too ill to do much."

Her face had grown softer as she spoke of her family. Daniel could imagine her as much younger, eagerly shouldering one responsibility after another.

"I liked keeping order, and I could usually find the information that was needed or a missing key or a correspondent's address. Papa called me a marvel."

Her gaze was far away. Obviously, she was remembering some of the happiest moments of her life. She'd been a different creature before her brother's troubles engulfed her, Daniel concluded. He was moved by the picture of her basking in her father's praise. A sharp pang of envy muddled the feeling.

"I learned from our man of business when he visited, and the tenants. After a while, I could explain the more complicated matters to Papa." She looked up and seemed to recall her surroundings. Her expression shifted. "So, perhaps it's fortunate I'm here," she said briskly.

"It certainly is."

The warmth in his voice startled them both. Emotion suffused the room, like mist drifting across the surface of a secluded lake. Daniel's chest tightened. It was not harder to breathe. He was imagining that. Miss Pendleton had been speaking of other people, other places. Nothing to do with him. She'd be shocked to know what he was feeling. This… whatever it was, would be appreciated by no one. He knew that from long experience. Ancient resentments stirred; he squashed them. "I'll go and give the orders about gathering papers," he said.

"Yes." As if she couldn't sit still, Miss Pendleton rose and began picking up the papers that had flooded out of the wardrobe yesterday. "They should stack everything on the inner side of the parlor, away from the windows," she said without looking up.

"Stack," Daniel echoed. The word implied mountains of papers and was probably hideously accurate. He moved toward the door.

"So we can begin our files on the other side and keep everything straight."

"I took your meaning," he replied. He wasn't dim, Daniel thought. On the contrary, he was very clever about some things. Obsessive sorting wasn't a sign of intelligence. Look at squirrels. Resentment tried to rise in him again. There seemed to be quite a large amount of it, looming, powerful. Wanting nothing to do with the sensation, he stalked out. He would take his time speaking to his housekeeper, and he wouldn't return until he was utterly composed.

When the door of the estate office opened sometime later, Penelope turned eagerly. "Look at this!" She held up a parchment she'd unearthed. Curlicues of antique writing adorned it. There was even a tiny illumination in one corner.

"Something about Rose Cottage?" Lord Whitfield asked.

"No. It's a grant of advowson from 1634!"

"Advowson," he repeated.

"The right to recommend a clergyman for a vacant post, or to appoint him. The latter, in this case."

"Right. I knew that. Which living is it?"

She'd become so engrossed in the hunt that she'd forgotten the way he'd left, as if he couldn't wait to be gone. Awkwardness flooded back when he looked at the parchment as if it was just a scrap of paper. Her fervor ebbed. "Why there was a two-hundred-year-old grant here in the desk I can't imagine."

"Can't you?"

He had no reason to be distant. She hadn't done anything. In fact, she was helping him. And herself, of course. How long would it take to find the information she wanted in this jumble? "You should keep current matters close at hand and store older documents elsewhere."

"No doubt."

Penelope stifled an urge to hit him. "That method is sensible, you see, because the older ones are needed less often."

"Yes, Miss Pendleton, I do see. Anyone would. The idea is obvious."

"And yet never used at Frithgerd, as far as I can see."

"After an hour of rooting about." Whitfield looked stung, which was curiously satisfying.

"Long enough to discover a complete lack of organization."

He started to speak. Penelope braced for a setdown. Then he shrugged and gave her a rueful smile instead. "I know. Can a horror of paper be handed down in families, do you think?"

Penelope had to smile back. There was the charm again, flashing like a dark lantern flipped open in the night.

"There's probably some Greek word for it. There generally is. Papyrophobia? The oddest fears are named in Greek. Were they pigeonhearted, do you think?"

"They won the Trojan War."

He stared at her. She stared back. It was like looking into a mirror of feelings, Penelope thought. He looked startled and amused and speculative. Just as she did, she was certain. They shared a silent communion. Then he nodded. Acknowledgment or dismissal?

"Give me a task," he added. "I'll pitch in."

Work, they were here to work. "You could look through the pile around the wardrobe."

He groaned but went to do so. They sorted in silence for a while.

"Oh my." The exclamation escaped Penelope.

"What is it?"

"A loose page from an accounting in Latin. From 1296, if I'm reading it correctly. How far back does your family go at Frithgerd?"

Daniel gladly abandoned his litter of papers. "The tale is that a Norman lordling came along after the Conquest and married a Saxon girl to get a chunk of the land hereabouts. He even took her name to ingratiate himself with the locals, since the Friths were so well established. He was a clever fellow or a greedy invader, depending on the side you take. There's a bit of the Saxon stonework left in the east wing."

"Really?"

He nodded. "Would you like to see it?" Daniel stepped closer. Viewing would entail a walk outside, which seemed like a godsend.

"Perhaps another time."

"Architecture doesn't interest you as much as documents?"

"No," she said absently. "Though I don't suppose the records go back nearly that far."

With a sigh, Daniel returned to his designated litter of papers. "I can only hope," he said. "Mrs. Phipps, my housekeeper, told me that there are trunks of records in the attics. I think she was keeping that from me to save my sanity."

Miss Pendleton laughed. It was a delightful sound, lilting and musical. If he could make her laugh, perhaps he could endure the sorting, Daniel thought. "She wondered if we wanted them down here *in all their dirt*," he continued.

"Of course we want them!"

"Just what I told her. They're putting the trunks in the blue parlor."

Miss Pendleton actually rubbed her hands together. They were dusty, Daniel noticed, and those odd sleeve covers hadn't prevented the skirts of her gown from acquiring a streak.

"I saw your father's will," she said.

It was on top of the desk, so of course she had. "It's not informative about Rose Cottage, as I'm sure you noticed."

She nodded. "It's so strange that there are no other documents about the place."

"I looked."

"Of course."

Her tone was…condescending? His family's disorganized papers had given her a false impression of him, Daniel thought. He was capable, just not an antiquarian. As he'd be more than happy to show her. Various improbable heroic deeds filled his brain.

"Was the cottage always part of your estate, or was it purchased at some point?" Miss Pendleton mused.

Daniel took the question as it was meant, rhetorically.

"There ought to be a history of the estate, with maps showing the original boundaries and any changes over the years. I compiled a volume of boundaries and deeds for Papa." She broke off, suddenly melancholy.

How would he feel if Frithgerd was suddenly gone? Despite Daniel's difficulties with his parents, it would be like losing a limb. She hadn't stood to inherit her father's estate of course, but she'd obviously loved her home. Daniel thought her dead brother must have been either a blackguard or a complete idiot.

❧

Three floors above, in the attics of Frithgerd, a great winnowing was taking place. Trunks and boxes were opened, examined, and left in place or hauled downstairs, according to their contents.

Kitty, Betty, and Tom had come along to help, one on orders and the other two out of curiosity.

Tom turned to discover two female rumps in the air as the girls rummaged through a trunk, skirts pooled on the dusty floor around them. They presented a striking contrast, Betty's figure plump and well rounded, Kitty's on the scrawny side. Tom took in an appreciative eyeful, then looked away.

"His lordship's taking a deal of trouble for your young lady," Betty said. "You think he's sweet on her?"

"Might be," replied Kitty, her voice somewhat muffled by the depths of the trunk. "How would I know?"

"You see them together when he visits."

"He didn't bring her flowers or nothing," said Kitty. "Is this a hat?"

"I still think he'll wed a grand lady from London," said Betty. "Daughter of a duke or some such thing. With bride clothes from the very best places. And a dresser who knows all the tricks."

"But not too grand to teach you," replied Kitty.

"I'll make sure she takes to me."

The two girls straightened, each holding a large hatbox.

"Lord Macklin's a dab hand at matchmaking," said Tom.

"The old lord?" said Betty. "I wouldn't think he'd take an interest."

"You'd be surprised."

The girls turned to look at him. "How'd you come to work for him?" Betty asked. "And what d'you do anyhow? Nobody belowstairs can figure."

"I make him laugh, mostly. I think he's lonely since his wife died."

"Don't he have any family?" asked Kitty.

"He does, but he says his children are right busy. He's taken me on like one of them court jesters, I reckon."

"A what?" Betty frowned up at him.

"I saw one in a pantomime in Bristol," Tom went on. "They dance around with bells and make jokes."

"You do that?" Betty gaped at him.

Tom looked contemptuous. "'Course not. But I'm not like anybody he's ever known, see. He's curious."

"You like being treated that way?"

"I don't mind. He's kind about it. And I get to see and do a mort of things I never would have otherwise. I'll move on after a bit."

"Where?" asked Kitty.

Tom shrugged. "Wherever I like. America maybe."

"It's full of wild Indians! And panthers."

"What a load of nonsense."

"There are!"

"Not in New York or Boston, which is where I'd land." Tom looked speculative. "Maybe I'd go and look for the wild Indians." He eyed the hatboxes. "You know there's no papers in them boxes, right?"

"We have to look everyplace," Betty replied. She and Kitty exchanged a glance and giggled.

They set the boxes down and opened them. Unsurprisingly, they contained hats, which the two girls promptly donned. Betty grinned from under the wide brim of a confection adorned with ribbons, feathers, and artificial flowers. A similar hat, with the addition of a stuffed bird perched on top, fell down over Kitty's nose, covering her forehead and eyes. "Whoever owned this 'un must have had a head like a pumpkin," she declared.

A footman passed by, returning for another trunk to haul downstairs. "What the deuce are you doing, Betty Fancher?" he said.

"Just checking boxes, Ned. As ordered."

"Dressing up ain't checking." Ned glared at Tom. "Being led astray by a vagabond, more like."

"Don't be daft," answered Betty. "He's just a lad."

"He's big enough to help carry, instead of larking around with you. *If* he wants to help, that is." The footman's tone suggested deep doubt.

"I don't mind," said Tom amiably. He moved to join Ned.

"I can't get this off," cried Kitty. "Somethin's stuck."

Betty set her hat back in its box and went to assist. She tugged at Kitty's hat.

"Ow! Ow! Ye're tearing my hair out by the roots."

Tom and Ned stepped closer. "It shouldn't ought to stick," said Ned. He grasped the brim and yanked.

Kitty shrieked.

Ned let go as if the hat had burned him and jumped back.

"Lemme see," said Tom.

"As if you'd know anything," said Ned.

"Sit down," Tom told Kitty.

"I can't *see*," she moaned.

"Here." Betty guided her over to a trunk and eased her down.

"Now then." Tom bent over the offending hat. He ran nimble fingers over the surface, peering beneath silk flower petals and lengths of ribbon and the feathers of the bird. "Ah." He reached, pulled, and withdrew a hatpin from the crown—eight inches of steel with a small golden ball at one end and a lethal point at the other. "Wait," he said. Further probing turned up another pin, just the same. "Try now," he said.

Kitty raised her arms and gently pulled. The hat came off, revealing her red and tearful face. A folded sheet of paper fell onto the floor.

"That was clever," said Ned. He gazed at Tom with new respect.

Kitty shoved the hat at Betty, who set it back in its box. Tom showed Kitty the pins before handing them to Betty so she could replace those as well, and then he picked up the fallen page.

"All papers to go downstairs," said Ned. He took the paper and dropped it into a nearby box waiting to be carried down.

"That was worse than a panther," said Kitty, smoothing down her hair.

Seven

In the kitchen of Rose Cottage, Kitty held up a small, brown oval. "What's nutmeg?" she asked. Her pointed face creased in a grin. "Could be a lass selling roast chestnuts. Getcher nuts from Meg in Market Square."

Penelope smiled. "It's a spice," she replied. "To flavor food."

"And that one needs to be grated," added Mrs. Hart. She handed Kitty the proper utensil.

Kitty held the nutmeg in one hand and the bit of perforated metal in the other, looking back and forth.

"Rub it across," said Mrs. Hart. "Here. I'll show you." She demonstrated the grating process. "All of it, mind. We don't want any waste."

The small, sturdy lady who came in half days to cook at Rose Cottage was a fanatic on this point. Penelope admired her iron frugality, particularly because it never compromised the luscious taste of her dishes.

Mrs. Hart put half a cinnamon stick in the mortar. "If you'd like to pound this out to a powder, miss," she said to Penelope. "Though I can easily do it."

She never quite believed that Penelope wanted to learn to cook with her own hands. Eventually, she'd convince her. Penelope took up the pestle and began to pulverize the cinnamon. Sweet scents wafted through the room.

"Ow!" cried Kitty. "This dratted thing bit me." She held up a bleeding finger.

Penelope watched Mrs. Hart restrain her impatience. Kitty was clumsy in the kitchen, from lack of ability or lack of experience, Penelope wasn't sure which. She knew Mrs. Hart often snatched an assigned task away from the girl and did it herself. Not when Penelope was present, since she knew Penelope wanted Kitty to learn. But she'd heard other exchanges. Their cook was a much better practitioner than teacher and struggled to endure mistakes, her professional pride warring with her natural kindness.

There was a delay while Kitty's finger was bound up, and then a muttered argument when the girl insisted she would keep on grating the nutmeg. Mrs. Hart very much wanted to take over, but at last she gave in. Kitty went back to it with exaggerated care.

Some minutes later, Mrs. Hart poured the prepared spices into a sieve with a pound of sugar. "Now we sift these together, miss." She held the sieve over the worktable and tapped the edge. "They should be well mixed, so the flavors are spread through the dough."

Sugar and spices rained down in an aromatic mélange.

"You can fetch three eggs and break them into that little bowl," Mrs. Hart said to Kitty. The cook kept sifting as Kitty obeyed. "Watch for bits of shell," she added.

On several occasions, Kitty had left a few when she cracked eggs. She peered into the bowl and fished some out. Penelope was glad to see that she didn't use her bandaged finger.

"Do you have that rosewater, miss?" asked Mrs. Hart.

"Yes, it's here." Penelope held up the bottle she'd procured at the farm where she bought milk and eggs. The farmer's wife had a notable stillroom as well.

Mrs. Hart nodded approval. "Pour a bit in with the eggs, and beat them."

"How much?" Penelope asked.

"Just a dollop."

Penelope hesitated, added a splash, then a bit more, before starting to beat the mixture.

The back door opened. Foyle looked in, then retreated with a disappointed expression. Penelope had noticed that her manservant hung about the kitchen when Mrs. Hart was here alone, but never when Penelope was having a lesson. She suppressed a smile and kept beating.

Mrs. Hart added her sifted ingredients to a large mixing bowl of fine flour and stirred it all together. She gestured with her wooden spoon, indicating that Penelope should put in the eggs, which she did. They were stirred in.

"Bring over our melted butter, Kitty," said the cook. "Carefully now."

The young maid used a corner of her apron to grasp a saucepan on the hob, carrying it as if the liquid butter might leap out and burn her at any moment. She set it on the worktable with visible relief.

"Perhaps you could pour some in the bowl, miss," said Mrs. Hart with a sigh in her voice.

Penelope wrapped a cloth around the hot handle and picked up the pan. "All of it?"

"No, miss. We want just as much as will make it a good thickness to roll out. Perhaps half at first." Penelope poured. The cook stirred. "A bit more," she said. "There, that's it."

"How can you tell?" asked Penelope. The dough looked the same to her.

"By the feel."

"May I try?"

Mrs. Hart handed over the spoon. Penelope stirred, trying to memorize the texture. She wasn't certain she succeeded.

The cook molded the dough into a loaf shape. "We'll let it sit for a little while before we roll it thin. Then your Shrewsbury cakes can be cut it into whatever shapes you like."

Kitty's eyes brightened. "Goats?" she asked. "Or lions?" She clapped her hands. "We could make them like Jip and Jum."

"The dogs may *not* come in as models," said Penelope, earning a grateful glance from Mrs. Hart. They were of one mind on the dogs' place in the household—outside, charming as they were. Kitty held to the other side of the issue and couldn't be trusted to heed the rules.

"You can cut them," said Mrs. Hart, forestalling disappointment. "Whatever shapes you like."

Penelope nodded. A beaming Kitty went to fetch the rolling pin and a paring knife, only to be diverted by a knock at the front door.

"I'll go," said Penelope.

"I should do it, miss."

"Never mind." Forestalling argument, Penelope went out and opened the door. Lord Whitfield stood on her threshold, looking powerfully athletic in a blue coat and buff riding breeches. Penelope was suddenly conscious of some streaks of cinnamon on her apron. She could feel that the heat of the kitchen had caused her hair to droop about her ears.

"Good day, Miss Pendleton," said Daniel. He'd expected to be greeted by the maid and to ask if her mistress was free. Perhaps these social conventions made no sense in such a small dwelling. Should he have sent a note asking to call? He hadn't really considered, he'd been so eager to see her.

Clearly he'd chosen an inopportune moment, because Miss Pendleton had flour on her nose. Daniel felt a nearly irresistible impulse to pull out his handkerchief and wipe it off. But he stayed his hand. She wouldn't like that. Better to ignore the smudge. Instead he took a folded sheet of paper from his inner pocket. "One of the shelves in that wardrobe collapsed. We have another flood of paper, I'm afraid. But this conveyance was caught in a crack at the back. My great-great-grandfather bought Rose Cottage about a hundred years ago."

"Really?" Her blue eyes lit in the way that always shook him as she took the page, opened it, and began to read. "What crabbed handwriting."

"Shall we go in?"

"Oh, of course." She moved back, and Daniel followed her into the parlor. She sat down, all attention on the document. He took the armchair. There was a spot of flour on the back of her hand as well. She looked utterly charming in an apron. The house smelled sweetly of spice.

"It doesn't say why he bought the cottage from this Addison."

"No. I expect the opportunity simply arose. My great-great-grandfather extended the estate in several directions. He was a notorious nipfarthing. Spent every penny he could scrape together on land."

She nodded and read on to the end. "I don't see how a transaction in 1713 can have anything to do with me."

"No," he replied, carefully not looking at the smudge on her nose.

"Still, it's a step along the way in solving our mystery."

"Yes."

"And it does tell us that the cottage wasn't part of your ancestral heritage, which would make it easier to give away, I imagine." She looked pleased with that idea.

"A good point."

"What *is* the matter?" she asked.

"The—?"

"You keep looking at me sideways."

"You have flour on your nose," Daniel admitted.

"My *nose*?" She swiped at it, merely spreading the smudge. "Why didn't you say so?"

"I didn't want to embarrass you."

"It's more embarrassing to know it was there all this time. Is it gone now?"

"Not quite." Daniel got out his handkerchief and offered it to her.

Miss Pendleton rubbed off the smudge. "Thank you." Handing back the square of cloth, she seemed to notice her apron. "Oh." She stood, untied the strings, and set it aside. "I was having a lesson with Mrs. Hart this morning."

"Mrs. Hart?"

"The kind neighbor who comes in to cook for us."

"Ah."

A burst of Kitty's giggles came from the kitchen. "That's daft-looking, that is," she said.

"We were making Shrewsbury cakes."

"*You* were?" Daniel asked.

Something in the question seemed to annoy her. "Why shouldn't I? I'm not a grand noble. I have a small household to run."

"I didn't mean…" Daniel cast about for words. "That chocolate cake you served on our first visit was as fine as anything my cook makes at Frithgerd."

Miss Pendleton gave him a rueful look, then burst out laughing. "Your cook *did* make it. It was in a hamper of food you had sent over when I arrived."

Her eyes crinkled up when she laughed. Humor lit her face in a way that made the whole room seem brighter. She didn't laugh nearly enough. He joined in. "That's why the taste was familiar."

"That sort of cake is beyond my skills so far. I'm starting smaller."

"I'm very fond of Shrewsbury cakes," he insinuated.

"I'd offer you some, but they're not baked yet."

"Perhaps I could help." He'd never had any interest

in cooking before, but this entrancing young lady had altered his views on a number of things.

"*You?*"

He waited, and then enjoyed seeing her realize that she'd used the same incredulous tone he'd employed. She smiled at him. Daniel's pulse began to race. What a fool he'd been to think her wan and sylphlike. She…glowed.

"Certainly *Lord* Whitfield," Miss Pendleton said. "I'll find you an apron." She picked up her own, put it on, and led him to the kitchen.

Mrs. Hart dropped a scandalized curtsy at their entrance. "My lord."

"Lord Whitfield is interested in how Shrewsbury cakes are made," said Miss Pendleton as she walked into the pantry. Her teasing tone clearly shocked the cook.

The young maid, oblivious, pointed at some blobs of dough lined up on a metal baking tray. "Mine are a right mess. Mrs. Hart's going to roll them out again so's I can make another try."

"We don't seem to have a fourth apron," said Miss Pendleton, reemerging. "You could have mine." Her eyes brimmed with humor.

"I wouldn't dream of depriving you," replied Daniel, trying to conceal his relief. Unsuccessfully, her expression told him.

"We can't have flour on your fine coat."

"We won't be getting any flour on his lordship," said Mrs. Hart firmly. With the air of a long-suffering parent marshaling her brood, she added, "Give me those, Kitty."

Kitty gathered up the blobs and passed them over. With a few deft strokes, Mrs. Hart rolled the dough out flat.

"We can each cut the shapes we like," said Miss Pendleton. "You must give us our own bits of dough to work with, Mrs. Hart."

The cook rolled out more and arranged three, not four, stations along the kitchen table. She distributed small paring knives, then stepped back to check the brick oven in the side of the fireplace.

"I've ordered the closed stove," said Miss Pendleton as they lined up to address the dough. "It should be here in a week or two."

"That'll be grand, miss," replied Mrs. Hart. She seemed uncomfortable with her ill-assorted staff.

"Knives at the ready," said Miss Pendleton. She held hers upright, like a fencing foil. Kitty giggled.

"Is it a race?" asked Daniel.

"An artistic competition. Mrs. Hart will judge which of us does best."

"Not me, miss," said the cook, holding up her hands, palms out.

"Well, we'll fight for the prize among ourselves." Miss Pendleton waved her knife in a little flourish. "And begin!"

They bent over the dough. Daniel decided he'd make scalloped edges with a circle inscribed in the middle. He'd had some Shrewsbury cakes like that once. But the plan was more easily imagined than done. This wasn't like drawing. The blade tended to drag the dough out of shape. His scallops were unsatisfactory. He glanced to the side. Young Kitty was frowning over more incomprehensible blobs. Miss Pendleton was cutting simple stars. Neat, straight lines were clearly a good idea, Daniel realized, as he watched her set her knife, cut, and then push sideways, easing the dough apart. He wished he'd thought of that. He noticed a smudge of flour on his coat sleeve.

Miss Pendleton glanced up, saw him looking, and smiled.

How many smiles did she have in her repertoire? This one was easy, mischievous, literally breathtaking. For a moment, Daniel's chest locked.

"Hellish thing," muttered Kitty. "That's no manner of tail."

A clatter from the hearth suggested that Mrs. Hart had dropped a sizable object.

Miss Pendleton's dancing eyes invited him to share in her enjoyment. Daniel's spirit expanded, and he smiled back wholeheartedly. Perfect understanding seemed to tremble between them, like a hovering kestrel ready to strike. Then she blinked, looked away, and turned back to her stars. Daniel's hand was the slightest bit unsteady when he addressed his scallops of dough once more. Perhaps he'd call them waves, he decided—tossed by a turbulent sea.

When they finished, Miss Pendleton was unanimously judged the winner, though Kitty complained that she would have gotten her dogs' ears right if she'd had more time. Daniel tried to see any trace of hound anatomy in her creations, and failed.

They put the baking in the oven. Daniel realized that he'd been at Rose Cottage far too long for a courtesy call. And he'd promised to ride out with

Macklin and show him a scenic overlook. "I must go," he said.

"You won't wait to taste your creations?" asked Miss Pendleton.

"I fear I can't. I have an appointment with Macklin."

"Too bad. We'll send your…waves up to Frithgerd. As a return for the cake." Her eyes glinted.

"Will you bring them?"

The words came out urgent. She looked startled.

Daniel moderated his tone. "Aren't you coming tomorrow to continue working in the estate office?"

"Yes."

"Well then." Daniel brushed at the flour on his sleeve as he walked around the kitchen table. Miss Pendleton followed him to the back door. "I'll go out this way to get my horse," he added.

"I suppose you took it to the barn when you arrived," said his hostess. "I hope Foyle tended to it."

"He said he would."

"With poor grace, I suspect. What a ramshackle household I have."

"I had a splendid time," Daniel said. It was true. This was the most fun he'd had in months. Perhaps ever? "Far better than a *ton* party."

Miss Pendleton raised her eyebrows, incredulous.

"I'm perfectly serious."

"Then you are perfectly silly. You cannot compare *this* to a brilliant drawing room and fashionable entertainments." She gestured at the bits of dough and scattered kitchenware.

Standing in the doorway, Daniel surveyed the

scene. Kitty, her apron festooned with swirls of brown and white, was grinning at them. Mrs. Hart had her back turned, but her stillness indicated a keen interest in their exchange. "Hostesses are always searching for ways to be original," he said. "But it's the quality of the conversation that distinguishes a society gathering, don't you think?"

"I don't know. I've never attended one."

"I didn't think you could have," said Daniel.

She stiffened. "Am I so rag-mannered?"

He shook his head. "I would have remembered you if you'd had a season in London." Satisfied with the effect of this remark, he bowed and went out.

Penelope watched the door close, hiding those intense brown eyes and the look in them that made her knees tremble. She turned to find Kitty gazing at her like an alley cat that had discovered a fish. Mrs. Hart, on the other hand, looked concerned. "We should tidy up," Penelope said.

"I'll do that, miss," replied the cook.

"I'll help."

Mrs. Hart held up an impervious hand. "Give me that apron, and go sit down. In a bit, I'll bring tea and some of your cakes."

"The ones I cut." She needed the wavy ones to take to Frithgerd.

Scraping dough from the table surface, Mrs. Hart spoke without looking up. "Yes, miss."

"And some of mine," said Kitty. "I wonder what Jip and Jum will think of them?"

"Don't you be giving pastry to those dogs," replied the cook. "What did I tell you?"

"I was only going to *show* them," replied Kitty, convincing no one.

Penelope left her apron and went to sit in the parlor. Had she actually been baking with a viscount? She smiled, recalling his arguments in favor of his misshapen Shrewsbury cakes. It had been fun. She couldn't remember when she'd enjoyed herself more. He'd brought excitement and laughter to her kitchen. He'd treated her like a…friend.

Penelope's mood plummeted.

What she was feeling wasn't wise. Her family was disgraced, her status ambiguous at best, tainted at worst. She was no partner for a peer. Very soon he must realize it, too. Unless he had some illicit connection in mind.

A hideous vision assailed Penelope—the viscount's mistress lurking in Rose Cottage like some latter-day Fair Rosamund in the bower. Whispers wherever she went, snubs and snide insinuations. Who would come with the dagger and the poison and offer her the choice?

"Don't be ridiculous," she said aloud. Gripping the chair arms, she added, "Idiotic."

He wasn't like that. He'd been unfailingly polite and respectful. And should he show any signs of misbehavior, which he would *not*, she'd refuse, naturally. And that would be the end of it. This was real life, not a medieval legend.

The trouble was, she didn't want to see the end of it. She wanted their association to continue, even though there was nowhere that it could possibly go. She wanted to laugh with him again, to learn more about him. Even perhaps to touch? Penelope remembered a saying her father had used when she and Philip were small. "This will end in tears."

She rose. "I'm going to take the dogs for a walk," she called and hurried out, forgoing bonnet and shawl. The dogs were delighted to see her, and she worked off her excess energy by pacing the back of the Rose Cottage property and then throwing sticks for them until they lay at her feet, panting in exhaustion.

Eight

IN THE WEE HOURS OF THE MORNING, AT THE TAIL
end of a wakeful night, Penelope decided not to
resist temptation. Why should she? What did she
have to lose? The ruin of her family had few advan-
tages, but one was that she didn't have to worry
about losing her position in society. That had already
gone up in smoke. She wanted to see Whitfield. She
wanted information that must be buried in his estate
records. She was going to get what she wanted.

And so she wrapped Lord Whitfield's Shrewsbury
cakes in a napkin, put them on the seat of her gig, and
set out for Frithgerd alone at the appointed time the
next day. A gray sky threatened rain, clouds scudding
through damp air. Birdsong was muted, making the
clop of her horse's hooves and the rattle of the wheels
seem louder.

Tom was at the gatehouse again, standing on the
bench this time, repairing a broken shutter for Mrs.
Darnell. The lad waved when Penelope turned in.
"Could I come along with you, miss?" he asked. "I need
more nails. I can take the gig around to the stables."

Penelope pulled up, transferred the napkin to her lap, and let him climb in. "You're often at the gatehouse," she observed when they were underway.

"Just helping out while Mr. Darnell is laid up."

"The gatekeeper? Is he ill?"

"Wrenched his back," Tom replied, his homely face solemn. "Feels like knives stabbing into his entrails, he says."

"Oh dear."

"He says it's happened before, and it gets better in a week or so if he don't move about."

"Is there no one else to help him?" On such a large estate, couldn't Lord Whitfield find someone other than a stranger to aid his gatekeeper?

"Loads of people," said Tom. "But I like to keep busy, same as you."

"Me?" Penelope was startled by this personal comment.

"I beg your pardon, miss. I didn't mean to presume."

"No, it's all right. I'm not offended. I do like to keep busy. I'm just surprised you noticed."

"Mr. Clayton reckons you know how to run a big house and don't have half enough to do at Rose Cottage."

"Does he?" Penelope was beginning to be amused. "Who is Mr. Clayton?"

Tom looked chagrined. "Done it again," he muttered. "Running my mouth. Hanging about with a lord is giving me bad habits." He hunched a shoulder. "Mr. Clayton is Lord Macklin's valet, miss."

"Ah. Not part of the Frithgerd household then."

"No."

"I suppose Lord Whitfield's servants wonder why I'm there so often." It was just as well to know the opinion of the staff, Penelope thought. Though she wasn't going to let it dictate her actions.

"Clearing up a mort of muck, Mrs. Phipps the housekeeper says." Tom ducked his head. "Not in just those words, miss. But she's right glad to have some bits set in order. I heard her tell Mr. Clayton the place ain't had a proper mistress in an age. Not since she was a girl fresh come to service thirty years ago."

"But Lady Whitfield died quite recently," said Penelope. Hadn't it been less than a year since the shipwreck that took Whitfield's parents?

Tom shrugged. "Dunno what she meant by it, miss," he said. "She did say it was a blessing that somebody was finally *paying attention*."

They had reached Frithgerd's front door. Penelope pulled up, handed over the reins, and climbed down with the wrapped cakes in hand. She'd expected a rather different reaction from the servants here. To be seen as a blessing was surprising, and surprisingly gratifying. She found she was smiling as she knocked on the front door.

It was opened by a man dressed as a valet. Oddly, Lord Macklin was with him. This, then, must be the Mr. Clayton who had so many opinions about her.

"Good morning, Miss Pendleton," said the earl, imperturbable, as if he often played footman at great houses. "Did you see Tom when you passed the gatehouse?"

"I did. He rode up with me and was kind enough to take my gig to the stables."

"Ah. Thank you. You've saved Clayton a walk." He nodded at the valet, who went out as Penelope came in. "On your way to the estate office," the older man added. It could have been a question, but wasn't.

"I am," answered Penelope. She moved on, and wasn't pleased when the earl came with her. Glancing over at him, she suddenly realized one reason he made her uncomfortable. He reminded her of the magistrate who'd first questioned her last summer at her home in Lancashire—the one who'd brought her the news of her brother's death. He had the same square jaw and broad brow, the same authoritative manner, as if command was as natural and unconscious as breathing.

"And you've brought a gift," he said, with another nod at the folded napkin she carried.

She wouldn't be intimidated. "Shrewsbury cakes."

"Indeed?"

He sounded benignly curious, but Penelope remembered how an innocuous tone could grow gradually harsher as the questions continued. And end in venom.

"I'm fond of Shrewsbury cakes," he said after a short silence.

Penelope kept walking. What did he want? She wasn't going to offer him one of the oddly shaped pastries she carried. Why was this corridor so very long?

"May I speak to you for a moment, Miss Pendleton?" he asked.

She froze. Mild phrases like that one had begun some of the most grueling sessions with Lord Sidmouth's men. "About what?"

"Nothing in particular. Merely to get better acquainted."

This earl wanted to stand about in a hallway, with her clutching a knotted napkin, and exchange pleasantries?

As if he knew how unlikely that sounded, Macklin made a dismissive gesture. "And about Whitfield. His situation. And yours."

"Situation?"

The older man looked vexed. Now it would start, Penelope thought. He would insinuate or accuse, and when she answered, he would twist her words. Such men always assumed the worst, and then used it against you.

"I'm not putting this well," Macklin said. "I don't suppose you'd like to go and sit. No, I can see that you wouldn't."

False sympathy. Did he imagine she hadn't seen it before?

"I became acquainted with Whitfield because I grew interested in the many forms of grief."

What sort of trick was this? Penelope wondered.

"And hoped to be of help, as I've experienced a good dose of it myself," he added.

This wasn't what she'd expected.

"You've heard that he lost his parents? In a shipwreck?"

She nodded.

"A sudden death is a great shock. As you must have felt."

Penelope stiffened. Here it was. "Lord Whitfield told you about my brother."

"He did."

"Must I say it again? I knew nothing about his activities or associates or political writings. Yes, it is strange that two people living in the same household could be so separate. But we were!" She bent her head. "As I was sad to discover." She'd regretted that distance in so many ways, not least in her failure to understand her only brother.

Lord Macklin took a step back. "I beg your pardon."

Penelope looked up, surprised. Where was the doubt, the barrage of questions?

The earl bowed. "I've upset you. Forgive me."

None of her questioners had asked forgiveness.

"I won't keep you any longer."

She hesitated briefly, not daring to believe, then turned and hurried along to the door of the estate office. "Good day, Lord Macklin," she said, and entered the sanctuary of the estate office.

The older man stayed where he was, pensive. Clayton found him there some minutes later. "I sent Tom off with the message," he said.

"Good. Thank you, Clayton." He still didn't move.

"Something wrong, my lord?"

"My conversations with Miss Pendleton don't go well."

"What are you aiming at, my lord?"

"That's the problem, isn't it? I'm not sure I know."

"She seems like a pleasant enough young lady," answered the valet. "The servants here say she's quality."

"But does she add up?"

"My lord?"

Arthur sighed. "I suspect she's been treated shabbily, and I'm sorry for that. But I'm really here for Whitfield. I'd like to see him happy. Is she the sort to make him so?"

"You should receive replies to your letters soon," said Clayton.

"Yes." Arthur gazed at the closed door of the estate office as he tried to be satisfied with this.

⁓

"They taste good even if they look ridiculous," said Daniel on the other side of the panels. He took a second bite of a Shrewsbury cake that he'd shaped so ineptly. The room seemed different with Miss Pendleton installed in a chair beside his at the desk. Fresh and lovely in a blue cambric gown, she transformed it from a place of dry drudgery to a chamber full of possibility. She'd seemed harried when she first came in, but the sight of his documents, and the donning of her oddly charming dust sleeves, had visibly settled her.

She finished her cake. "That's the great thing about pastry," she said. "It's still delicious even when you've sat on the box. Although eclairs are rather a challenge in that regard."

Daniel raised an eyebrow. "That sounds like wisdom drawn from direct experience."

Miss Pendleton nodded. "The…rather squashed-looking Shrewsbury cakes reminded me."

"I must hear the story."

Her smile was pensive, a little distracted. "As a special treat, my mother and I sometimes visited a bakeshop in a town near where we lived. Mama used to say the owner was an artist of the oven. On this particular day, I insisted on carrying the box with its wonderful pink string. I was so proud, like an altar boy bearing the chalice." She glanced at him. "I was four years old, you understand. I put the box on the seat of the carriage while I climbed up. Mama stepped in after me and sat on it." She shook her head. "I hadn't thought of that in ages."

Daniel imagined how his own austere mother would have reacted to this misstep. "Was she annoyed?"

"Oh, worse than that."

He had visions of a thundering scold, even a boxed ear.

"She burst into tears," said Miss Pendleton.

The picture in his mind underwent a quick revision.

"She'd picked out a lemon tart, one of her favorite things in the world. She was looking forward to it as much as I was to my éclair. More, perhaps. And now they were both ruined." She made a melancholy face. "So I had made my mama cry."

"Difficult." Daniel started to point out that it wasn't entirely her fault. Her mother might have been more careful about where she sat. But Miss Pendleton went on before he could speak.

"Utterly tragic for a small girl."

"You might have gone back to the shop and replaced them."

"I suppose. We didn't. Perhaps there was a reason Mama had to be back. But in any case, she soon recovered. She was wonderful that way. She turned setbacks into…festivals."

Rather like her daughter did with an upended life, Daniel thought. "How does one redeem squashed pastry?"

"Ah." Miss Pendleton's smile was impish now. "We took our flattened box to her sitting room and hid it away until a maid had brought tea for Mama and a glass of milk for me."

"Hid it? Why?"

"We didn't want to hurt Cook's feelings by letting her know we'd bought pastry. She was very skillful, but not with sweets. So we always ate our treats in secret."

"That was kind," said Daniel. Had his parents had any such concerns about Frithgerd's cook? Or any of the servants? He didn't think so.

Miss Pendleton blinked rapidly. "My mother was extraordinarily kind." She took a deep breath. "When the coast was clear, we spread open the box and ate spoonfuls of the…contents. We decided to call it an 'eclart.' Which I still think is a very fine word."

"Like a burst of excitement in your mouth," he replied.

"Exactly!"

As their eyes met, alternative meanings for this phrase seemed to unfold between them. Daniel was suddenly conscious of the beautiful shape of *her* mouth, not far away at all. He wasn't aware of leaning forward until he noticed that she'd done the same. They were inches apart. He wanted to wrap his arms around her, pull her close, and kiss her passionately, repeatedly, until they were both dizzy. He could just barely make himself sit back. The effort left him rigid, in more ways than one.

Penelope caught her breath. She hadn't touched him, but it felt as if she had. The sense of connection had been as intense as an actual caress. She'd never experienced anything like it. She was suffused with longing. Did it show on her face? Was he wondering what was wrong? Her hand twitched. Their fingers brushed, and another bolt of sensation coursed through her.

Whitfield moved his hand away. He raised it, left it hovering in the air for a moment, then reached for another Shrewsbury cake.

Penelope ordered *her* hands to stop trembling, and they obeyed. She'd learned to hide her feelings in the past year, as she discovered that a person being questioned by the authorities, particularly a woman, had to appear calm and rational at all times. Emotion roused suspicions and drew contempt. Interrogators might shout and be seen as forceful, but they would pounce on the slightest tremor in their prey and call it instability. Not that Lord Whitfield was like that. She was muddling two very different things. She had to get hold of herself.

Picking up a page from one of the piles she hadn't yet investigated, Penelope scanned the contents. "Are you installing a bathing chamber at Frithgerd?"

Whitfield leaned over to look, and the page shook slightly in her grasp. "I forgot about that," he said. "I met a fellow in London who promised we could have hot water at will and all sorts of other conveniences. He made that drawing."

Penelope ran her eyes over the diagram, interest growing as she understood the various elements. "Do you have a water tank in your attic?"

"Not now. We have a rainwater cistern, but it's dependent on the weather, of course."

"And a mill-wheel pump?"

"No. We'd have to build that part. Unless the servants carried the water up to the tank."

"Which would be at least as much work as hauling cans of hot water," said Penelope.

Lord Whitfield nodded.

"Imagine turning a spigot and having hot water!" Penelope looked more closely at the drawing. "The water would be heated in the wall beside the kitchen fires?"

"The fellow said that was the way, because they're always lit. People would have to come downstairs for a bath."

"It would be worth it!" She met his eyes, thought of naked limbs lolling in a luxurious bath, and looked away. "You'd have to lay in a good many pipes."

"You're very clever with architectural plans."

"Philip was interested in all sorts of mechanisms." It was easier to say her brother's name this time. Perhaps, eventually the pain would fade? "He used to explain new inventions at the dinner table, with illustrations." She turned the page over. "A water closet, too?"

"That was the plan."

"You should install it," said Penelope, imagining a world in which no one had to deal with chamber pots.

"I don't know." Lord Whitfield surveyed the cluttered room. "There's so much else to do."

"You'd only have to supervise. I'm sure you know the best workmen in the neighborhood."

"I do. But they've never built anything like this." He gestured at the plans.

"You could get advice from the person who made these."

"I've forgotten his name."

She pointed to a neat signature at the bottom of the page. "Andre Fontaine. With his address as well."

Whitfield smiled at her. "You're very enthusiastic."

The warmth in his eyes made Penelope feel as if she'd stepped close to a roaring fire. "My family has... had a mechanical bent," she managed.

He leaned closer again to examine the drawing. His brown hair curled slightly at the nape of his neck. Penelope was seized by an intense desire to run her fingers through those strands.

"All right. Yes, let's go ahead. If you'll take charge."

"What? Me?"

"You're so efficient."

"Efficient," Penelope repeated. It was the sort of compliment she'd sometimes wished for when a dance partner had praised her fine eyes or her grace. Now, it seemed less than satisfactory. He couldn't know how her heart was beating.

"I'm sure all would go smoothly under your direction," Whitfield added. "I'm continually amazed at your abilities."

Penelope couldn't help herself. She leaned into his warm brown gaze, basking in the admiration she saw there. They were close, closer, and then their lips brushed. A soft, glancing kiss. Fleeting, but volcanic as a rush of desire shuddered through her.

Whitfield jerked back. "I beg your pardon," he said, sounding breathless.

"You do?"

"I should. I must. You're a guest in my house, a young lady. I would not offer you insult for the—"

"I believe I kissed you. I think I did."

She had. Those brief sentences brought the experience back in every detail. How could there be so much to remember in such a brief caress? The surge of longing that followed was overwhelming.

"Did you like it?" she asked.

Daniel groped for words. One didn't speak to young ladies about such matters. It wasn't done. They would be scandalized and offended. Or so he'd always been told. Miss Pendleton did not seem to be either. She appeared simply inquisitive. She wasn't like other young ladies. Unless they were all like this, and he'd just never had the opportunity to find out. She wasn't going to walk out in a huff; that was obvious. Little else was, at this moment. Except that Daniel was seriously interested in Miss Penelope Pendleton. He would have liked to hear that she felt the same. He did want to hear it. "Very, very much. Did you?"

She looked away, straightening a stack of documents on the desk. "Yes."

Exultation raced through his veins. The muddle of his papers suddenly seemed more a blessing than a burden.

"What shall we do about that?" Miss Pendleton asked.

It seemed an honest question. She spoke as if there might be an answer lurking out there somewhere. He ought to promise that kisses would never happen again. He didn't want to. But he couldn't expose her to gossip and disrespect. "I suppose it would be best if we get back to work and forget what happened," he said.

"I don't think I can forget."

The heat in her blue eyes thrilled him beyond measure. No, forgetting was right out, Daniel thought. "Ignore it then. Obviously we can't be in here kissing when we're supposed to…" A vivid picture of embraces silenced him. Her expression suggested that she shared his imaginings, which was the most enflaming idea of all. "To be keeping our minds on the task at hand," he finished weakly.

She blinked, breaking the lock of their gaze, and looked down. "I do want to find information about Rose Cottage," she said. "And of course help you bring order to your papers, as I promised. It would be fascinating to supervise construction of the bath."

He wanted to continue enjoying her company. And kiss her again. He thought of having her here for the rest of the day. Of sitting down to dinner with her and talking afterward in the drawing room. Her presence would brighten a humdrum evening, which all of them tended to be lately. And when the time came for bed… Ah, what was he thinking? He couldn't take advantage of her innocence. But he couldn't let her go either. He had to make sure she would be here tomorrow, and the day after. "So, we're agreed. We'll go back to the way things were before the… Before."

Penelope gazed at him. This was *not* a disappointment. On the contrary, it was the only choice, unless she wanted to leave Frithgerd and never return, as a respectable young lady would undoubtedly do. What would he think of her otherwise? What did he already think after the way she'd behaved? She looked down at the papers on the desk. Order suddenly seemed such a dull thing, such an overrated ideal. "Very well. We'll say no more about it."

"Agreed." He seemed about to offer a handshake; then he didn't.

They sat in silence. Having told herself to forget the kiss, Penelope of course thought of nothing else. Echoes of longing still reverberated through her. "Perhaps we should have a look at the trunks they brought down." She needed to move, to put some distance between them, or she was going to kiss him again. What would a longer, deeper embrace be like? She rose and stepped away. "To see what we have."

Daniel stood when she did. They walked to the parlor where the trunks had been placed, with some distance between them, like two people who were barely acquainted. He found it maddening.

Miss Pendleton moved around the room, opening all the lids. Then she stood back and gazed at the trunks. "I don't suppose it matters where we start. We can pick a trunk and go clockwise from there."

"Very methodical." He hadn't meant to be sarcastic, but he was frustrated at her withdrawal, even though it had been his suggestion. She gave him a sharp look. Daniel turned to the nearest trunk and picked up a sheaf of paper.

"I've forgotten my notebook," said Miss Pendleton. She turned and left the room.

Despite the trunks, the parlor felt empty and barren without her. Daniel realized that he'd begun to think of her as part of his home, part of his day. He looked forward to her arrival. He thought of things to tell her when she wasn't here, set aside items to show her. He enjoyed that. A new estate agent would be a damned nuisance, he realized. He'd put off hiring a new one until…until he decided to do so.

She'd been gone quite a while. Could she be as unsettled as he was? He hoped so. Daniel put the pages back in the trunk. His thoughts were as disorganized as his dashed estate records.

The object of his perplexity returned with her small notebook. "Lost your pencil?" he asked.

"What? No."

"Thought you might have been looking for it."

"I keep it with the notebook," she replied, frowning at him.

"Of course you do." Who would have imagined that efficiency could be adorable, Daniel thought. If anyone had asked him a few months ago, he'd have sworn the idea was ridiculous.

"We'll assign numbers to the trunks," Miss Pendleton declared. "Then we'll glance through them quickly, and I'll record a general idea of their contents."

He nodded.

"A bit of chalk would be helpful," she murmured as she surveyed them. "But eight isn't too many to remember. The trunk on this side of the door shall be one, and we will go from there."

"Clockwise," said Daniel. Could she switch to business so easily? Or had her extended absence to fetch the notebook provided time to subdue her agitation? He hoped for the latter.

She gave him a sidelong glance as she pointed at the other trunks, designating them two through eight.

Then they dug in. Their shoulders brushed as they began to riffle through the stacks of paper, and Daniel nearly caught hold of her. His mind wasn't going to settle on these new documents, he thought. But a general idea of the contents of these trunks would be the same jumble as everywhere else.

"This is odd," said Miss Pendleton.

"What is?"

"It seems to me… I don't know." She went to another trunk and sifted through the contents, tried a third.

"What?" Daniel repeated.

"I almost think these documents have been mixed up. As if they'd been quickly searched and shoved back in. See, part of this stack is upside down, and another section is reversed compared to the rest."

He looked. "Perhaps they were just dumped in by someone clearing out the estate office." Daniel frowned. "I don't remember that ever happening though. The room has been much the same for as long as I can recall."

"This account is twenty years old," she said, indicating a page at the top. "The one below it is three decades older. And then, facedown and reversed, comes a hundred-year-old receipt." She turned it over to match the order of the pile. "Which hardly needed to be kept," she muttered. "Five shillings to the blacksmith."

"You think the records were gone through and put back out of order?" Daniel asked again because it was such a strange idea. Who would care to do that?

Miss Pendleton nodded. "These trunks were all in the attic?"

"Yes."

"So someone could search them without being noticed."

"Not just anyone. They'd have to get into the house and…" Daniel shook his head. He couldn't see it. "Perhaps my father's estate agent was looking for a particular record. Rather as we are about Rose Cottage. And he went mad over the disorganization. Had to fling papers about to relieve his feelings." He could see the appeal. "Perhaps that's why he left."

"Possibly."

She smiled, and Daniel felt a spark of triumph. He wanted her smiles. Nearly as much as he wanted her kisses. Nearly. "I'll write and ask him."

"If he went mad and tossed papers about?"

Daniel smiled back. This was better. "If he went through the trunks."

"A good idea. You might inquire how he kept track of transactions, too. This top one had to have been placed here when you were a boy."

"Briggs wasn't here then. That would have been old Garrity."

She sighed. "The label 'old Garrity' does not fill me with confidence."

"You're very perspicacious. Garrity worked for my grandfather for many years, and my father kept him on. By the time I knew him he was… 'Doddering' is the word that comes to mind." Daniel looked at the trunks. "That might account for this mess. Papa kept him on until he died."

"Sitting at the desk in the estate office, I suppose," said Miss Pendleton. "With a quill in his hand and a blotted parchment. And so he haunts the chamber still, mixing up the records to thwart his successors."

Daniel laughed. "At his cottage in his sleep, I'm afraid. Though your tale is much more exciting."

She closed her notebook. "There's no simple way to record what's in these trunks. We may as well give up. And I should go."

"It's pouring rain," he said. Water streamed down the windows.

"I see that it is."

"Better wait till it clears. That gig of yours won't keep you dry."

"That could be hours."

Their eyes met. That kiss would remain between them whatever their resolutions, Daniel thought. Until, perhaps, another sweeter one replaced it.

"Lord Macklin will be wondering where you are," she added.

He'd forgotten his noble guest. He kept doing that. The lovely Miss Pendleton drove everything else from his mind.

"I must go." She sounded determined, or resigned. He couldn't tell which.

"A little longer."

"No, I really must." She hurried out, leaving him alone with his muddled heaps of history.

Nine

PENELOPE DID GET WET DRIVING HOME. THOUGH Whitfield provided an oilcloth to spread over her skirts, and the servants raised the gig's folding top, the rain drove in under it. The horse seemed aggrieved; his hooves threw up clods of mud, some of which whizzed past her ears. Kitty would raise a fuss when Penelope got home, but she had needed to get away from her beguiling neighbor before she flung herself into his arms again. She wanted to do that as much as she'd ever wanted to do anything in her life. The thought of their brief kiss kept her warm in the rain. But that wouldn't do, would it? He wanted to observe the proprieties, because he was a gentleman. And that was *not* a melancholy thing to be. How could she think so?

Reaching Rose Cottage, she drove around to the barn and left the horse with Foyle. She ran through the rain to the back door and up to her bedchamber, shutting the door on Kitty's hand-wringing. Solitude, quiet, space. As she changed out of her wet gown, she noticed that none of these seemed to help. Her thoughts—her heart?—remained at Frithgerd.

There was a knock at the door, and Kitty looked in. "I'll hang your wet things by the kitchen fire, miss."

"Thank you, Kitty." Penelope handed over her discarded clothing.

"Are you all right, miss? You look a bit peaked. I hope you haven't caught another chill."

"I'm fine."

"If that cough should come back, where would we be then? You shouldn't ought to drive out in the rain."

"I'm fine," Penelope repeated. "I'll be down in a few minutes."

Kitty took the damp garments and departed with a lingering backward glance. Penelope turned to the window and watched the rain fall from the gray sky. The garden and countryside looked less green in this weather, but Penelope felt more alive than she had in months and months. More than she ever had, perhaps. She *wanted*. She wanted to go where she liked and do as she pleased and work and learn. She wanted, especially, to kiss Lord Whitfield again. Her fingers curled at the memory of his touch.

She'd promised—what had she promised? To ignore what had happened between them. Not to forget it. Which was fortunate because she would never forget. She'd had to go off to another room and wrestle with the tides of yearning that rushed through her in his presence. Forgetting was impossible.

And she hadn't promised never to do it again.

An almost feral smile lit Penelope's features. Whitfield thought he had to observe the proprieties. But must she? With no family and no standing in the community, she wasn't hemmed in by the social restrictions that had ruled her youth. No society matrons would be monitoring her behavior at assemblies and evening parties. The local social round wouldn't include her, so she couldn't lose her place in its ranks.

Hard-faced government men, with their endless questions, had taken that position from her. They'd given her a lesson in vulnerability she would never forget. But she'd endured; she'd made it through, fought them off with the truth. And here, on the other side, she became aware of a fierce determination to grasp what she wanted with both hands. She would not be cowed. She would not see her life as wrecked. She'd pay them all back by enjoying herself while she had the chance.

Penelope blinked, not seeing the rainy landscape any longer. Lord Whitfield would bring home a bride from the next London season, or the one after that. Nothing was more likely. That was what viscounts did. It was the path she'd expected to take herself before things came crashing down around her. She might have met him at a ball or evening party and made his acquaintance—in quite a different way of course. And who could say it was a better one? She wouldn't know him as well from a few dances and rides in the park. She wouldn't have spent time alone with him or shown him her organizational skills. He wouldn't have been *amazed at her abilities*. She wrapped her arms around her chest as if to hug his admiration close. They had this time together. She would savor it. And if she wanted more, she would dashed well have it.

Another knock heralded Kitty's reappearance. "Are you all right, miss?" the girl asked, looking around the doorframe. "Only I thought you might've fainted dead away. I'm thinking I'll ask Mrs. Hart about poultices tomorrow. I expect she knows."

"Poultices?"

"A mustard plaster for your chest." Kitty seemed to relish the idea. "That'd be the thing. Draw out the flan."

"The what?"

"That stuff you cough up."

"Ah. I haven't any phlegm." Penelope moved toward her. "See, I'm coming downstairs with you. Perfectly well."

Kitty eyed her as if she might burst into a paroxysm of coughing at any moment.

Penelope led her down the steps. "If you'd like to learn about poultices from Mrs. Hart, you're welcome to do so, but none will be tested on me."

Kitty looked resigned. "Do they use them on dogs?" she asked.

"I don't know. They're put on horses' legs sometimes. Or is that a fomentation? Foyle would know."

"Eh. Don't reckon he'd tell me. He thinks I'm stupid."

Penelope hadn't been sure if the girl had noticed this. "Foyle has always been irascible."

"I 'spect that means grumpy as a bear with a thorn in its paw. But there's no thorn to take out, is there?"

Quite a clever summation, Penelope thought, and far from stupid. "Not that I've ever discovered."

"Mebbe Mrs. Hart'll find one. He's not so *rascible* with her."

Meeting the maid's twinkling eyes, Penelope saw that she hadn't imagined Foyle's interest in their cook. She'd have to discover Mrs. Hart's views on this subject.

Kitty went into the kitchen. Penelope lit the kindling in the parlor fireplace and settled down in the armchair as the fire caught. Her thoughts drifted back to Whitfield, and a good bit of time passed in pleasant reverie.

Kitty came in. "Mrs. Hart left a beef stew, miss."

Something had made the girl more anxious than usual, Penelope thought. And Kitty tended to worry. "How was your day? Did you see your friend Betty as you hoped?"

The girl shook her head. "It was her half day, but she went out with Ned. He's a footman up at Frithgerd, miss. They're courting and mean to marry and go up to London and get fine new positions."

Penelope heard envy and resignation in her voice. Kitty's position was a bit like her own, with fewer options. Penelope had a sudden vision of the two of them fifty years from now, old ladies moving about the place with much greater difficulty. There were such households. She shook her head. Her life would be more than that. Kitty's, too. She'd see to it. She sat straighter. "The stew smells wonderful." Indeed, the luscious aroma permeated the small house.

"Shall I make up your tray?"

"Yes, please, Kitty. And don't worry."

Blinking in surprise, the girl went out. She returned so quickly that Penelope knew she must have had the tray waiting. As the only inhabitants of a small house, they might have eaten together, but Kitty wasn't comfortable with the idea. She'd practically squirmed when Penelope suggested it. For her part, Penelope didn't like sitting at the large table in the other room alone. A tray before the hearth was their compromise. Kitty set it across the arms of the chair.

A scrabbling noise came from the kitchen. "Did you let the dogs in?"

"No, miss, I wouldn't."

A muffled woof and the tick of paws on floorboards contradicted her.

The girl was lonely, Penelope realized. And who could blame her? So was she. She'd have to see what she could do about that as well. For now, she could pretend she hadn't heard the noises and not give her usual order to put the dogs out.

Kitty scuttled from the room as if eager to evade those very words.

❧

Daniel had just finished numbering the trunks in the blue parlor with a bit of chalk from the billiard room when Macklin came to find him. "I've received some answers to my letters of inquiry," he said.

"Ah."

"Shall we sit in the estate office?"

"Let's go upstairs." The estate office was *her* spot. "You look grave," Daniel added as he led the way to the drawing room.

"I'm bemused," his guest replied as they sat down. "Miss Pendleton's brother seems to have gone out of his way to insult people. He actually printed up copies of Byron's Luddite poem and sent it around to everyone in the government."

"Poem?" Daniel frowned. "*Don Juan*? *The Corsair*? The ministers of the crown were offended by bombast?"

Macklin smiled. "Not those. Byron's 'Ode to the Framers of the Frame Bill.' Came out in the *Morning Chronicle* several years ago. You may not remember it. Rather a masterpiece of sarcasm, dripping with contempt for Liverpool and the rest of the government. It was one of the reasons Byron fled the country."

"I thought that was down to debauchery."

"That, too." Macklin's smile faded. "The point is, reviving that piece was a foolish thing to do. Philip Pendleton sent it around with a signed letter condemning current policies."

"Which put people's backs up."

"An understatement. It was unnecessarily incendiary. And in their anger, his targets paid less attention to his arguments."

Daniel nodded.

"A man may disagree with certain laws," Macklin continued. "*I* do. But one of my correspondents said that Pendleton seemed more interested in spewing outrage and destroying his opponents' reputations than in real reform."

Daniel wondered how such a man could be related to Miss Pendleton. He sounded completely unlike her. "Perhaps he was misunderstood."

"He commissioned a broadside listing all the Prince Regent's mistresses and debts, going back to his youth, and arguing that it was past time to abolish the monarchy."

"Ah."

"It included a caricature of the king suffering a fit of madness."

"Prinny must have been livid. I'm surprised Pendleton wasn't arrested."

"His sponsorship wasn't proven until after the Manchester incident." Macklin shook his head. "The man seems to have been a political idiot. If I listed all the ways one could antagonize the government, he would tick every box. Without anything to offer to replace them but ranting."

"Reform is brewing, I think." Daniel had never delved too deeply into politics, but he knew that much.

"And I'm behind it," replied Macklin. "Change is necessary, and inevitable. But I dislike stupidity. And it doesn't do to tear everything down all at once. We saw where that leads in France. Do we want another Terror?"

"Obviously not."

"I don't think Philip Pendleton would have agreed. He seemed intent on mayhem. The 'Cry havoc and let slip the dogs of war' sort of thing. I wonder if he was a bit unbalanced?"

"Can Miss Pendleton know all this?" Daniel still had trouble reconciling these two radically different people. Scurrilous broadsides and fiery rhetoric just didn't fit with the young woman who'd sat by his side organizing documents. And kissed him so sweetly that his spirits still reeled.

"I expect she does, by this time."

"This time?"

"She was questioned after he was killed. They

would have shown her their evidence at some point, trying to get more information."

"She told me about the investigation," Daniel said.

"About being locked up?"

"What?"

"The aftermath of the shooting was chaotic. Miss Pendleton was taken from her home and...secured in Manchester for a while."

"Secured! They imprisoned her?"

"More of a house arrest. Or hotel arrest." Macklin shrugged. "Her brother was thought to be one of the ringleaders. Because of his rank, I suppose. Some imagined he was the head of a network of revolutionaries, and that his house would be a treasure trove of information. They wanted free rein to search the place. As it turned out, they found nothing. She was soon released, but forbidden to leave Manchester until the inquiries—which is to say interrogations—ended."

Daniel was horrified. When she'd spoken of an investigation he'd imagined something like the local magistrate's court, over which he presided. Stern, but courteous; just, but kindly. Now he saw her hemmed in by frowning men shoving broadsides into her face and demanding facts she didn't possess. "My God."

"It must have been very difficult for her," said Macklin.

"Difficult!" Daniel's hands curled into fists. It was all he could do to sit still. He wanted to go to her and comfort her and assure her of...what?

"You're right, worse than difficult. A friend of mine who is familiar with the case was shocked and outraged by the way she was treated. He said some of

Sidmouth's men went much too far in the aftermath of Peterloo. It was soon clear that Miss Pendleton had nothing to do with her brother's activities."

"As she told them!"

"In their defense, they may have really believed that a revolt was imminent."

"By the daughters of baronets? I wonder she doesn't lay an action against them in court."

"She may wish to forget the whole matter, insofar as she can."

She'd certainly been reluctant to talk about it. And what would his efforts to comfort do but reveal that he and Macklin had been poking into her past? A vast frustration descended on Daniel. He wanted to be… something to her.

A knock on the door heralded the entrance of young Tom. "Another letter's come, my lord. Clayton would've brought it, but he's out." He handed the folded sheet to Macklin.

"Thank you, Tom."

"I thought I'd walk up into the hills. Unless I can do anything for you, my lord?"

Macklin merely waved him off, breaking the seal and beginning to read his letter. With a grin, Tom went out. "Ah," said Macklin after a while.

"More ill news?" The older man's expression suggested it.

He tapped the page. "This is from Cranbourne. The man I mentioned who is deep in government councils. He suggests that Miss Pendleton may be seen as a way to catch rioters who are still at large."

"How? Why?"

"Sidmouth's people have been working to eliminate their refuges. Should any of her brother's supposed confederates apply to her for help—"

"But she didn't know anything about them!"

"And from what we've learned, her brother probably had none. No sensible radical would want to ally with an inept firebrand. But agents never believe they've found the whole truth. Deception is their profession. They see it everywhere."

"So Miss Pendleton is being watched?"

"That seems possible."

"Well, you must write your friend and put a stop to it at once."

"He works in the Foreign Office and has no power to end such an investigation," Macklin replied. "Nor do I. Sidmouth and I are not friends. I'd be happy to vouch for her character, if I thought it would help. But that might not be a good idea."

"Why not?"

"In an agent's mind, a character reference implies a need for justification, and thus some secret wrong."

"That's preposterous."

"When you live in a world of suspicion, everything is suspicious."

"We can't just do nothing! When Miss Pendleton has been staked out as bait."

"I believe you're overstating the case, Whitfield."

He didn't care. He was filled with a burning desire to help her.

"I wonder if any strangers have arrived in the area recently?" said Macklin.

"I'll find out." Daniel was glad of some action to take.

"I think it would be better for Tom to ask. He's a stranger himself and would naturally ask questions. You or your servants will attract attention."

Daniel struggled with the wish to do it himself. But in the end he had to acknowledge Macklin's logic. "Do you think the lad is up to such a task?"

"I do. He's clever and can be surprisingly subtle."

Thinking of the homely, grinning youngster, Daniel doubted that. Yet he trusted Macklin's judgment, and the earl knew Tom far better than he did. "If any spies are found, I can send them packing."

"Not behind Miss Pendleton's back. I've learned my lesson on that sort of interference."

"She'll be happy for the assistance," Daniel said.

"Will she?"

"Why do you look so dubious? You can't suspect her of deceit." The thought outraged Daniel.

"Not deceit."

"You think it's unusual to know nothing of a brother who lived in the same house all your life?" Daniel was far too familiar with that sort of sensation.

"I think assistance is sometimes a hard thing to define," Macklin said.

Daniel scarcely heard him. "I scarcely knew my parents," he retorted. "They might have been acquainted with any number of revolutionaries, and I would never have known."

Macklin gave him a long look, but he said no more.

Ten

WHEN PENELOPE ARRIVED AT FRITHGERD THE FOL-
lowing afternoon, she discovered that someone—it
had to be Whitfield—had numbered the trunks in
the blue parlor with chalk, just as she'd ordered.
This tangible sign that he appreciated her ideas and
remembered them when she wasn't here lightened
her spirits. She had a place in his mind, as he did in
hers. They were linked. And she was glad. "Glad,"
she murmured. "So there."

"Who are you talking to?" asked the gentleman in
question.

Penelope whirled and found him in the doorway.
He wore a blue riding coat and buckskin breeches
today, and he looked ready to take on the world. "My
better self," she replied. "Or worse one. I'm not really
certain." She repressed an errant laugh.

He came closer.

"You numbered the trunks."

"As decreed." He gave her a mock salute.

Whitfield wasn't conventionally handsome,
Penelope thought. His features were too blunt, his

bone structure too rugged. She tended to forget this fact because when his face was animated, as it was now, he was rivetingly attractive.

"Are we going back to the trunks?" he asked. "I thought we'd decided to leave them for later."

She couldn't stand here gazing at him, enjoyable as that was. He'd think her a mooncalf. "I woke in the night certain I'd missed something," she answered.

"In the night." He smiled at her. "Was it a nightmare about the papers? I've had those. Sometimes they smother me. There was one where documents rose up like a great wave ready to break over my head and bury me. I had to fight them off with a cricket bat." He mimed a swing, put a hand to his brow, and pretended to watch something fly off over her head.

She laughed. "Nothing like that. This was a nagging sense that I'd noticed something without fully taking it in."

"What?"

"Well, that's the question." Penelope went to the trunk she'd been sorting through yesterday, opened it, and looked down at the stacks of documents. They were just the same—columns of figures, blocks of text, ornate signatures and seals, all jumbled together. There was too much to notice and nothing at all. She frowned, remembering what she'd done yesterday. She'd leafed through the pile at the end, reached down to take out part of it, then put it back. She repeated these actions.

As she finished, she felt it. The cloth lining of the trunk bulged out at this end, a small irregularity that one couldn't see but could feel. She ran her fingers over the square, flat shape. "I think there's something hidden here."

He came up beside her, his shoulder brushing hers. "Hidden?"

Penelope took his hand, and then had to pause at the thrill that went through her at his touch. He noticed the brief hesitation, meeting her eyes. Warmth washed through her. With an accelerated pulse, she guided his fingers over the shape.

"Ha. I see what you mean." Whitfield took a penknife from his waistcoat pocket, unfolded it, and slit the buff lining.

"Wait." It was too late. The cloth gaped open, revealing a bit of dark leather. "I wanted to see how it had been put in there," Penelope added.

Whitfield shrugged. "Sorry." He reached behind the lining and pulled out a slender notebook.

It was an oblong the size of a piece of notepaper, bound in dark calf. The cover looked worn, as if it had been well used. There was nothing extraordinary about the object, except its hiding place and the fact that Whitfield was staring as if it might bite him. "Is something wrong?" Penelope asked.

"My mother always had a notebook like this," he replied in a distant voice. "Carried it everywhere. She bought a dozen at a time. I remember my father rushing off, on one of their visits to London, to pick up a fresh supply for her. Had to do that instead of having lunch with me. Obligatory, he said."

"A diary?"

"I just realized that I've never found any of them since they died." He tapped the cover. "Until this."

He looked around at the trunks of records. "What's become of all the others?"

"Perhaps she destroyed them?"

"Why would she do that?"

"Well, if they were diaries, they might be private."

A spark lit his dark eyes. He grasped the cover.

"Perhaps we shouldn't read it?"

He gave her an incredulous look and opened the notebook, flipped a few pages, frowned.

Penelope tried to restrain her curiosity and failed. "Is it a diary?"

"I haven't the least idea." He handed it over.

The pages were full. Lines of text covered them, written in a strong, distinctive hand. But there was no clear narrative. The words were more like notes, random jottings. There were scraps of sentences listing birds and weather and vegetation, little drawings in the margin, French phrases, whole lines of tiny doodles. None was unusual in itself; the odd thing was that they went on and on. Penelope flipped a few pages. The whole notebook was full of this…gibberish, remarkably repetitive. "There are dates and places," she said, latching on to something she could identify. "This one is headed Jamaica."

Whitfield bent over her shoulder. She could feel his breath on her cheek. "It's so disjointed."

Penelope nodded. "I wonder what she meant by it?"

Daniel turned away. "You will never know." He set his jaw. "As usual," he muttered.

But she heard him. "Usual?"

"My mother was not a forthcoming person. She

didn't speak about…anything really." Would he never learn? Daniel wondered. She'd had nothing to say to him in life. Why would death be different?

"It's certainly odd." Miss Pendleton was practically rubbing her hands together. Clearly, she loved a puzzle. "I wonder if there are more."

They checked the other trunks and found eight similar notebooks, hidden in the same way and equally cryptic. When they were sure they had them all, they took the pile to the estate office.

"Fascinating," said Daniel's lovely companion. They sat side by side at the desk looking over their finds.

He'd never met anyone who was more so.

"There are patterns." Miss Pendleton glanced from one notebook to another. "Repeated phrases, but I can't make any sense of them." She closed the slim books and set them aside. "We must keep working, as tempting as these are."

Tempting? Daniel hadn't fully understood the meaning of the word until he spent so much time with her. He longed to fold her in his arms. He wanted to keep her from all harm. Which was impossible, of course— the folding and the keeping. Yet he could think of little else.

"Frithgerd is full of mysteries," she said.

"Like Rose Cottage."

"Precisely. You are right to keep me on track."

"I…to keep you?"

"That is the advantage of a team."

Her smile ravished him. He hated to think of her in danger.

"What *is* the matter?" she said.

"Matter?"

"You've been looking at me oddly today. And... hovering."

"No, I haven't."

"You have. And you stare as if you've discovered I have a fatal disease."

"Nonsense."

She examined him. "Well, perhaps it's more as if you have a guilty secret."

"Wanting to kiss you again," he replied, a truth and a diversion in one.

"Oh, *that*."

With one short word, Daniel was thrilled and bewildered. She'd sounded offhand, unperturbed. Because she felt the same?

Miss Pendleton peered deep into his eyes. "I don't think that's it."

How strange. He liked the idea that she could see into him.

"I wish you would tell me."

He couldn't deny her, and the truth was, she deserved to know. Even though the news was not happy. "Macklin received replies to the inquiries he sent out."

She stiffened and moved a little away. "I see."

"I didn't understand how dreadful it was for you. I wish—"

"I don't want to talk about the investigation," she interrupted. "Yes, it *was* dreadful. But it's over and done. I'm through with it."

"Yes." The word escaped him because he so wanted it to be true.

"Why do you say it that way?"

"What way?"

"As if you doubted me." She turned away. "Ah, you do. That's the way of these conversations." Her voice trembled. "Can you believe I was never really doubted until my brother's death? Not in any serious way. About anything important. I was considered a very honest person, a model of integrity."

"I do *not* doubt you."

"And then suddenly, overnight practically, everything I said was met with skepticism and contempt. As if I'd always been a liar. I couldn't take it in at first. I kept thinking they'd see—"

"I absolutely do not doubt you," Daniel declared. "Not one iota."

Tears pooled in her blue eyes. She tried to blink them away, and Daniel couldn't stand it. He pulled her into his arms. She was rigid and trembling. He thought she might pull away. But then she relaxed into his embrace, rested her head on his shoulder, and allowed herself to cry. He knew that was the proper phrase. He felt both her resistance and her capitulation. He held her; she wept. And Daniel didn't feel the least bit reluctant or awkward. Indeed, he was sorry when she pulled away.

"I don't usually do that anymore." She got a handkerchief from her reticule, wiped her eyes, and blew her nose.

"Anymore." He hadn't meant to repeat the word. But the history it had evoked cut him to the heart.

She didn't look at him. "There was a time when I nearly despaired. But I endured, and now it's in the past."

"The thing is…" Daniel didn't want to tell her. He wanted to see happiness light her face, laughter rather than apprehension.

"What?"

"It may not be quite over."

Miss Pendleton shook her head. "No, I convinced them, finally. I was assured of that. They agreed that I had no hand in Philip's activities."

He could see how much stock she put in the idea. He wanted to let the matter drop. But it would be worse if government agents showed up at Rose Cottage unexpectedly. He had to tell her. "One of Macklin's correspondents suggested that you may be seen by the government as a…lure for rioters who are still at large. And a way to catch them if they come looking for help."

She went so still that he feared for her. Then she burst out, "I have tried very hard not to dislike my brother, but sometimes I am so angry!"

"He seems to have been reckless—"

"Reckless? He was idiotically rash, uncaring, *bumbling*. He flailed about and shouted and accomplished nothing but his own death. Such a dreadful waste." She gripped the inkwell as if she might throw it across the room, but she didn't, though her fingers whitened with strain.

Daniel put a hand over her free one. "Was he always so?"

She shoved the inkwell away. "The truth is, I don't know. He went off to school when I was seven years old, and he often spent his holidays with friends. He was my brother, but not my companion.

Or my friend." She sounded sad as well as angry now.

Daniel knew something of distance from family members.

"When he *was* home, he did talk about new inventions and change and poverty. But his talk was never systematic. He said nothing to predict what happened. He jumped from one topic to another. He seemed just a young man full of random enthusiasms." She swallowed. "Papa didn't like it when he criticized the government. They had one blazing row about that, and Papa forbade him to mention the topic again in his hearing. Philip complied. And stayed away from home even more often.

"I told the agents all of this. I told them everything. Which was really nothing, because I knew nothing. I didn't know Philip's friends, if he had any. He must have had some, surely?" She looked at Daniel, her expression desolate. "But after that row with Papa, he would have told them his family wasn't sympathetic. They would have no reason to apply to me."

But would the government know that? Daniel wondered. She wasn't the problem; they were.

"Philip saw me as Papa's pet," she continued. "He resented it. He did tell me that once. And I was with Mama much more than he was. She was an invalid. I was her daughter. I helped care for her." She looked down at her now tightly folded hands. "Philip tired her out. She tried to hide it, but she wasn't good at dissembling. She was glad when his visits were over, and I know he saw it."

In her face, Daniel saw a girl struggling to bridge an irredeemable gap that had opened in her family.

"The sad truth is, I scarcely knew my brother. Do you think that can't be? That I had to know? That's what the agents believed," she finished bitterly.

"I'm well aware of what it is to be a stranger to your family," Daniel said. "Ties of blood are meaningless if people ignore them."

Penelope turned, moved by the emotion in his voice. His eyes held sympathy and an understanding she'd never thought to encounter again.

"Or if they refuse to reciprocate," he added. "One can make all the overtures in the world, but if they're ignored, there's nothing to be done."

"Or repulsed, yes. After a while, Philip pushed me away. Can you really know how that is?"

"All my life I was treated like an acquaintance by those most closely related to me."

"Your parents." When he looked surprised, she added, "You said you were at odds with them."

"I did?"

"When we began our search through the papers." Her easy recollection seemed to startle and then to move him.

"'At odds' is too strong a term. I shouldn't have said that. It implies disputes. We didn't dispute. We conversed. We *chatted*."

He said the last word as if it was unbearably offensive.

"The last time they were home before their trip to India." He glanced at her. "They were killed in a shipwreck on the way back."

"I remember."

"You do?"

"I remember everything you've said to me."

He blinked as if she'd said something astonishing. He started to speak, then pressed his lips together and swallowed, obviously overcome by strong emotion.

"I'm very sorry about your parents," Penelope added. Fleetingly, she remembered Lord Macklin's talk of grief.

Whitfield nodded—more an acknowledgment than an acceptance of sympathy. He cleared his throat. "On that last visit—I didn't know it was the last, of course. But I was determined that we should do better. We'd been a family for more than a quarter century. I hadn't seen them in five months. I thought they must, in their hearts, want a closer connection as much as I did. I arranged for us to attend a lecture on African wildlife. It was the sort of thing they liked to do."

"And you don't," said Penelope.

"How do you know?"

"It was the way you said 'lecture,'" she explained.

He gazed at her as if she was an exotic creature herself. The hint of a smile tugged at his lips. "Well, I don't, as a rule. I'd rather be doing than listening. But the joint outing was the point. The three of us went, and heard the fellow, and agreed that it had been a dashed informative talk. And then they said they had to go. I'd arranged dinner, which they knew quite well. But they said that an important engagement had come up, a man they had to meet."

"More important than—" Penelope broke off.

"Important as opposed to not important at all. That

was my impression. It was necessary for them to dine with this person. And entirely *un*necessary to do so with their son."

"Who was he?"

"I don't believe they said. Which was typical. If they mentioned a name, I don't recall. I was annoyed."

"I expect so!" How could anyone treat him that way? Penelope wondered. Let alone his parents. How could they not want to spend as much time with him as possible? She'd only known him a short time, and she wanted that.

"People don't call it cruel when others are simply...absent," he added in an emptily even voice.

Penelope nodded. "My mother's illness made her selfish in later years. She was in pain and had no patience for other people."

"Pain is a terrible burden. One can't help but sympathize. But my parents were not in pain." Whitfield's jaw tightened. He looked away. The fingers of his right hand, resting on the desktop next to Penelope's left, tapped the wood in a nervous rhythm. The sound somehow felt like the drag of retreating waves, pulling everything in their path out to sea.

Penelope leaned over and put an arm around him. Whitfield went still, like a man in the presence of some rare and breathtaking animal, who doesn't dare move for fear it will bound away. Then, slowly, he bent his head until the side rested against hers.

Temple to temple, shoulder to shoulder, they sat for several minutes. Penelope felt his chest rise and fall under her arm, along with a sense of kinship unmatched in her life till now. Gradually, his muscles eased.

The atmosphere in the room shifted. Penelope's hand on his coat sleeve went from comfort to caress.

He turned a little toward her. "We can't—"

She put her other arm around his neck and pulled him closer.

He kissed her. Or she kissed him. Both, Penelope decided, while she could still think. What did it matter?

His arms slipped around her. She melted against him. Her heart pounded as the kisses multiplied in urgent bliss.

And then his hands closed on her waist and moved her away from him. He scooted his chair back to increase the distance.

"No," said Penelope.

"Yes," said Daniel. His breath caught on a laugh. "There's a reversal." He was aching with desire, grasping the tatters of control.

Miss Pendleton—Penelope—watched him. Her blue eyes were soft with longing. Her breath, coming fast, made the rise and fall of her bosom entrancing.

"You should go." If she stayed... She couldn't stay. He wouldn't be able to resist her. "I can't be answerable," murmured some pompous part of him.

She gave him a startling smile. "And if I don't wish you to be?"

"What?"

"Answerable."

"What?" he asked again. Didn't she understand that his good intentions were hanging by a thread? He wanted her so much.

The inexplicable Miss Pendleton laughed. "May I take these with me?" she asked. Her hand—the one that had caressed the back of his neck moments ago—was now resting on his mother's notebooks. "Perhaps I can decipher them."

Daniel frowned at the notebooks. His mother had cared for them as if they were the most precious things in her life. Far more precious than a son, for example. Miss Pendleton could throw them in the refuse heap for all he cared. "All right."

"I'll keep them safe."

"Do as you like with them." The statement came out harsh.

She gave him another strange smile, as if she knew things he couldn't imagine. And then she was up and gone before he could rise to bid her farewell.

Daniel sank back into his chair, body aching with desire, mind whirling with confusion. He'd done the right thing. Why did it feel like he'd been a fool? And that Miss Penelope Pendleton had some lively plans for him? A riot of sensual pictures crowded his brain at the idea. But she hadn't meant *that*. Of course she hadn't. Couldn't have. But the look on her face when she'd said she didn't want him to be answerable! Daniel had difficulty breathing for a moment.

She remembered everything he said. Daniel contemplated this admission for a while. The thought made his throat tight in a different way. His eyes felt hot, and he had to blink. Like a child unwrapping a gift and not daring to hope that it was the thing he really wanted, he thought. And what the deuce did that mean?

He was still sitting at the desk and wondering twenty minutes later when Macklin appeared in the doorway. His tall, dark-haired houseguest looked about the room as he came in. "Has Miss Pendleton gone?" he asked.

"She went home. I think. Yes, she must have."

Macklin glanced at him. Had he sounded wrung out? Daniel wondered. He certainly felt it. He stood.

"I thought we could discuss inserting a few questions about newcomers into Tom's rambles about the neighborhood," said the earl.

"I see no need for discussion. By all means, set him to asking. You say people have grown used to him."

"They have," said Macklin. "And he's a positive magnet for confidences."

The small part of Daniel's mind not fixed on Penelope Pendleton found this dubious. "Miss Pendleton was very unhappy, naturally, to learn that agents or friends of her brother might be lurking and watching her."

"Ah, you told her that?"

"Did you imagine I wouldn't?" He would not have her suspected, Daniel thought.

"I advised you to do so," replied the earl. His glance was uncomfortably acute.

Daniel acknowledged this with a nod. "Let us have Tom do it." He had to do something. He didn't want her agitated again; he didn't want her threatened. "This is my land. I'm the magistrate, taxed with keeping the peace. I have every right to gather information."

"True."

"Well then?"

"I wonder if government agents might have a duty to report to you." Macklin shook his head. "This is Sidmouth's covert corps, I suppose. They wouldn't observe such niceties."

"The Home Secretary is not above the law."

"I agree. Sidmouth might counter that he *is* the law."

"Not on my land," replied Daniel grimly.

Eleven

PENELOPE PUSHED THE HEELS OF HER HANDS INTO A mass of bread dough on the kitchen table, leaning forward to increase the pressure. With practice, she'd learned to feel when the dough took on the springy texture that signaled it was ready to be set aside to rise. She folded, turned, and kneaded again.

Lord Whitfield didn't want to be *answerable*. Very well, she would take charge of things then. She'd certainly had plenty of experience *answering*. Penelope paused, startled. This was the first time she'd made a joke, if only silently, about her months of interrogation.

"Oh, it's all spoilt," said Kitty, bent over a pan on the hearth.

It was indeed, Penelope thought. Whitfield seemed to forget that she was already ruined, her status snatched away with her old life. She'd had no choice at all then. She swore she would now. She pounded the dough.

"A lighter hand there, miss," said Mrs. Hart, who stood beside Kitty overseeing the preparation of a blancmange. Penelope obeyed. But inside, her determination continued to build. The cook turned back to Kitty and said, "You just have to keep on stirring."

Penelope turned the dough and pushed it down. Matters with the alluring viscount were definitely stirring.

"How do I make it go stiff?" said Kitty.

Penelope snorted.

Mrs. Hart glanced at her again. Penelope bent her head over her task. "The gelatin we put in will set when it cools," the older woman answered.

What might she stir up, Penelope wondered, if she took what *she* wanted?

"Will it wiggle?" asked Kitty.

A laugh escaped Penelope. Mrs. Hart looked, appeared to catch the scandalous tenor of her thoughts from her expression, and raised her eyebrows. "It'll be firmer than a jelly," replied the cook.

"I like to make them wiggle," said Kitty, stirring.

Mrs. Hart coughed, or choked on laughter. Penelope wasn't sure which. She rather hoped it was the latter.

The dough was ready. She smoothed it into a ball and put it in a large bowl, covering it with a cloth before she set it aside to rise. She pumped water into a basin to wash her hands.

"What comes next?" asked Kitty.

That was up to her, Penelope thought. Whitfield would tie himself into knots behaving like a gentleman.

"Pour it into the molds," said Mrs. Hart. "Carefully now."

Could she give her life a new shape? She had her own money, her own home. If she threw the old rules out the window with her girlhood, what were the new ones?

"Oops!" Kitty said. "That wasn't my fault."

Whatever Penelope did, she had to make it clear she wasn't Whitfield's *responsibility*. She didn't want to be any such thing. A confidante, a delight perhaps, but not a burden.

"What if it goes wrong?" Kitty asked.

There were always consequences, Penelope thought, no matter what one did. Even when one did nothing at all, as she had been doing when Philip's recklessness had brought the world crashing down on her. She simply had to accept them.

"It'll be fine," said Mrs. Hart. "Put the molds over here where it's cooler."

Should she wait until she was calmer to decide? Only, Penelope didn't know when that would be. Whenever she thought of Whitfield, she felt she might go up in flames.

Filled with the energy of her inner debate, Penelope left the kitchen. There was a pile of mending. She'd planned to wash the windows upstairs. She couldn't expect Kitty to do all the cleaning. Foyle had left her some bills for fodder and harness to look over, as well as suggestions for a stiff letter to the owner of the goats. He wanted to threaten the man with the law, which would mean appearing before the local magistrate—who was Lord Whitfield. Even had she wanted to antagonize her neighbor, which she didn't, that wasn't a scene Penelope cared to enact.

A knock on the front door broke into her musings.

"I'll go," Penelope called before Kitty could emerge, and went to open it.

A tall, lanky workman stood on the stoop. He pulled off his cap at the sight of her. "I've come to see Miss Pendleton," he said.

"I am Miss Pendleton."

"Miss," he said with a respectful nod. "My name's Henry Carson. His lordship said I should speak to you."

"Lord Whitfield?"

"Yes, miss."

Penelope took in the man's straw-colored hair, powerful shoulders, and craftsman's hands. One of them held a roll of paper with familiar markings. "About the bathing chamber?" she said.

"Yes, miss," he said again. "He said you'd be over-seeing the building of it."

He looked dubious, but Penelope didn't mind that. It was a typical attitude when laborers discovered that a young lady was in charge of their work. In her experience supervising projects on her father's estate, eight out of ten could be won over by treating them with respect, demonstrating comprehensive knowledge of the task at hand, and paying them fairly and promptly. The other two had to be told that their services were not required, which sometimes changed their tune.

"Come in." She ushered Henry Carson into the dining room rather than the parlor so that they could spread out the plans on the large table. She weighted down the corners with books and indicated that he should sit opposite her. "I don't suppose you've con-structed anything like this before? Almost no one has. It's a new design."

This frank admission seemed to reassure him. "No, miss. I've built cottages and barns, done a good deal of repairs at Frithgerd."

"Stonework as well as carpentry?"

He nodded.

"What about pipes? Like putting hand pumps in scullery sinks?"

"Not so much. But I know a fellow who does."

"I think we'll need him. You understand what we mean to do?" She tapped the plan with one finger.

"Get water from the stream up to a tank in Frithgerd's attic," he replied with a skeptical frown. "And then down again, through a firebox, and into a tub." He ran one finger over the requisite part of the plans as he spoke.

"Precisely." Penelope was glad to see that he could read and understand architectural drawings. Indeed, she was impressed at his quickness.

"And that works, do you think, miss?"

It was vital not to claim more knowledge than she had. She'd learned that early on. "The designer promises that it will."

"Architects," said Henry Carson. He did not spit, but Penelope got the impression that in other circumstances he might have.

"Have you noticed anything that you're certain *won't* work? In your opinion."

He looked both thoughtful and gratified to be consulted. "Not as I can spot, miss. But as you say, this is a new sort of construction. And you never do know with these grand schemes until the roof falls on you, do you?"

She raised her eyebrows.

"They had a fancy London architect in to put a ballroom on Paine Hall," he added. "That's a matter of five miles from here, miss. He was dead certain he knew how to frame a dome in the center. Only he didn't. We ended with a pile of rubble and Ron Carroll with a broken leg."

"Oh dear."

His nod this time was portentous. Bending over the plan, he added, "This'll take a deal of pipe. I should start in on that. I know a cooper can make a big water tank, but the mill wheel—"

"Perhaps there's a mill nearby where we can consult?"

"Aye." Carson looked relieved. "Reckon the miller might know about pumps as well. Or who to ask anyway."

"Good idea."

He sat back. The uneasiness had reappeared in his expression. "I do think I should speak to his lordship before I go ordering a load of work."

"Because he will be paying the bills," said Penelope with a smile.

"Yes, miss."

"Perfectly understandable. Why don't we go and see him now?"

"Now?"

The thought made Penelope happy, remembering the fire in Whitfield's gaze when she'd left him the last time. She so looked forward to igniting it again. "Why not?" She rolled up the plans and handed them to her companion.

"Perhaps I should make an appointment, miss."

"I'm sure Lord Whitfield would like to hear about the progress we've made." She gave him no time to protest but went to tell Foyle to ready the gig. Kitty was elbow deep in flour with Mrs. Hart, so Penelope drove the short distance to Frithgerd escorted by Henry Carson.

They found the viscount in the front hall, just back from the stables. He wore riding dress and looked ruddy with exercise, a figure who could take on anything. "I didn't know you meant to come today," he said to Penelope. His obvious appreciation at seeing her warmed her to her toes.

"We came to tell you about our construction plans. Mr. Carson and I have been discussing what needs to be done in order to put in the bath."

Daniel nodded to Henry Carson, who had often worked at Frithgerd, but he was diverted by the animation on Miss Pendleton's face. She positively glowed with excitement. Over pipes and pumps? Or could he hope that seeing him had some part in it? Either way, he wanted to impress her. "Drains," he said. "People are always nagging me about drains. They seem sadly prone to stopping up or smelling. We must make certain any new drains installed work properly."

"A good point." Miss Pendleton jotted a few words on her ubiquitous notepad and looked at Carson to make sure he took the suggestion on board. "Have you chosen the room where the bath will be installed?"

The necessity had slipped Daniel's mind. "I was waiting for your opinion."

"Next to the kitchens," she declared.

"Because the fires are always lit there, and they will warm the water." He remembered that.

Carson looked at Miss Pendleton and then back at Daniel. His expression was bemused. Possibly, most likely, he'd never met a young lady like her, Daniel thought. And he'd probably never encounter another. She was enchantingly unique.

"But we don't want to interfere with the cooking," she replied. "That wouldn't do."

They trailed after her as she headed toward the back premises, rather like staff officers supporting their commander on an inspection, Daniel thought. A startled housemaid stood against the corridor wall as they passed, arms full of clean linens. In the kitchen, the cook and her helpers stopped work and turned to bob curtsies and stare. Macklin's lad Tom rose from a chair in the corner, in the act of biting into a buttered scone. "Good day, Mrs. Jensen," said Daniel to the cook. "We've come to examine the rooms hereabouts. I've decided to put in a bathing chamber at Frithgerd, and it needs to be near the kitchen fires."

The cook looked confused. "Bathing, my lord?"

"A tub," he said. "With pipes for hot water."

The cook looked at the hot-water reservoir on her closed stove and frowned.

"How?" asked Tom. The scone had been devoured in three huge bites. The lad's homely face was bright with curiosity.

Before Daniel could reply, his housekeeper arrived in a rush. Word of their incursion was obviously spreading through the house. "I wasn't told that you needed anything, my lord," Mrs. Phipps said. Reproach tinged her tone.

Daniel repeated his announcement.

"Bathing chamber." His housekeeper repeated the words as if they were in a foreign language.

"It's a new invention," said Miss Pendleton. "The very latest thing." Gesturing with the roll of plans, she gathered the attention of everyone in the room. "Water will be pumped up to a tank in the attics," she continued. "Mr. Carson will fit pipes to bring it down to a smaller tank next to the fire, where it will be heated, and then brought into the chamber. After that, it will be a matter of simply turning a spigot and running a hot bath." She made a twisting gesture with one hand. All eyes followed it. "And no one will have to carry countless cans of heated water upstairs to fill a tub again."

"Champion," said Tom.

"I don't believe it," said Mrs. Phipps.

Miss Pendleton turned to the housekeeper. "I daresay some visitors won't wish to come down to bathe and will still prefer the old way."

"I should say so," she muttered.

"People will be traipsing naked through my kitchen?" asked the cook. She frowned at Daniel as if he was proposing to shed his clothes here and now.

He met Miss Pendleton's eyes, ready to laugh, and encountered a look that turned his thoughts in quite a different direction. Might she come and make use of his new bathing room? Surely she would wish to test her creation when it was finished. And what if she wanted company in that steamy luxury? The unprecedented, outrageous idea made his breath catch.

She looked away. "Not naked," she answered, her voice a bit high. "In their dressing gowns perhaps. But we'll make certain they don't disturb you here by choosing the right location. What is on the other side of the chimney?"

That was the ticket, Daniel thought. Keep pressing forward before objections could pile up.

"A set of storerooms, miss," answered Mrs. Jensen.

"We should look at those. This way, is it?" Before anyone could protest, she was through a brick archway and gone. Daniel went after her, with Henry Carson, the housekeeper, the cook, and Tom on his heels. The narrow corridor on the other side was immediately overcrowded.

A row of four small chambers backed up to the great chimney. "We use these for storing things that need to be warm and dry," said the cook. "Flour and such."

Miss Pendleton paced to the small window at the far end and looked into the fourth storeroom. "This would do," she declared. "We could close off the corridor here." She drew an imaginary line on the floor with one foot. "And open up a new entrance here." She patted the rough plaster of the wall opposite the rooms. "I wonder what's on the other side."

Daniel visualized the geography of his home. "That would be the blue parlor, I believe. Where we put the trunks." This wasn't the worst news, as the room wasn't much used. But he hadn't realized they'd be ripping through walls.

"That'd let us run the pipes down the outside of the house from the attic," said Henry Carson. He looked relieved. As well he might, Daniel thought, if he'd been wondering how to fit pipes through thick walls and ceilings.

"Much easier," agreed Miss Pendleton. She stepped into the storeroom. Daniel followed. "Oh good, there's a window here," she said, waving at the small opening. She put a hand to the far wall. "It's warm."

Daniel mirrored her pose. The bricks were indeed warm from the kitchen fires. He looked down at the storm—in the guise of a lovely young lady—that he'd unleashed on his peaceful dwelling. Her answering gaze was eager, arrested, and then intensely arousing.

"So." Miss Pendleton cleared her throat. "The water heated here and the tub sitting below."

He could almost see her stepping out of veils of steam, like Aphrodite emerging from the foam. He would always long to see her so. Wasn't there some myth like that? With the goddess Diana, he remembered. But that story hadn't ended well. The young man who caught sight of Diana bathing had been transformed into a deer and torn to pieces by his own hunting dogs. Not the thing at all.

"Quite revolutionary," he said, and was stirred by the brilliance of her answering smile. Who would have imagined such a heady mixture of beauty and ingenuity and sheer competence? Not he, until he met her. Daniel became aware of a bouquet of interested faces gazing at them from the doorway. "Where does one buy a bathtub, I wonder?"

"The Prince Regent's staff will know," she replied. The spark of mischief in her blue eyes, and the murmurs of awe from the corridor, told Daniel she knew exactly what she was doing.

"Shall we go and survey the attic?" she asked. "Find the best site for the water tank?"

"I could do that, miss," said Henry Carson. "No need for you to bother."

"I like to have a firsthand view of everything," she replied.

"Of course you do," said Daniel.

This earned him a sharp glance, but he hadn't intended any sarcasm. "Very wise to make sure of every detail," he added. He fell in beside her, thinking this was far more amusing than bending over fusty documents.

They shed the servants as they went back through the kitchen, but Tom asked to come along and "see how it all works." And so they found a second lantern for him to carry, and the four of them walked upstairs together and into Frithgerd's extensive attics.

"We want the end nearest the kitchens," Miss Pendleton said.

Combining Daniel's knowledge of his home with periodic looks out a window, they found the appropriate location. The roof dipped lower here, and the flooring ran out to show exposed rafters and great criss-crossing roof beams. Henry Carson declared this just as well. "We need to see what sort of supports we've got to work with," he said. "Water's right heavy."

Miss Pendleton walked out onto a rafter, showing no sign of apprehension.

Daniel couldn't restrain himself. "Be careful."

"My balance is secure," she answered. "I think

there's sufficient room for the tank in this spot, Mr. Carson."

The man made his way out to join her. He held up his lantern, surveyed the area, and nodded. "No beams to be cut obviously. Floor to be reinforced first. This ought to do it."

"Splendid." She tripped back as if the surface below her was perfectly solid. "We should make a list of tasks."

A groan escaped Daniel.

Miss Pendleton laughed. "Yes, Lord Whitfield, another list. But I shall have charge of this one, and every task will be well done."

He had no doubt of it at all.

❧

Penelope drove back to Rose Cottage bursting with high spirits. There was nothing like the feeling of getting things done—planning, arranging, approving the result. In a few weeks, Lord Whitfield would have his new tub. Such luxury, a whole room just for a bath. She could see it in her mind, with him standing in the steam like a statue of a Roman god. Gloriously unclothed. She flushed but refused to dismiss the idea.

They'd had baths—the Romans, not the gods. Though perhaps their gods had them as well? She had no idea. Penelope laughed as she drove her gig up to the barn. Her mind was flitting about like a flea.

Kitty emerged from the house. The two dogs came out with her, Penelope noticed. She'd let them in again. "Mr. Foyle's gone out," Kitty called as Jip and Jum pranced over to greet her. "He walked off with Mrs. Hart and left me here all alone." She came over to help Penelope unharness the horse and tend to him. "I might have been killed by robbers," Kitty said.

"There are no robbers hereabouts."

"We don't know that, do we? They'd be stealthy."

"It's a very safe spot." Penelope set the water bucket where the horse could reach it. "So Foyle escorted Mrs. Hart home?"

"No, they went to some sort of talk at the chapel. About missionaries in Africa."

"Foyle did?"

Kitty grinned at her. "Could have knocked me over with a feather, too, miss. I reckon he's courting her. 'Cause Mr. Foyle ain't one for preaching."

Penelope could only agree as they walked to the house together. The dogs trotted behind, clearly intending to follow them into the kitchen. Penelope gave them a stern look, which she transferred to Kitty when Jip and Jum sloped off to their outdoor quarters.

"Mrs. Hart left a steak-and-kidney pie for dinner," said the girl quickly. "Will I ever be such a dab hand with pastry, do you think?"

Penelope doubted it, but she didn't like to say so. Instead, she pumped water and washed her hands at the sink.

"Are they really building a great fountain over at Frithgerd?"

"Fountain? No. Lord Whitfield is installing a bath."

Kitty cocked her head. "Mrs. Hart said there was to be pipes all over the place."

Stories spread like wildfire in the country, Penelope thought. And just as haphazardly. Once again, she explained the plan and how it would work.

"Hot water at a touch," Kitty marveled when she'd finished. "You really think it'll work, miss?"

Lord Whitfield's bathing room would become a wonder of the neighborhood, Penelope realized. Unless it didn't work, in which case it would be a famous folly. But it would work; she had no doubt about that.

They ate their pie. As the day faded, Penelope tried to settle to some mending, but her brain craved more activity. The notebooks she'd brought back from Frithgerd sat in a pile on the large table in the front room. She went over, spread them out, and opened them all, in three rows of three. Looking back and forth, she compared the texts. She turned pages.

These were such odd documents. Any diary she'd ever seen had spoken of familiar happenings. What the writer did in a day, meals and visits and companions. Sometimes there were notes of monies spent. Lady Whitfield's notebooks were totally different. Fragmentary, cryptic, and yet they nagged at her. Penelope turned more pages.

Some commonplace phrases were repeated from page to page and notebook to notebook. Lady Whitfield had been interested in birds, apparently, and trees. She'd often recorded the numbers and types she'd observed, and made drawings of them. Then there were notations that looked like words, but weren't known to Penelope. And some odd symbols, too. Not signs Penelope was familiar with, like Greek letters or numbers. They were more like tiny drawings.

She read more closely, moving from one notebook to another. So many drawings of birds. Crows and gulls and owls were recognizable. They looked like English birds, however, not exotic species Lady Whitfield might have seen on her travels. The same was true of the tiny pictures of trees. They ran along in lines, interspersed with symbols and an occasional letter. The text didn't coalesce into meaning, no matter how much she concentrated. Yet it seemed far too complicated and…persistent over such a long time to be nonsense.

All at once, Penelope began to wonder if the notebooks were written in a code, with all the drawings and phrases and symbols standing for something else. The journals were so intricate. They *felt* so portentous. And they'd been hidden so carefully. Unless Whitfield's mother was mad, which she'd never heard, they must mean *something*. Lady Whitfield had clearly thought them important. Were they the secret record of her innermost thoughts?

Penelope turned a page, and another, then sat back and rubbed her eyes. If it was a code, there must have been a key—a list of correspondences that explained the symbols and phrases. There was no understanding these notebooks otherwise.

Penelope's spirits sank. She'd been so eager to decipher them. But how would she and Whitfield ever find the key—one or two sheets of paper perhaps in the sea of documents at Frithgerd? They could search for weeks. If it was there at all.

Then she rallied. The person who created these notebooks had been astonishingly meticulous. She would have a system. Penelope concentrated. What would she have done in the same circumstances?

Lady Whitfield wouldn't have hidden the key with her notebooks, she concluded. That would be stupid. So not in the trunks then. Somewhere not at all like them, under the writer's control, readily at hand. Lady Whitfield's personal possessions would the best place to start. Penelope stood, ready to race to Frithgerd and begin a search, but realized that the hour had grown late as she'd pored over the journals. The house was silent. Kitty was asleep. She'd have to curb her impatience for a bit.

Twelve

DANIEL OPENED THE GATE AT THE BACK OF Frithgerd's gardens and ushered his party through. The walk to see the site for the new mill wheel and pump, which Daniel had anticipated as a chance to spend more time with Miss Pendleton, had somehow turned into an expedition. Henry Carson was with them of course, but Macklin and young Tom had attached themselves as well. The latter was full of questions for Carson about building methods and materials, which was no great matter. But Macklin had taken the position at Miss Pendleton's side that Daniel had begun to think of as his rightful place. She was ethereally lovely in a muslin gown the color of peach blossoms with just a shawl over her arms on this warm summer morning.

"I'll go ahead and find the miller," said Carson after a while. "He's to meet us by the stream."

The builder strode ahead up the slope behind the house. When he was out of earshot, Macklin said, "We have some news. I believe Whitfield told you about the possibility of watchers?"

Miss Pendleton's face grew shuttered, and Daniel nearly cursed. She'd been looking so happy these last few days, full of plans and even jokes. The past should be left in the past, he thought. Raking it up never did any good.

"Tom has been roaming about the neighborhood," the older man added. "It's a habit of his, and everyone is used to it by now. They scarcely notice him anymore. So he's ideally placed to keep an eye out for strangers."

Miss Pendleton frowned at Tom, whether in concern or disapproval Daniel couldn't tell.

"And he's spotted someone," Macklin continued. "Tell them what you told me, Tom."

The lad nodded. "It's a fella staying above the tavern in the next village over," he said. "Toward Rose Cottage. Said he's here to study butterflies."

"Butterflies?" Daniel found the excuse unlikely.

Tom nodded as if he felt the same. "But he don't seem that sort of person, if you know what I mean. More like a military man, I'd have said. And he don't know much more about butterflies than I do. I asked him about those little purple ones, and he didn't seem to know which ones I meant. He walks the fields with a net and a case. But when I watched him for a bit, he didn't catch any butterflies."

"What is his name?" asked Miss Pendleton.

"He told the tavern keeper Jake Wendell, but I didn't believe him."

"Why not?"

"I just didn't." Tom shrugged. "Growing up on your own, you get a feel for liars. Or you get in a mort of trouble." He received their sympathetic glances with a shrug.

"What does he look like?" Miss Pendleton's face showed the anxiety that Daniel had hoped was eased.

"Tall and well set up," replied Tom. "Long, sharp nose and a chin to match. Black hair but light eyes. The kind of fella you don't want to cross, in my opinion. Like the bully boys in Bristol."

"Does that sound familiar?" Macklin asked her.

"No. I don't remember anyone like that." She crossed her arms and gripped her elbows protectively.

Daniel longed to wrap her in his arms and shield her from harm. Which he had no right to do. Or ability? What could he do about a suspicious visitor? "He was the only stranger in the neighborhood?" he asked.

"The only funny one."

"You should keep an eye on him, see what he does."

"But be careful not to let him see you following him," said Macklin.

"He won't, my lord."

"This isn't the streets of Bristol."

"I'm used to the country now." Tom sounded confident.

"Really," said Miss Pendleton. "These people are not gentle or patient. Do not put yourself in jeopardy on my account."

"No need to worry, miss."

"That is what you think," she replied, almost too quietly to hear. "And then you discover how naive and ignorant you were."

It would be vastly satisfying to thrash the men who'd made her feel that way, Daniel thought.

He realized that Macklin was watching him. He unclenched his fists.

They rounded a clump of trees and saw Henry Carson standing beside the stream with a short, plump man in buckskin breeches, an old-fashioned skirted coat, and a tricorn hat. Daniel recognized Walter Simpson, the local miller. They'd met before on estate business, and he'd found Simpson brusque but extremely competent. Daniel moved forward to greet him and introduce the others.

Simpson nodded with the air of a man who valued manners but had no time to waste. "You've got a decent head of water here," he said. The stream was fifteen feet across at this point, tumbling over good-sized rocks. "And it runs pretty strong all year, as you know, my lord."

"Quite a spate when it rains," Daniel replied.

"Which is why you need the right bit of bank for your wheel," said Simpson. "And I've found you one."

He led them upstream to a spot where the riverlet narrowed between two rock outcroppings and dropped in a picturesque waterfall. "You wouldn't even need a dam here," said Simpson. "You could fit an overshot wheel right in there. The fall has hollowed out a space behind, y'see."

They all peered into the dim space behind the cascading water.

"And the water here is deep enough to fit your pump," the miller said, indicating the pool below.

"I had thought of that bigger pool near the house," said Henry Carson.

"Aye, but that's where all the kiddies hereabouts

swim this time of year and the young people picnic," said Simpson.

Daniel met the miller's sharp green eyes, impressed that he'd taken this into account.

"You don't need too tall a wheel for a pump, my lord." He turned to Carson. "You just have to figure how to cut off when your water tank up at the house is full."

Simpson and Carson fell into a discussion of shafts and gears and levers. Carson made notes and drawings on a slate he'd brought along. Tom leaned over the diagrams with eager curiosity.

"Perhaps your young friend would like to be a builder," Daniel said to Macklin.

"Waterworks is certainly an up-and-coming discipline," the earl replied. "We'll see if Tom's interest lasts. He's always taken by new ideas. But he tends to move on once his curiosity is satisfied."

On the walk back to the house, Daniel managed to get Miss Pendleton to himself by the simple expedient of moving slower and slower until the others had pulled well ahead. Yet solitude didn't bring her back from far away. "It's fortunate Simpson knows someone who can design the millworks."

"What? Oh, yes."

She'd been immersed in details of the project, full of enthusiasm, laughing with him as Carson's helper took a sledgehammer to Frithgerd's corridor wall. But now she'd gone muted, guarded, and suspicious as she'd been when they'd first met. Daniel loathed the change. "I'd feared the water wheel would take longer," he tried. "Two weeks is much better than I expected."

Miss Pendleton merely nodded. She scarcely looked at him.

An image flashed on Daniel's inner eye, repeating as quick as an eyeblink. A carriage driving away, with no acknowledgment from the passengers as the vehicle grew smaller and smaller until it disappeared around a bend in the road. Again, and again, without mercy. "Don't go."

"What?" His companion turned, stared, her attention definitely caught.

Had he spoken aloud? Surely not. The pictures had been momentary, barely grasped and then gone. And they made no sense whatsoever. Of course she would be going. She didn't live here. She wasn't *with* him in any conventional sense. And thus she would be leaving. In her gig, not a traveling carriage. As she always did. Desolation was inappropriate. Desolation? Ridiculous.

Miss Pendleton touched his arm. "Lord Whitfield?"

He'd stopped walking. His chest felt tight. What the deuce? He moved, a step and then faster. "We should make sure Carson remembers to engage the bricklayer."

Puzzled, Penelope strode after him. They both knew that Henry Carson needed no reminders; he'd proved his competence over the last few days. So what had caused the strain in Whitfield's face and the urgency of his tone? She felt a leap of sympathy even though she didn't understand. Had he said, "Don't go"? She wasn't sure now. He'd muttered. The pain in his face had distracted her.

Penelope's dark memories, the despair she'd felt at the idea of watchers looming over her, receded a bit. She hurried to catch up with him.

"What news on the piping?" he asked when she reached his side.

"Elm is recommended. The pipes can be made from trees in your woods." He knew this. She'd told him.

"Tom wants to see how they are bored out."

"So you said."

"Did I? You have a marvelous memory. I don't know how I got anything done without you."

Penelope found his joking tone irritating. But if he wanted to pretend the last few minutes had been just as usual, she couldn't stop him. He wasn't obliged to explain himself to her. Pushing aside a brush of hurt, she said, "I wanted to talk to you about your mother." She'd been trying to find a time to tell him her theory.

Whitfield started and looked at her as if she'd said something bizarre. "My mother?"

What was the matter with him today? "I have an idea about her notebooks," she replied.

"Notebooks?"

It was a perfectly simple word. There was no need to look at her as if she was daft. "I think they might be in code."

He couldn't have looked more astonished. "Code?" he repeated.

"Or call it a private writing system," Penelope went on. "Some people invent those to keep their personal thoughts private. There's Leonardo da Vinci's mirror writing, for example."

Once again, he stopped on the path. "You cannot be comparing my mother to da Vinci."

"Well, no. Or only in this one sense. Creating a hidden way of writing."

"But why would she do that?" Whitfield looked bewildered, then annoyed. "Would she go to such great lengths to keep from revealing herself? Was that really necessary?"

Penelope blinked at the anger in his voice.

"To be deliberately incomprehensible," he continued, voice rising. "And then, as if that was not enough, to hide her notebooks in the lining of trunks where I was bound never to find them. She must have known I never would. Was she insane?"

"Well, perhaps she had some reason," Penelope began.

"What possible reason could she have had?" He started walking again, very fast.

Penelope nearly had to run to keep up with him. "And anyway, you did find them."

"*You* did. She didn't count on you. Nobody could have imagined you." With a humorless laugh, Whitfield strode down to the garden gate, opened it, and started back toward the house.

She trotted after him, wanting to ask what he'd meant by that last remark. It hadn't sounded like a compliment. Nor had it seemed to be a criticism exactly. She gazed up at him as they raced along. His face was grim and closed. Perhaps it would be better to drop this subject. But she was driven to solve the puzzle of the journals. He must feel the same, surely? They contained his mother's thoughts. "So, if it is a code, which I really think it is, there must be a key."

"A key? To unlock what exactly?"

"Not an actual physical key. It would be a list of the phrases and symbols that she used over and over again. She did, you know. You can see the repetition if you look through the notebooks. So the key would have an explanation of what each one stands for. Substitutions."

"Substitutions," Whitfield echoed. His sidelong glance was darkly skeptical.

"Yes." In her hurry, Penelope tripped on a stone in the garden path. She stumbled, trying to catch her lost balance.

Whitfield caught her, effortlessly holding her upright with one arm and pressing her close against his chest. He felt like a bulwark. There were his lips, inches from hers. There was the line of his jaw and the breadth of his shoulder. The anger drained from his expression as he stared down at her. "You really believe they're meant to be...deciphered?"

"I think it's a strong possibility." She was breathless. Her hands had gripped his upper arms as if they belonged there. She didn't want to let go.

"You do know how strange that sounds."

The cloth of his coat was smooth under her fingertips. She couldn't look away. And seemingly, neither could he. "The notebooks are rather strange."

He gave a bark of laughter. "An understatement, Miss Pendleton. And why, we ask? Uselessly."

"We might learn the reason if we decode them."

He let her go. Did he regret that as much as she did? Penelope inhaled the sweet scent of some flowering bushes at the edge of the path. The heady perfume would always remind her of him.

"How do you propose to do that?" he asked, his voice gone flat again.

"By finding the key, of course."

"Finding. We haven't had much luck at that so far. Nothing about the Rose Cottage legacy. Just a mountain of moldering paper."

Something had certainly soured his mood. Penelope wanted to raise it. "I think the key would be among your mother's personal things." She explained her reasoning to him.

"My parents' possessions were packed up and stored in the attic," he said when she'd finished.

"Shall we go and look at them?"

Daniel was reluctant. He didn't want to go through his mother's things. Nor did he care what her diaries said, or so he told himself. When had anything gone right with his parents? But Miss Pendleton was practically vibrating with curiosity. The bright enthusiasm was back in her face, and he couldn't deny her. Daniel nodded and walked on.

They made a brief stop to question his housekeeper and snag a branch of candles, and then he led the way upstairs to the attic.

"Mrs. Phipps said they put my mother's things over here when they cleared out her room." He walked around bits of old furniture and stacks of boxes to the west side of the main attic. As his housekeeper had promised, he could easily identify the recent additions to storage. To one side was his father's old shaving stand. He hadn't wanted to look at it every day, and anyway he had a newer, more efficient one. "These should be hers," he added, indicating a neat row of trunks and boxes and a dressing table that he hadn't wanted to see again either. He lit the candles, augmenting the light from the dormer windows, and put them on the dressing table. Melancholy threatened. He pushed it aside.

"Right." Miss Pendleton surveyed the prospects like a workman rolling up his sleeves. "Do you want to—"

"You look," said Daniel.

Sympathy and uncertainty seemed mingled in the glance she gave him. She opened a trunk and began lifting out gowns swathed in linen. Unfolding the coverings, she examined each one. "No pockets," she said. "You have no idea how lucky you are to have so many pockets in your clothes."

The scent his mother had used drifted over them. Daniel was besieged by fragments of memories, glimpses of his parents flitting in and out of his life. Mostly out. Without a backward glance.

Miss Pendleton replaced the gowns and repeated the process with a second similar trunk. She looked through a box of shoes, gloves, handkerchiefs, and reticules, turning out the latter and shaking each one. She sorted through ornaments from his mother's room and mementos from her travels. Her enthusiasm appeared to dim as she found no sign of what she wanted.

The last two trunks held hatboxes. She looked inside them all, and the hats. "Nothing," she said. She sat down on a closed trunk, surrounded by sheaves of tissue paper and ornate headgear.

"Her dressing case and more personal items went down with the ship," said Daniel. He was ready to leave this shadowed room and the weight of the past.

"She wouldn't keep the key with her," declared Miss Pendleton.

"Why not?"

"That would have defeated the purpose of a code. Anyone might have found it and deciphered the journal she carried. No, the notebooks were hidden here at Frithgerd. The key would have been, too."

"You may be making far too much of this. Perhaps my mother just had an addiction to…inane scribbling." Had the contents of her mind been as jumbled as the estate records, Daniel wondered. Was his heritage nothing but muddle?

"I don't think it can be that. I *feel* the notebooks are important."

Conviction and curiosity lit her face. She wouldn't give up; she wouldn't turn away. Daniel felt as if he could look at her forever.

She sighed. "But there isn't even a scrap of paper."

He roused himself and looked around. "My mother had a writing desk. Its contents should be with the rest of her things."

"Oh!" Miss Pendleton spread her hands. "We're idiots! We had all the papers taken downstairs. Whatever was in her desk must be among them." She grimaced. "If only we'd known from the first, this might have been much easier." She wrapped tissue around a hat, nestled it in its box, and replaced the lid. When she bent to place the container in the open trunk, she said, "What's this?" Setting the hatbox aside, she reached into the bottom of the trunk, coming up with a small flat case covered in velvet.

"Looks like jewelry." Daniel held out his hand. "That should have gone to the strong room." She handed it to him, and he opened it. A sapphire and diamond necklace sparkled in the candlelight. He'd never seen his mother wear this. But then he'd seen so little of her. Daniel looked up. The sapphires were just the color of Miss Pendleton's eyes. "This would suit you."

Penelope's frustration flamed into a violent revulsion. She wasn't angling for jewels. Mistresses got jewels, were continually greedy for them by all accounts. Did he suppose she was helping him to augment her fortune, to cajole rich gifts out of him? "I don't want a necklace."

"I merely observed that sapphires are your—"

She barely heard him. "I need no largesse from you."

"*Largesse*? What sort of word is that?"

"The sort used by sanctimonious prigs who patronize the poor and *downtrodden*." She'd been looked down upon by too many insulting men in the last year. She wouldn't tolerate any more.

"What the deuce is wrong with you?"

"I don't want your necklace!"

"I wasn't offering it to you!"

"But you said—" She broke off in confusion.

"That sapphires would suit you. Not that you could have my mother's necklace."

Penelope felt the blush spread from her cheeks down her neck and across her chest. She was certain the crimson was visible even in the dim light. She'd allowed unhappy memories to control her. She'd vowed never to do that. Still agitated, she said, "I decide what suits me and whether I shall have it. Not you."

"Undoubtedly. But that does not give you the right to—"

"My *desires* are not your responsibility."

Whitfield blinked.

She'd silenced him, Penelope saw, enjoying the sensation. And yes, this was about far more than a necklace. It was about a year of being chivvied about and mistrusted and frightened, whenever her captors could manage that. They'd intimidated her for quite a time. Perhaps they meant to try again, by sending someone to lurk in her new neighborhood and spy on her. She couldn't stop them. But she could refuse to follow the steps they laid out, like the lines of a dispiriting play.

The light in Whitfield's dark eyes shifted as she gazed steadily into them. Her past trials weren't his fault. But her future wasn't his responsibility either. Her decisions were her own. He would have to learn that.

She stepped closer and set a hand on his shirtfront. She could feel his heart beating against her palm. She moved closer still.

It was like setting a spark to tinder, or plying the bellows to make a fire flare. She could rouse him with a gesture, she thought, and she gloried in that power. Penelope slipped her arms around his neck and kissed him.

His arms and lips received her with only an instant's hesitation. Then he was holding her, and their kiss went from gentle to probing to urgent.

A great wave of certainty rose in Penelope, riding the sweet sensations that shook her whole body. She wanted this. She would have what she wanted. She pressed against him. His hands slid over her, promising delights.

"My lord Whitfield?" Tom's voice floated up the stairwell. "Miss Pendleton?"

Whitfield pulled away as if he'd been stung. Though he looked dazed, he took two quick steps back. His boot heel caught on an uneven floorboard, and he stumbled briefly.

Tom's homely figure appeared at the head of the stairs. "They said you was up here. Mr. Carson needs you to approve the size of the new doorway before they frame it in."

Whitfield muttered something—possibly a curse. Penelope was pleased to think it was, at any rate.

Thirteen

SOMETHING HAD TEETERED IN THE BALANCE BEFORE
that intoxicating kiss, Daniel thought, grasping the
tatters of his dignity as Tom came over to them. Not
the nonsense about the necklace—something more.
"My *desires* are not your responsibility," she'd said.
He could still hear the conviction that had vibrated in
her voice. He could feel her hand on his heart. She'd
commanded him in that moment, and it was beyond any
thrill he'd experienced before.

"Just a moment," Miss Pendleton said. Daniel was
pleased to hear the tremor in her tone. She was as
shaken as he was, and he was fiercely glad of it. She
picked up an elaborate hat to place it in its box.

"Watch out for that one," Tom said. "It's got some
wicked pins in it. Sharp as a knife."

She turned back, holding the wide brim of a
confection adorned with ribbons, feathers, artificial
flowers, and improbably, an entire stuffed bird. "I saw
them. But how do you know?"

"Ah, well." Tom shifted from foot to foot. "We
were larking about when everyone was hauling papers

down from here, and Kitty put it on, meaning no harm, miss. She tried to take it right off again, but them pins stuck in her hair."

Miss Pendleton nodded. "It doesn't matter."

"Or it might have caught on the paper that was inside," Tom added.

"Paper?"

"It fell out when we pulled the hat off Kitty."

Her face lit with excitement. She leaned forward. "What sort of paper?"

"We didn't look, miss. It was folded up in the hat."

"Where is it now?"

Tom took a step backward, clearly intimidated by the intensity of her question. "Ned put it into a box. Following orders. All papers to go downstairs." He looked worried. "That's what we was supposed to be doing."

"Yes, of course you were. Tell me about the box."

"The box, miss?"

"The one Ned put it in."

She was worrying the boy. "It's all right," Daniel told him. "There's nothing wrong. Just tell us whatever you remember."

"Yes, my lord." Tom frowned. "I wasn't paying any particular attention to Ned. I believe the box was wooden, sitting right about there." He indicated a spot next to the trunk. "Mebbe so big?" He held his hands shoulder width apart. "I'm not sure."

"Did it have any special markings?" Miss Pendleton asked.

"I didn't notice any, miss. Was it somethin' important? Nobody told us."

"That box must have held the contents of my mother's desk," Daniel said to her. "Papers. That's why it's not here."

"And that's the one we have to find," she replied. As one, they turned to the stairs.

"What about the doorway?" asked Tom.

"What doorway?"

"They've finished breaking through the wall down by the new bathing room. Mr. Carson wants you to have a look at the doorway. In case you want it bigger."

"Right," said Daniel. "We'll do that first."

Once they had, they consulted the housekeeper, who confirmed that the contents of his mother's desk had been packed up into a box that was wooden, as far as she recalled. She couldn't remember anything distinct about it, however.

And so they set about examining all the wooden boxes that had been brought down from the attic and put in the blue parlor and another room beyond it. The day waned as the pile of those that were *not* the one they wanted grew. Sandwiches were brought in lieu of dinner, and the search went on. At last, a final box was discovered. This one had been shoved behind others, had tipped over, and been hastily repacked. It did contain papers, in a jumble.

"This looks like the things from her desk," said Daniel. "Yes." He lifted out an empty inkwell, a crystal paperweight, and some small ornaments. "This is the one."

He carried it back to the estate office and, once he'd removed the larger items, upended it onto the desk.

A litter of receipts and correspondence and household accounts rained down. Daniel poked through them. A packet of letters tied with a black ribbon sat on top. Miss Pendleton leaned over his shoulder. He breathed in her light scent and felt as if he'd gone molten. Everything fled his brain except those kisses.

"That's odd," she said.

Odd that she could set him afire by mere proximity? But she couldn't mean that. "What is?"

"That looks very like my mother's handwriting." She picked up the packet of letters. "And her notepaper. It *is* her notepaper." She untied the ribbon and spread the letters out. "This is her hand. And this one. And this. What are letters from my mother doing here?" She read one of the addresses. "Who is Miss Serena Walsden?"

"That was my mother's name before she married," replied Daniel. He bent closer. "This one is her handwriting. And this." Quickly he separated the missives into two piles, one written by his mother and the other apparently by Miss Pendleton's.

She sat down beside him. "Katharine Keighley," she said, touching the address on a letter. "That was *my* mother's name before she married."

Side by side, they stared down at the preserved correspondence.

Daniel shuffled through the piles, examining each one. "They seem to date from 1792 to 1811."

"My mother died in 1811. Her letters must have been sent back to her correspondents. Papa and the solicitor took care of all that sort of thing."

Daniel tried to remember anything particular about

that year and his mother. Nothing came to mind. He would have been eighteen and in London.

"So here is the connection between our families," Miss Pendleton murmured. "Our mothers were acquainted. Friends."

He looked down at the scattered letters.

"Do you suppose the reason I have Rose Cottage is in there? It must be. Can we read them, do you think?"

"They were in her desk, not hidden or secret," Daniel replied. "I think we can." He was curious but also a little apprehensive for some reason.

Miss Pendleton nodded. Daniel thought she looked as if she felt the same. She sorted the missives. "We should go in order by date." She checked each letter and laid out the two sets in order.

He smiled. "Always methodical."

Seeming too unsettled to smile back she handed him a letter. "This is the first. From your mother."

Slowly he unfolded the page. Nearly thirty years old, the ink was a little faded. "Dear Kate," he read.

"No one called my mother Kate."

"Apparently *my* mother did." He acknowledged the bewilderment in her gaze, suspecting his face mirrored it. Looking down, he began reading aloud again.

Dear Kate,

And so we are to be married in the same year, very nearly in the same month. I certainly wish you great happiness. Isn't it odd to do so by letter from far away when we spent every day of the last three

*years together? And can it have been only three?
Somehow, though our school years were brief, they
made me feel as if I've known you all my life. I am
well aware that my existence BK (before Kate) did
not include you, and yet I expect you to recall every
detail. Perhaps because I was always pouring out
confidences, whether you wished to hear them or not!*

*I hope this Sir Jared fellow is worthy of you and
understands what a gem he is getting. Tell him I
will make him sorry if he does not!*

*Your ever friend,
Serena*

Daniel raised his eyes and gazed at his lovely companion. She seemed transfixed by what she'd heard.
"They were at school together," she said.

"Apparently."

"Mama never told me much about her school
days."

"Neither did mine." Of course she'd never told
him anything.

"I had the impression she enjoyed them."

Daniel said nothing, because he had no *impressions*
to share.

Miss Pendleton blinked, unfolded the first letter in
her pile, and read, "Dear Serene Serena."

"Ha," said Daniel. He wouldn't have called his
mother serene. Cold, perhaps. Indifferent. But not
serene.

"What?"

"Nothing."

Too curious about the letters to wonder at his stern expression, Penelope read on.

Dear Serene Serena,

I was so surprised to hear that you are marrying after all. How often did you vow that you never would? And you are to be a viscountess! I must imagine you in an ermine cloak and coronet. Splendid, I'm sure, but what about the life of adventure and dark intrigue you plotted? Nay, insisted upon. You had such plans! I hate to think you have given them up in just one (glorious, I'm sure) season. However, I don't wish to sound critical. I will be delighted with anything, or anyone, who makes you happy. I trust you to judge what that will be.

And of course I wished to hear your confidences. As you know very well. Just as you welcomed mine. Did we not both marvel at how easily we fell into friendship? And what a rare gift it was, to find a kindred spirit.

Your forever friend,
Kate

"A kindred spirit. But Mama never even mentioned her to me." Penelope found this omission surprisingly hurtful. She'd thought of herself as her mother's closest confidante, and believed she'd known the important things about her. "I knew she went to a young ladies' seminary in Bath."

"I never heard even that much." Whitfield's tone

was harsh. "'Adventure and dark intrigue.' What nonsense." He picked up the next letter in the sequence,
frowning at it, and read.

Dear Kate,

*How I miss your jokes. No one else in the world
calls me Serene Serena—for very good reason, as
we know! I can almost hear your laugh as you
say it. I wish I really could. But you are miles
away in Lancashire, and I am fixed in London
for the present.*

*As to that, the season was not glorious but
tedious in the extreme. I hope you are not still sad
about missing it. Society is a wasteland of time
frittered away and money lavished on trivialities. I
cannot tell you how many evenings I simply gritted
my teeth and endured, like Prometheus chained to
his crag with the eagle ripping at his entrails.*

"That sounds more like her," Daniel interjected.
"My mother was fond of exaggerated comparisons.
Spoken with genial contempt. And very amusing to
her, if no one else."

"And she didn't care for society apparently," said
Miss Pendleton.

"No. She made a point of avoiding it." And her
home and her son, Daniel thought. He read on.

*Be assured that I have not abandoned my
plans. I simply discovered how little scope one
has as a young lady on her own, at least of the*

sort I want. Marriage seems to be a necessity. Fortunately, I have found just the sort of husband I require. I've exacted a promise from him that I shall have my adventures. I've also spoken with my father's friend, as I told you I would. He was most interested in my idea, particularly when he saw how carefully I'd laid it out. And heard of the alliance I have engaged myself to make. I shall get what I want, have no fear.

Your ever friend,
Serena

Daniel scowled down at the page. "It sounds as if she was simply making use of my father," he said. At some point, early on in his life, he'd decided that theirs was a love story for the ages. They were always off traveling together because they were a charmed twosome, he'd concluded, a world complete unto themselves. The idea had even reconciled him, a little, to being always on the outside. Now the phrase *the sort of husband I require* seemed to contradict that theory.

"Or she'd found someone who shared her interests," said Miss Pendleton.

He remembered what Macklin had told him about the way his father changed after his engagement. That didn't sound like sharing.

"The next letter is from a whole year later," his companion continued. "I wonder if all their correspondence is here?" She began to read.

Dear Serene Serena,

Congratulations on the birth of your son, though I must scold you for not having sent me word yourself. Am I really to hear such news from Letty Crane?

We are following in each other's footsteps once again as I had a boy as well. We have named him Philip. Jared is pleased and proud, as I'm sure your viscount is as well. Men set such store in handing along their titles.

They don't quite tell you how difficult childbirth is, do they? Or perhaps they do, but one can't really know until the time comes. I hope you are not as worn down as I have been.

It seems a long age of the world since we met. When I think of our endless talks at school, I get quite teary. Perhaps we can arrange a visit soon. Jared is not averse to a trip to London once I have recovered. And naturally you are always welcome here.

> *Your forever friend,*
> *Kate*

"I don't think they ever visited," Miss Pendleton said. "I never heard about it if they did."

"Nor I," replied Daniel. But then he probably wouldn't have. He took up the next letter.

Dear Kate,

I am sorry to be slow in answering your letter. I've been languishing in my bed. Me! Can you imagine it? "Difficult" is a pale word to describe childbearing. You teased me about mentioning Prometheus, but I now know precisely how he felt as the eagle ripped at his entrails. You were right. A society party is not nearly that bad. Giving birth assuredly is! Our son—we have called him Daniel—had no easy passage into the world. Indeed, the doctors tell me I shall never have another child. I must say that this news was a relief. I certainly don't wish to endure that agony again.

I'm sad to say that a visit is not likely just now. As soon as I am fully recovered, we are departing for the West Indies. My plans begin to take form at last!

Your ever friend,
Serena

Daniel wondered whether his mother had held the pain of his birth against him. She'd never mentioned it, any more than she'd told him why he had no siblings. He tried to think of one confidence she'd shared with him, and came up empty. The final lines sounded like the parent he remembered, more eager to set off for new places than to see her old friend.

"There must be some letters missing," said Miss Pendleton. "There was no teasing about Prometheus in these." She turned over the rest of the papers that had come from his mother's desk. "I don't see any others."

"Perhaps some were lost, or thrown away." His voice sounded distant, Daniel thought. He was feeling odd. None of his imaginings of growing closer to his parents had been like this. Miss Pendleton gave him a sidelong glance as she unfolded the next letter.

Dear Serene Serena,

I hope you are feeling better. I'm sorry that you will have no more children. I should like several, if my health allows. I'm determined it shall, though I've had another of my wearisome bouts of fever. Indeed, I find I am too weary to write much now. I will do better next time. May your journey be all you hoped for.

Your forever friend,
Kate

"My mother was often ill," Miss Pendleton said. "She had a recurring fever, which weakened her lungs. The least ailment sent her to her bed. For weeks sometimes."

"And mine didn't write back to her for more than a year," Daniel replied, looking at the next letter in the sequence. "I suppose she was traveling and too busy for a friend. That would be like her."

"There might be other lost letters."

"I doubt it." He pushed on with reading before she could reply.

Dear Kate,

I weep every time I hear that you've been poorly again. If only I had not dragged you into those dreadful marshes, and you so full of pluck, keeping watch while I tried to find that sailor's shack and extract his story. When you fell ill afterward—I swear I've never regretted anything more. If I could go back and change that day, please believe that I would do so in an instant.

Daniel looked up, met Miss Pendleton's shocked gaze, and dropped his eyes again. He was disturbed by the emotion that vibrated through this passage. His mother had clearly been concerned about her friend. He hadn't thought she cared deeply for anybody except his father. Now he found that there were others. Which made her treatment of him all the worse, in his opinion. He set his jaw and read on.

I've never forgotten the moment we met, quaking new arrivals at Miss Scofield's Academy. I would have set all the teachers' backs up if you hadn't stepped in and smoothed things over. As you continued to do for three years. I never had a better friend.

Warn your family that if they don't cosset you, I shall descend upon them in clouds of wrath and put some stick about, as my father used to say.

> *Your ever friend,*
> *Serena*

"Marshes," said Penelope. Her brain whirled. "What can your mother have wanted with a sailor in the marshes? What story?"

"I suppose it was some *adventure* that she thought more important than endangering a friend," replied Whitfield.

"But is this the origin of Mama's illness?" Penelope leaned over to reread the last letter. His shoulder against hers was at once a thrill and a comfort.

"It sounds so. People do contract relapsing fevers in the marshes. And she seems to have caught one in my mother's *service*."

His tone was so curt. Though she knew it wasn't directed at her, Penelope hid a wince. "She was sorry."

"She says she was. But then she never visited. Actions speak louder than words."

Penelope picked up the next letter. She was both curious and daunted. The mother of these letters wasn't the woman she remembered, and the contrast was vastly unsettling. She took a breath and read.

Dear Serene Serena,

Such a time since I heard from you. I suppose you are off on your travels again with not an instant for correspondence. I wrote to the Boston address you gave to tell you about my new daughter, Penelope, but I'm not certain that letter got through. Did you receive it, I wonder?

I adore the embroidered shawl you sent me from New Orleans. I showed it to Penelope, and she was eager to chew on the fringes, which of course I did not allow! She is such a dear baby.

I would say this to no one but you—we have always kept each other's secrets, have we not? I

*prefer her to Philip. I know a mother isn't sup-
posed to admit such preferences, but he is a loud
and unruly child. His favorite word is no, and he
becomes absolutely furious when thwarted. Angrier
than I thought a child could be. I often don't know
what to do with him, but Jared only laughs. I hope
that school and a crowd of other boys will improve
his temper.*

*He will be more like you than me, I expect,
standing up for his friends like Joan of Arc. Or some
hero, I should say, in Philip's case. I suppose you
are doing something very like that with your secret
missions. I can only say—bravo!*

*Your forever friend,
Kate*

Penelope blinked back tears. She'd known her
mother favored her. It had been an uncomfortable
feeling for most of her life. On the one hand, she
cherished her love. On the other, it wasn't fair. And
Philip had, inevitably, noticed and resented it.

"Secret missions," said Whitfield. He sounded
puzzled and contemptuous. "Is that some kind of joke
between them?"

"Her notebooks may tell us," replied his companion. "I'm even more convinced they're in code."

He made an impatient sound. "There's a gap of
several years before the next letter."

"Because some were lost," Penelope said. She
wanted to believe that Serena had kept up the connection in those years when her mother had been often ill.

"Perhaps. This is the last one we have."

Penelope bent closer to look at the date. It was a week after her mother's death. She'd never received this missive from her old friend. It had been gathered up with the others and returned.

"I've just remembered. My parents took a long voyage to the East around that time," Whitfield said as he unfolded it to read. "I suppose she didn't bother to write until they were back. A letter sent from there would have been slow to arrive."

Dear Kate,

Remember how we talked about what a different world it would be if young women had property of their own? I have seen such terrible inequities in the last few years. You really can't conceive. Far worse than we imagined in our privileged youth in our little school. I don't even want to tell you.

I cannot change all that, but I am going to see to it that your daughter has what we never did. I suppose she won't need it. And it might simply pass to her husband if she's wed, but I don't care. She shall have a cottage from the estate here, free and clear. And we will arrange things so that her benefactor is a secret. She won't have to be beholden to anyone. She can do whatever she likes with the property. Might it be a godsend? A refuge? I hope so.

John has agreed, though he doesn't fully understand. I must say he is the most reasonable man. I am very fortunate to have found him, my second piece of great luck in the person department.

Your ever friend,
Serena

"Her second piece of luck," said Whitfield. "Not her third. No thought given to the heir and what I might think of the legacy." He let his fist fall on the page. "Reasonable. This is all she has to say about my father?"

"It explains why I have Rose Cottage," said Penelope. She understood his upset, but she was still trying to take in all she'd learned from the correspondence. Her mother had never known of this generous gesture. That was sad. She would have appreciated such a significant sign of their friendship.

"Indeed." He put the letter with the others. "I thought she loved him. Him, at least." His face had fallen into hard lines.

"Your father, you mean?"

He nodded. "But he seems to have been a mere... instrument for her schemes."

"That seems harsh."

"Can you say so when she treated your mother the same? Allowed her to ruin her health, killed her in fact?" He pushed the pile of letters away.

Penelope's impression was different. She'd pictured two girls conspiring together—foolish, yes, but not calculating. The accident of the fever made her sad, but not angry. "She didn't mean to. Everyone makes mistakes."

His response was silence, his expression closed. He

seemed an icy stranger. The correspondence, which might have brought them closer together, had opened a distance instead. Moved by the link with her mother, Penelope felt it keenly.

She wanted to put her arms around him. And she feared that his next words would be a request for her to leave. "We've forgotten our purpose," she said. "We were looking for the key to your mother's notebooks."

He shrugged.

"I'm sure they're related to the secret missions my mother mentioned."

"Schoolgirl blather," he replied.

"They're too intricate. I think your mother was gathering information on her travels. But for whom? The Foreign Office?"

Her host stared at her, incredulous.

Penelope shuffled through the mass of papers on the desk. "We must find that page from the hat."

"Gathering information for the Foreign Office," Whitfield said as if he thought the idea incredible.

She nodded as her hands automatically set the papers in order, unfolding, reading, sorting, stacking. She was nearly at the bottom of the pile when she came upon what she wanted. "Ah, here. This looks like it." She bent over the page, trembling with excitement. "Yes, I recognize phrases from the notebooks." She reached for one of them to compare. And was stopped by a hand laid on top of hers.

"Are you imagining that my mother was a spy?"

"I don't think I'm imagining it." Penelope savored the warmth of his fingers on hers. "Yes. Look at this." She put a fingertip on one line of the key. "Clouds mean ships. Because of their white sails, do you think?" She smiled at him. "Thrilling, isn't it?"

"It's…unbelievable." Withdrawing his hand, he sat back as if poleaxed.

She opened one of the notebooks and compared entries to the key. "A flock of crows signifies regiments of troops. That's rather funny. There are little drawings for numbers, which might have been suspicious if she listed them, I suppose. She used real places and dates at the head of each entry, so she could easily prepare a report from her notes."

"This is insane," said Whitfield.

"It was a risk," Penelope replied. "We realized there was a code. Others might have as well if they got hold of her notebooks. That's why she hid them, I wager."

Her host stared at her. "We? You did. I never would have thought of it in a thousand years."

"Men don't expect a woman's diary to be important," Penelope acknowledged. "Particularly powerful men. That was the beauty of it for her, I'd say. I'm sure she still kept them well hidden when she was traveling, as she did here. And I bet she could talk gibberish to match her entries if necessary."

"All the traveling was for this," murmured Whitfield.

Penelope turned back to the letters and rechecked a date. "Look, it seems your parents were in Boston around 1808, after the troubles with that American ship."

At his blank look, she added, "I've forgotten its name, but the Royal Navy stopped it looking for deserters, and the Americans were very angry. I had a history lesson about it."

"Americans," he repeated.

"You do remember the war with America in 1812?"

"Of course."

"There you are then." She spread her hands.

"What I do not remember, or say rather comprehend, is the idea that my mother was gathering information about them."

"And your father, of course."

"Of course?"

"He must have been helping. Well, the letters said as much. She…enlisted him."

Daniel felt as if his world had been turned upside down. In a matter of minutes, his parents had gone from self-absorbed vagabonds to government spies. The absences he'd resented had a purpose larger than his individual concerns. The conversations he'd always found vacuous were in fact diversions. But had it been necessary to divert *him*?

Miss Pendleton was leafing back through the letters. "This friend of her father's that she mentions. Perhaps he was in the government."

"My maternal grandfather had political connections."

"That would explain it."

"They might have told me, given me some hint at least." Not when he was a child and liable to let something slip, but later. Why had they never trusted him?

"I suppose they developed a habit of secrecy," said Miss Pendleton.

"What?"

"Well." She spoke slowly as if thinking it through. "They would have had to learn to hide in plain sight. To seem guileless, so they would be quickly dismissed.

I imagine that such a pose could become…engrained. Perhaps it had to."

"So they were never genuine for a moment." Bitterness tinged Daniel's tone. He couldn't help it.

The charming little wrinkle that appeared in Miss Pendleton's brow when she was puzzling out a problem deepened. "If your parents were quite different when they were at home, someone might have noticed. London is full of travelers. And as I have reason to know myself, once suspicions are aroused against you, they run wild."

Daniel considered her point. It made sense. And yet it didn't make him feel better. "It's rather worse knowing that they had important secrets and didn't confide in me. When I thought they were simply shallow, I could…shrug them off."

She put a hand on his arm. "I would guess they thought they were protecting you."

Or themselves, Daniel thought. "They might have given me credit for some intelligence, and discretion." This new information felt like another layer of judgment reaching out from the past to condemn him.

Miss Pendleton shrugged. "My father always saw me as a child, even when I was managing his estate better than he could."

Her hand remained on his sleeve, a spot of warmth. Her head was bent over the scatter of papers on the desk. Daniel took in the lovely line of her cheek, the grace of her slender frame.

"It's strange that our mothers were such good friends," she said. "It feels like a…link, doesn't it? Even though we never knew."

The warmth spread through him, gaining heat as it rose. Daniel noticed that the house was quiet around them. The mantel clock showed that the servants would be off to bed soon. They must be wondering about Miss Pendleton's continued presence. Wondering and whispering perhaps. Exchanging sly grins or raising eyebrows in disapproval.

When she looked up and met his eyes, desire flashed though him. He wanted all the things the gossips whispered about, and more. He wanted to sweep the damned papers from the desk and lift her onto it. He wanted to cover her with kisses. He wanted... everything. "My *desires* are not your responsibility," she'd said. Very well, but what about his own? They were, and he had to keep a rein on them.

They'd been behaving with a reckless lack of formality. Some would interpret that as disrespect. Or careless, confident possession. Fury filled him at the idea of anyone seeing her that way. He had to take more care. Which did not mean folding her in his arms and shielding her from all harm, much as he wished that it might.

Daniel stood. His chair rocked with the force of his movement, and Miss Pendleton jumped. "I must get you home," he said.

"*Get* me home."

"At once." He started for the bell rope, then didn't ring. Why draw more attention to their long tête-a-tête? "We'll go to the stables. You have your gig?"

Miss Pendleton rose, her hands resting on the desktop as if for support. "And if I don't wish to go?"

"You don't understand—"

She cut him off with a gesture. "My understanding

has never been in doubt, whatever else was suspected about me. I know very well what I mean when I say I would like to stay a while. Here. With you."

Every fiber of his body leapt at the invitation in her blue eyes. If he touched her now, there would be no going back. "People will think—"

"*People* have thought I was a dupe or a liar or an outright traitor to my country. People are idiotic."

"Some are," he acknowledged.

"Quite a large proportion. I have decided to disregard them."

"That is more easily said than done," Daniel replied. "We live within society." If he took what he wanted— what they both wanted?—she would be ostracized.

"I do not. I have no social position. All that is lost to me. So I can do as I please." Her voice wavered slightly on the last word.

He had to turn away from the appeal in her face. It was one of the most difficult things he'd ever done. "Nonsense." The word came out harsh.

Miss Pendleton stepped back.

"You don't know what you're talking about."

"*I* do not?"

"No, you don't." He wanted to mend matters, not bring further ruin upon her. "You are still a baronet's daughter. What would your father, your mother think?"

She flinched as if he'd hit her.

Daniel's hands reached out of their own accord. "Miss Pendleton." He hadn't meant to say that last bit. Emotion choked him.

She picked up the bonnet and shawl she'd tossed onto one pile of boxes and strode out the door.

Fourteen

STOMACH KNOTTED, EYES HOT WITH HUMILIATION, Penelope eased her gig through the gates and onto the lane that passed by Frithgerd, following a mounted stable boy holding a lantern. The head groom had insisted on sending this escort, saying milord wouldn't like it if they let her go off on her own, and Penelope hadn't been foolish enough to argue. She'd never driven alone at night. Fortunately the lane was familiar, and her horse steady. Reassured by the light ahead, he clopped placidly along. Unfortunately, that left her free to remember how Lord Whitfield had practically shoved her away. She'd offered herself to him, and he'd refused! Her cheeks burned. The look on his face… What had it been before he turned his back? Disapproval? Revulsion?

Penelope's nails dug into her palms. Propriety! Men used the rules to manipulate others, and then ignored them when they became inconvenient. She'd thought Whitfield was different. She'd been feeling so close to him, after reading those letters together. She'd assumed he felt the same. Hadn't she learned by now never to assume? Hadn't a host of assumptions fallen about her ears over the last year? People she trusted had abandoned her. Rights she'd relied on had proven flimsy as wet paper. And now this man she'd come to care for—yes, she had to admit it—had turned away. *Miss Pendleton* he had called her, as if that girl still existed, and yet he'd wanted to sneak her out of the house like a disreputable secret. Where had she gotten the ridiculous idea that she could ever have what she wanted?

The stable boy raised the lantern higher, illuminating the turn at her own road. Penelope guided the gig onto it.

What could she have? He'd taunted her with her birth. Yes, a baronet's daughter was an acceptable, if not brilliant, match for him. But her brother's disgrace had altered everything. Perhaps that was it. He'd realized that a connection to her would taint him as well. Society wouldn't reject a viscount, but they would titter and whisper. And if he had any political ambitions... Penelope made a throwaway gesture. Her pride, trampled and tattered though it was, reared up and rejected that picture. He was right. No sort of liaison was possible. She would erase the idea from her mind.

Penelope blinked. She was not going to cry. She was done with tears. Determination, independence, anger—these were there to sustain her.

Rose Cottage appeared ahead, its stone walls pale in the light of a half-moon. Penelope drove her gig around to the barn, thanked the stable boy, and endured Foyle's scold as she climbed down. Kitty gave her more of the same when she went inside, piqued that her mistress had gone visiting without her. Penelope promised never to do so again and escaped to her bedchamber. There, tossing down her shawl, pulling off her bonnet, she looked at the familiar furnishings, a bit large and grand for her new dwelling. She was lucky to have this refuge. Things might have gone so much worse for her. She ought to be grateful. She was. Yet it was so hard not to yearn for an impossible more.

❧

In a cozy parlor at Frithgerd, at that moment, the Earl of Macklin was curious and restless. To a man used to the bustle of London society, or of large country house parties, the place seemed very quiet. His book didn't hold his attention. Instead, he was staring at the open page, wondering what mysteries preoccupied his host and their pretty neighbor. Beyond the obvious, of course. Was he wrong to leave them so often alone? Miss Pendleton wasn't his responsibility. Whitfield was his main concern. And she'd made it clear she didn't want advice from him. Yet she excited his ready sympathies as well. Her situation was unusual, perhaps more than she knew.

Arthur sighed, closing his book. Interference didn't come naturally to him. Among his family, he generally waited to be asked for aid before stepping in. His impulse to help a set of young men visited by grief had surprised him. He smiled. It had surprised everyone who knew anything about it and mystified countless others who didn't. A duchess whose renowned summer house party he'd skipped this year was convinced he was concealing a scandalous intrigue. One old friend had asked if he was ill; another had posed oblique questions about financial reverses. Arthur's "disappearance" from his customary haunts kept tongues wagging even now. On top of that, helping had proven more complicated than he'd imagined. Still, the transformation of his nephew in the spring had been extremely satisfying.

Buoyed by that thought, Arthur set his book aside and made his way to the estate office. He discovered Whitfield there on his own, hunched over the perennial litter of papers on his desk but not reading any of them. Arthur spoke his name twice, with no effect. Finally, he tapped the younger man on the shoulder. Whitfield lurched upright as if he'd been struck. "You were a thousand miles away," said Arthur.

"Not quite so far." Whitfield looked like a man who'd sustained a stunning blow and was struggling to recover.

"Miss Pendleton is not here?"

"She went home some time ago." He checked the mantel clock as if calculating the interval.

Arthur surveyed the scattered letters and notebooks before him. "Are you making progress?"

"Ha, we've wandered into the realm of fantasy. Further in, I should say."

"What do you mean?"

Whitfield sat straighter, visibly gathered his faculties, and tapped the notebooks. "It seems that my mother was a spy."

"What?"

Arthur's host launched into a tangled story of codes and correspondence. "So we've solved the mystery of the Rose Cottage legacy," he finished. "But we've uncovered another." He frowned down at the desk. "Or a fairy-tale adventure. There seems little mystery about it."

"May I see this key?" Arthur asked. Whitfield handed it over. Arthur ran his eye down the page, compared phrases in one of the notebooks, then another. He was puzzled, then astounded, then concerned. "I think you should put these in your strong room until we can make some inquiries." He examined the younger man's blunt features. "If you will allow me? I have a trusted friend who would know if there's anything in these speculations."

"Castlereagh?"

"An associate. Better able to keep things quiet."

Whitfield hesitated, then nodded. "Yes, I would like the truth. As soon as possible."

"I'll draft a discreet inquiry. We can send a messenger tomorrow."

"Thank you."

Arthur waited for more. When none came, he added, "Miss Pendleton is very clever."

"Not as clever as she thinks, perhaps."

"What do you mean?"

"A pair of fools," Whitfield muttered.

"You and I?" Arthur knew he hadn't meant this, but he wanted to hear more. Whitfield was obviously laboring under a weight of emotion.

"What? No."

"You and Miss Pendleton then?"

"What are you suggesting?" The younger man's tone had gone belligerent.

"Suggesting? Nothing. Wondering? A good deal."

Whitfield glared at him for a fiery instant. Then he looked down, his jaw tight, fists closed. "Damn it all," he said. He pushed his chair back so hard it nearly toppled over, then sprang up and strode from the room.

He'd forgotten his mother's notebooks and their revelatory code. Arthur gathered up the pile and carried it to his bedchamber, where he made use of the key in the writing desk there to lock all away until they could be transferred to the estate strong room. Sitting down to write the promised letter of inquiry, he wondered uneasily about the prospects for a truculent viscount and the ruined daughter of a baronet.

❦

Penelope didn't return to Frithgerd the following day, nor for several days after that. She received Henry Carson at Rose Cottage and conferred with him on the progress of work on the bath. She attended to her own affairs, baked an apple tart with Kitty and Mrs. Hart, joined the dogs on their patrols of her property. And through it all, she tried not to think of her beguiling neighbor. Without the least vestige of success.

Her mind was full of him—bent over estate records, chasing goats, cutting pastry with boyish concentration. And kissing her, of course. Caressing her until her senses swam. And lastly, refusing her *advances*.

That word burdened her when she thought of their most recent encounter. It made her cheeks burn.

What did he think of her now? That last was terribly important, because—left alone to reflect—she'd realized that she cared very much about his good opinion. About him. The stark truth was, she'd fallen in love with her unexpected viscount. And she wanted much more than stolen passion.

Walking with the dogs, she would fall into a daydream of a future with him, smiling at the notion that she was better at running his estate than he was. He would admit it. Indeed, that was part of his charm. He had no difficulty doing so. On the other hand, he was more at ease in the world. He could show her the way to go on among notables like Lord Macklin, who still intimidated her a little. And so they would pass their days. Then there were the nights, of course. She couldn't leave out the nights. Dreams of his touch haunted her sleep. She would happily spend her life with Lord Whitfield. Daniel.

At this point, her fantasy always came tumbling back to earth. No one was talking about marriage. The idea, which would have been implicit had they met at a round of *ton* parties, had never arisen. *He* wasn't thinking of it. *She* shouldn't be. And even if he did, it was impossible. Yoked to her social ruin, Whitfield would be pitied at best, rejected at worst. Penelope knew how it felt to have acquaintances edge away, turn their backs. She'd had a bitter taste of that when she moved out of her father's house. She wouldn't bring such a fate down on him. And was she to give him his cottage back as a dowry? Every feeling revolted. She needed to become accustomed to the life she had, rather than some castle in the air. If she worked at it, she would find contentment in her lot. And she would *not* yearn. She refused to yearn!

On the following day, however, the object of these reveries came to see her.

"I beg your pardon," Whitfield said when she opened the front door.

He clearly hadn't expected her to answer his knock. But Kitty had walked to the nearby farm for milk and eggs. Foyle had taken the gig into the village to look for some bit of ironmongery he needed. Penelope no longer had the scope, or the staff, to turn away visitors with the fiction that she was not *at home*. The pretense would be ridiculous without the insulating layers of a great house. No, he was here, and they were alone together.

Whitfield strode into her parlor and stood before the fireplace, slapping his riding gloves against his leg. As usual, the room seemed smaller with him in it. His energetic presence filled the space, even as it eased an ache in Penelope's heart. A joy that she shouldn't have allowed to take root expanded in her chest. She was so very glad to see him. Dangerously glad.

Daniel shifted from one foot to the other. It had been only a few days since they met, but he'd missed her dreadfully. The estate office seemed dusty and vacant without her stimulating presence. The construction project had lost its savor. He'd had to see her. And now he didn't know what to say. The memory of their last encounter vibrated between them. He'd made a mistake. And yet he'd done the right thing. He was having difficulty reconciling those two facts. Of course he'd had to refuse when she'd offered to stay.

No tinge of dishonor could be allowed to touch her. But oh, how he wanted her! He'd thought of nothing else ever since. One part of him called the rest an idiot for missing the chance to make her his own.

She stood there looking at him. The lovely lines of her face and form were so familiar now. She'd become an integral part of his world. She hadn't asked him to sit. This was all her fault for speaking their longing out loud. They should just go back to the way they'd been. And was pretending that he didn't desire her with every fiber of his being really what he wanted? Damn this confusion. If he'd lost her, he didn't know what he was going to do. "Some of the things I said the last time we met were…inappropriate."

"Which things would those be?"

Of course she wasn't going to make it easy for him. She never did. Daniel realized that, oddly, this was one of the things he liked most about her. Which didn't help him come up with an answer. "Those that implied that I have any right to dictate—"

"We completed our task," she interrupted.

"Task?"

"We found the information we were looking for," she said.

"Information?" Yes, just keep repeating a word from her sentences like a dashed parrot, Daniel thought. That made a fine impression.

"About Rose Cottage, why it was left to me. That was the reason we began. And we have succeeded."

"So now that you know, you're abandoning me?"

"Abandoning?"

He'd gotten her doing it. She looked incredulous.

But all that Daniel could think was that she was going to leave him. He had to stop her. "You said you'd help me set the estate records in order. You promised."

"'Promise' is rather an overstatement."

"And the bathing chamber. You said you'd supervise."

"I can consult with Carson from here."

"You like to see each step of the process for yourself. You said so." He had to find the right argument to keep her. There had to be one.

"I think it's not wise for me to be at Frithgerd. You as much as said so yourself."

"But I'm an idiot." His thoughts were muddled by the attraction she exerted—like the swift current of a river about to hurtle over a precipice. They were alone in the house. She could run to his arms, demand more of those intoxicating kisses. He would never be able to refuse her again.

To his everlasting relief, she laughed. "You do know that you should hire an estate agent," she said. "A really competent one since organization is not your forte."

"Forte," he repeated before he could stop himself. He loved the way she spoke.

"Not one of your natural skills."

"I know what the word *means*." It wasn't the vocabulary. It was the style.

She nodded. "There's no shame in admitting that one's particular talents do not lie in…certain directions."

For some reason, this innocuous phrase filled the room with heat. Daniel's thoughts went in the direction of lusciously fulfilled desire, and he was certain that hers did as well. But they mustn't talk about that, or she would withdraw again. "Fortunately your talents do."

She blinked. He'd made it worse. "I need you," Daniel blurted out. And clamped his teeth on the last of the phrase. He hadn't meant to say that. All at once, he felt exposed. People hurt you the most when you admitted this.

Penelope felt a pang. Her guest sounded wounded. There was no mistaking the set of his lips, the flicker in his brown eyes. The desire to comfort him was nearly overpowering. "You must see that I cannot—"

"Cannot?"

She very nearly said, "Spend more time with you when I can't have you." The words jostled in her brain, tangled on her tongue.

Whitfield stepped closer.

She would have so enjoyed setting that mass of paper in order. Sorting it had been a deeply satisfying process. But Frithgerd was none of her business. Lord Whitfield's engrained, rather endearing inefficiency was not her affair. The longer she held on, the harder it would be when all was ended by, for example, the arrival of a lovely new viscountess in those chambers she'd frequented. But the concern in his eyes—and something that looked very like tenderness—was too much. "All right," she heard herself say.

He leaned closer. "All right?"

"I did say I would help you. With the records."

The relief flooding his expression was nearly palpable. "You did."

"So I...I will."

He smiled. "Splendid. Wonderful."

He looked so very glad, as if her agreement had filled him with joy. Elation flooded Penelope. She couldn't help it. Perhaps a fleeting pleasure was better than none at all?

"But I mustn't—"

Whitfield was interrupted by a chorus of barking behind the cottage, followed by shouts and then a metallic clatter. Penelope turned automatically toward the window, but she couldn't see the barn from where she stood.

"What the deuce?" her guest said.

She needed to ask him what it was he mustn't do. But the barking intensified. So did the shouting. He started toward the door, and she followed.

They found Jip and Jum poised before the entrance to the barn, hackles raised, voicing defiance. A few feet away, Kitty was toe-to-toe with a boy, trying to wrest a large stick from his hands. An overturned basket spilled eggs at their feet.

After a moment, Penelope recognized the boy as the goatherd Sam Jensen. Which was a puzzle. She'd thought the goat problem was solved. The flock had returned several times after the dogs' arrival and been chased away. It was some time since they'd appeared. So what was Sam doing here?

Whitfield went over and took hold of the stick, pulling it away from them. "What is all this?" he said.

"He was going to hit Jip and Jum," replied Kitty indignantly.

"I come to get the goat they stole away."

"Stole?" said Penelope and her visitor at the same moment.

Penelope turned to the hounds and said, "Quiet!" Heeding the voice of authority, the dogs stopped barking. They continued to eye Sam Jensen balefully, however. "Sit," said Penelope. They did so.

"We don't come in your garden no more," the goatherd said. "Nor on your property at all. But we have to pass by sometimes." He sounded aggrieved.

"Don't see why," said Kitty.

"There ain't no other way to go," replied Sam. "And your dogs got no call to give me the evil eye. When I got back to the farm yesterday and found I was a goat short, I knew they'd took it."

"More likely you lost it," said Kitty.

"I looked everywhere!"

"Couldn't have."

"I did! All the places we went. And why are they so keen to keep me out of the barn?"

"Because they're good watchdogs," said Kitty. "They don't let anybody skulk about."

"I wasn't skulking!"

Penelope looked at Jip and Jum. Had they eaten a goat? That would not do. It would, in fact, be a serious problem. "Wait here," she said.

Whitfield set the stick down and followed. The light was dim inside the barn, but when she peered into the stall where Jip and Jum slept, Penelope glimpsed a patch of white. Heart sinking, she went closer. A small spotted goat, perhaps four months old, gazed placidly up at her. When she stepped nearer, it stood and came to meet her, sniffing at her outstretched fingers. Whitfield's horse looked on from the next stall, benignly curious.

Penelope ran her hands over the little animal and found no hurt.

"What is it doing in here?" asked Whitfield.

"I have no idea." She picked up the goat and carried it out into the yard.

"I told you," cried Sam as soon as she appeared.

Jip and Jum jumped up and came to push at her legs, as if to herd her back into the barn. As an experiment, Penelope set the goat down. Immediately, the hounds' attention turned to the little creature, pushing at it to go inside. The goat butted playfully at them in return as it complied.

With Whitfield once again at her heels, Penelope followed the three into the barn and watched Jip and Jum chivy the goat into the stall and resettle it. They then lay down on either side, tongues lolling, looking quite pleased with themselves. She turned to find that Kitty and Sam had joined them. "What're they about?" asked Sam.

"They seem to have adopted a goat," replied Whitfield.

The boy gaped up at him. "Adopted?"

"Like a stray pup you find in the street?" asked Kitty.

Sam shook his head. "I never heerd of such a thing in all my born days."

"Neither have I," answered Whitfield. "But I believe the evidence is before us."

They all gazed at the three animals.

"They can't keep it," said Sam. "I got to get it away from them." He stepped closer, eliciting a deep growl from Jip.

Penelope put out a hand to stop the boy. "Wait."

"They stole it," he protested.

"I wonder if there's some strain of collie or sheep-dog in their bloodlines," said the viscount.

Penelope met his gaze. His eyes were dancing. She was also suppressing a laugh.

"Them are foxhounds," said Sam. "They ain't sup-posed to do no herding. And I'll be in trouble over that goat. I got to have it back." He moved toward the stall. Both dogs rose and growled.

"Perhaps your master would sell it to me instead," said Penelope. She ignored a choking sound from Whitfield. "He does sell goats sometimes, doesn't he?"

"Now and then." Sam couldn't seem to tear his eyes from the stall. "But you're saying you'll buy a goat for your dogs? That's daft." He ducked his head. "Begging your pardon, miss."

"When you put it that way, it does sound odd," Whitfield said.

"So let's not put it that way," replied Penelope. "Just ask your master what price he wants, will you, Sam?"

After a bit more staring, Sam went off to inquire. "You wouldn't think Jip and Jum would like those devil eyes," said Kitty. "What are they going to do with a goat?"

"My question exactly," said Whitfield, his voice brimming with humor.

"I wonder, rather, why they added the creature to the things that they guard," replied Penelope, contem-plating the new member of her household. The goat's eyes were indeed very different from the steady brown regard of the dogs.

"They recognized it as their own," said her guest.

Shaken by the intensity of his tone, Penelope made the mistake of meeting *his* gaze. And then she couldn't look away. Breathing suddenly seemed far more difficult.

"Because they all have black and brown spots on their backs?" asked Kitty. She squinted. "Huh, the shapes are alike."

"Perhaps that's it," said Penelope when she could find her voice.

"There's a brindled cat over at the farm," Kitty added. "I wonder if they'd take to her, too?"

Whitfield laughed. The sound—deep and warm and easy—seemed to shiver across Penelope's skin. It drew a grin from Kitty, who showed no sign of going about her duties.

The sound of hooves heralded a vehicle approaching the barn—Foyle returning, no doubt. Half an hour ago, she'd been noting her lack of staff, Penelope thought. Now there seemed to be all too many of them. She led the way outside and found her conclusion correct. Foyle had returned. Moreover, Mrs. Hart sat beside him in the gig.

Kitty went to crouch over her fallen basket, exclaiming over one broken egg. "But I couldn't let Sam hit Jip, could I?"

Foyle drew up in front of them. He scowled at Lord Whitfield. "What are you all doing out here?"

"Jip and Jum have a-dopted a goat," Kitty told the newcomers.

Foyle turned his glare on her. "What sort of nonsense are you spouting now, girl?"

As Kitty related events, Foyle climbed down and turned to help Mrs. Hart. "And so we're buying the goat," the girl finished.

Foyle frowned at Penelope. She shrugged and nodded. The man shook his head as if he thought himself surrounded by lunatics.

Mrs. Hart reached into the gig for a bundle set behind the seat. "I've brought the chicken," she said. "Mr. Foyle passed me walking and kindly offered me a lift." When Penelope said nothing, she added, "You wanted to learn how to pluck fowls, miss."

"The deuce you did!" exclaimed Lord Whitfield.

Mrs. Hart's interested gaze shifted to him. "I've said over and over that I'm happy to do it myself, my lord."

"I'm sure you have."

Foyle turned his scowl back on the visitor. Kitty, too, seemed to be waiting for some intriguing new twist in their ridiculous saga.

"I should be on my way," Whitfield said.

Under the current circumstances, Penelope had to agree. As she watched him ride away, she was acutely aware that she hadn't found out what he mustn't do. But she vowed that she would.

Fifteen

DANIEL TOOK A ROUNDABOUT ROUTE BACK TO Frithgerd, enjoying the idea that he would soon be seeing the enchanting Miss Pendleton again. And again. Even now, after just a few minutes, he was craving the company of this indomitable young lady. Who else would buy a goat for her dogs? As he rode up the drive to his home, Daniel smiled at the memory of the scene he'd just witnessed. Leaving his horse at the stable, he wondered if she would come tomorrow. Surely she would.

Inside, he was greeted by the news that two strangers had arrived and were talking with Macklin in the drawing room. Joining them, Daniel discovered that the answer to Macklin's inquiry at the Foreign Office had come more rapidly than either of them had expected.

The two very serious gentlemen flanking his houseguest looked more like war-hardened military officers than Foreign Office functionaries, but they bore a letter of introduction from Castlereagh himself, along with a request to give them all assistance. The document did not mention their names.

As soon as Daniel had looked the letter over, one of the men said, "We've come to take charge of the materials mentioned in Lord Macklin's message."

"Take charge?" Daniel didn't care for his tone. The fellow sounded like a supervisor addressing a bumbling subordinate.

"Take them away, you mean?" asked Macklin.

He received only a brisk nod in reply.

"They were written by my mother," said Daniel.

"In order to produce reports for the Foreign Office, to which they now belong."

Once again, the man spoke as if the two noblemen were servants and he an impatient master. His companion put a hand on his arm, but the gesture had no effect that Daniel could see. Still, he had to ask. "She did travel for His Majesty's government then? To gather information."

The man hesitated, then offered another nod. It seemed as if giving out any information at all pained him.

Daniel blinked. He realized that he hadn't fully believed in this fantastic story until now, despite all the evidence.

"You will hand them over to us, along with every scrap of notes, at once." The man held out an imperious hand. His eyes were hard, his mouth set.

Anger surged through Daniel. He felt himself squaring up, as if he'd stepped into a boxing ring for a bout.

The second gentleman from the Foreign Office stepped between them. "Your mother's reports were a marvel," he said. "Detailed, meticulous, and invariably proved accurate whenever we had an opportunity to test them with other sources. We didn't know how she remembered it all. I can't tell you how much she was admired."

A thread of something like pride, or perhaps amazement, tempered Daniel's rage. Here again was a glimpse of a very different parent than the one he remembered. Here was a reason for her many absences, if not an excuse. He found he didn't want to relinquish all evidence of her exploits before he'd had a chance to adjust to these revelations. "If you have the reports, I don't see why you need her notebooks."

The first man snorted as if he couldn't believe his ears. "Because they contain information that must remain secret," he said.

"Not only facts, but when and how they were discovered," added his companion solemnly. "That could have serious diplomatic consequences."

"Nothing that can be understood without the key." Daniel started to say that he would give them that, but he found that he remained reluctant. These strangers were asking for the sole link he had into his parents' hidden life. He wanted some time to explore it. "I'll consider your request."

His unpleasant visitor took a step toward him. "It isn't a request. It's a demand from your sovereign's government. You have no right to withhold these documents."

Daniel felt a strong desire to punch the fellow. "If this is the Foreign Office's idea of diplomacy, no wonder we've had years of war."

"What would a pampered aristocrat like you know of war?" the man replied.

His companion pulled him aside, even as Macklin laid a hand on Daniel's shoulder. Daniel struggled with his temper as the second Foreign Office representative remonstrated quietly with the first.

His efforts were shaken off. "This matter has been bungled from start to finish," said the first man. "Dawson ought to have found these things after the woman's death as he was sent here to do."

It took Daniel a moment to absorb the implications of this remark. "You searched my home?" He hadn't really heeded Miss Pendleton when she suggested that the trunks had been rifled. But she'd seen the truth.

The second man made a placating gesture. "When a…person in your mother's position dies unexpectedly, it's customary to make certain nothing sensitive is left behind," he said.

"And rather than *asking* me—"

"We try to keep such information from wagging tongues," interrupted the first man. "As should be blindingly obvious."

Here was the attitude that had caused his parents to hide any hint of their activities from him, Daniel thought. "Get out," he said. "Get out of my house."

"Not without what we came for."

The second man spoke before Daniel could consign him to perdition. "Please think about what we've said. This is a matter of great importance. We'll come back tomorrow." He gripped the other visitor's arm and pulled him from the room.

"Insufferable," said Daniel. "Intolerable."

"He was." Macklin looked thoughtful rather than annoyed. "And I'm curious about why the Foreign

Office sent that particular agent. And gave him free rein to act with so little tact."

"Tact! That fellow doesn't know the meaning of the word."

"Castlereagh has made mistakes," Macklin replied. "But, really, he doesn't employ graceless oafs. I suspect there was some calculation involved. Perhaps they thought they'd get more information by making you angry."

"What?" Daniel turned to look at the older man.

"Thinking that in the heat of anger you would let things slip."

"There is nothing to *let slip*. We told them what we found."

Macklin nodded. "Yes. But as I've said before, when you live in a world of suspicion, everything begins to look suspicious."

"What could they possibly suspect me *of*?"

"That must be a frustration for them," his guest replied. "Knowing their secrets, I suppose. If you had read through the notebooks with the key—"

"That would take days." More hours spent in a sea of paper, Daniel thought, making a translation as deadly dull as mathematics. Except that it might be a window into his parents' life and thoughts. That idea gave him pause. Could he simply give that up?

Macklin nodded. "I'm a very curious person, but I'm not sure I would care to make the effort."

"No." And was there anything personal in that mass of cryptic phrases? Or would he find only dry facts and figures? Another sort of distance to add to the gap that already existed.

"Perhaps they know of something dangerous in the entries. Or fear there may be such a thing."

Daniel considered this idea. He still found it difficult to see his parents in this new light. "Well, the notebooks are quite safe in my strong room for now."

"I doubt those two gentlemen will be satisfied with that."

"They'll have to be. Until I decide otherwise."

There was a soft knock on the drawing room door. When Daniel bade the person enter, Tom slipped through the doorway, closing it carefully behind him. "That Jake Wendell feller is outside."

"Who?"

"The butterfly man. Who ain't any such thing, unless I'm mistaken."

This was the stranger sneaking about the neighborhood, Daniel remembered. "He's here?"

"With another man, mounting up to leave." Tom moved over to the windows and looked out. "They're going."

"The other is pale-haired and stocky?" asked Macklin. "With military side-whiskers?"

Tom nodded as Daniel went to join him and watch the two Foreign Office men depart. "The dark one is Wendell?"

"So he says," replied Tom.

Daniel looked at Macklin. "It seems our lurker is one of the gentlemen from the Foreign Office."

"He was nosing about Rose Cottage last night," said Tom. "Till he roused the dogs and had to leg it."

"What?"

"I was coming to tell you when I spotted him," Tom added.

Daniel turned toward the door. "I must go and tell Miss Pendleton."

Macklin held up a hand. "Wait."

"She will wish to know."

"No doubt," replied Macklin. "But we shouldn't upset her unnecessarily. We need to think this through."

They *needed* to keep her safe, Daniel thought. He remembered her descriptions of the interrogations she'd endured—the tremor in her voice, the distress in her face. What he really wanted was to go and fetch her, bring her to Frithgerd, and watch over her from now on. Which he couldn't do. "Think about what precisely?"

"What's going on," said the older man. "What is best to do about it." He turned to Tom. "Could you follow them and discover where they go from here?"

"Yes, my lord."

"Very carefully, mind. These are not men to trifle with. And they are on the lookout for conspiracies."

The lad nodded. "The butterfly fella hasn't noticed me. I'm good at keeping out of sight. Or out of mind. Depending." He grinned.

"See that you do. I mean it, Tom." Macklin waited for another acknowledgment and then sent him off with a gesture.

"He seems confident," said Daniel.

"As am I. I wouldn't ask him to do this otherwise." The earl looked thoughtful. "You may not be able to keep your mother's notebooks from the government in the end, Whitfield. The Foreign Office probably does have some right to them."

"And if the matter had been broached properly, we might have reached agreement on that." What had they expected to accomplish by treating him so rudely? "Two weeks ago, I didn't know they existed." And how his life had changed since a certain young lady arrived in the neighborhood! "I would like to look them over. Learn something about my mother's endeavors."

"And that is what worries the agents, I suppose," said Macklin.

"They cannot imagine I would reveal anything damaging to my country."

"I have found that such people can imagine the most extraordinary scenarios. It is, at once, their strength and weakness."

"Well, we will just have to show them the right of it." Daniel frowned. "Did you have any inkling of my parents' true reason for traveling, Macklin?"

"None whatsoever."

"I'm still finding it hard to take in, even with all evidence before me."

"I feel just the same."

They finally decided that Daniel should send over a note asking that Miss Pendleton definitely come to work on the estate records tomorrow morning. They would decide together what should come next.

❧

Though it had been only a few days since she'd visited Frithgerd, she'd missed the place, Penelope acknowl-edged the following day. "I have an idea about our filing system," she said to Whitfield when he joined her in the office. "The estate system, I mean. It would mean building some shelves."

He nodded, looking distracted. Yet he had asked her particularly to come.

"I think work on the bath is going well? Are there any problems?"

"No. The new doorway is finished, and the wall closing off the corridor is well under way."

Henry Carson tapped on the open door at this opportune moment and came in. "I've found trees for the pipes," he said. "They were cut last year so they're well-seasoned. The man's asking a steep price for them, however."

"How much?" asked Penelope. When Carson gave her the figure, she frowned. "That is high."

"We don't want green wood," said the builder. "It's liable to shrink and crack."

"I'll talk to him," she replied. "Leave me his name and direction."

Carson nodded. "I also need the smith to make me a larger auger to bore them out."

Penelope looked at Whitfield. He hadn't participated in the conversation, and now she wondered if he'd even heard. "Tell him his lordship would appreciate a speedy job."

"Yes, miss."

The builder departed, passing Lord Macklin coming in. The earl rarely joined them in the records room. Penelope began to suspect that something was wrong.

"Our two visitors from yesterday are back," Macklin said to the viscount. "They insist upon seeing you."

"Insist?" echoed Whitfield, obviously offended.

Though it was none of her affair, Penelope was bothered by the air of tension that had entered the chamber. Over the past year she'd become acutely sensitive to such shifts. "What two visitors?" she asked.

Whitfield turned away from her. "Never mind. I'll speak to them. You stay here."

"Why wouldn't I?"

The two men went out, leaving Penelope prey to a sense of foreboding. She had no reason for it, but she felt that something bad was about to happen. She made herself sit down to work.

Daniel met the Foreign Office representatives in his drawing room again. They looked as grim as before. Perhaps more so. He heartily wished them away.

"It has come to our attention that a known subversive has had access to Lady Whitfield's notebooks," said the one who called himself Jake Wendell.

"A what?"

"A connection of a traitor to the crown," said the man with blond side-whiskers. He might have been amending his comrade's accusation, or simply elucidating. "Miss Penelope Pendleton."

"This is a terrible breach of security," said the other agent before Daniel could speak. "I don't know whether you're careless or stupid or something worse, but—"

Generations of noble ancestors reared up in Daniel and lent their hauteur to his icy "I beg your pardon?"

"This woman frequents your house," continued Wendell, unaffected. "She is given free rein to examine your records. She has had the notebooks in her possession."

The way he said *this woman* filled Daniel with rage. "Have you been questioning my servants?"

"We question everybody," the agent replied curtly.

"You need to be more careful who you associate with," said the blond Foreign Office man.

Daniel wasn't actually going to throttle a pair of government officials. He didn't need Macklin's hand on his arm to restrain him.

"Miss Pendleton was cleared of any involvement in the unfortunate events in Manchester," said the earl.

"That what she told you?" answered Wendell.

"The Home Office did so."

Wendell scoffed, but Daniel thought the side-whiskered agent looked a little uneasy.

"We demand that you hand over the notebooks and any other materials of your mother's that you may possess," said Wendell. "They must be moved to a secure location in London."

"By you?"

"That is what we were sent to do."

"Not collect butterflies?"

Daniel saw Macklin make an involuntary gesture and silently acknowledged that he shouldn't have mentioned the butterflies. Revealing that they'd been watching him would no doubt heighten Wendell's suspicions.

The man's expression confirmed this.

"Possibly some arrangement could be made," murmured Macklin.

"Nothing could be simpler," said Wendell. "Give them to us now."

"I'm not going to do that," declared Daniel. "You may as well stop asking." At Wendell's scowl, he held up a hand. "You've set my back up, whether by design or accident, I don't know. But I don't like your attitude. And I won't put my mother's notebooks in the hands of two nameless men who march into my house without warning."

"We brought a letter from Castlereagh!"

"Perhaps. I've never received one before, so I can't identify his hand."

"Are you suggesting that we *forged* our credentials?" Wendell was the picture of outrage.

"You don't enjoy being suspected?" Daniel was aware of Macklin's steady gaze, but he couldn't help the sarcasm. He'd rarely disliked anyone as much as he did these two.

"You will regret this," the one with the side-whiskers began.

But his companion silenced him with a raised hand. "What do you propose to do?" he asked Daniel.

"The right thing. For my country and my family and myself. I may consult Castlereagh in person."

"A waste of time," muttered Wendell. "He will only tell you what we've already said."

"And in the meantime?" asked the other man.

"I'll take great care."

"As you have so far," sneered Wendell. "Handing them over to a traitorous—"

"I have nothing more to say to you," Daniel interrupted. Jaw set, he loomed over his unwelcome callers.

"I'll see you out," said Macklin, herding them.

Playing the footman to keep him from exploding? Daniel wondered. In other circumstances, it might have been amusing.

Under the unyielding gaze of two peers of the realm and practically being pushed out by the more impressive, the men went.

"I shouldn't have mentioned the butterflies," Daniel said when Macklin returned. "I hope I didn't put Tom in jeopardy."

"We may need to call him off, now that they know we've been watching."

Daniel nodded.

"Are you really going to speak to Castlereagh?"

"Perhaps." He wanted to do what was best for the much-maligned Miss Pendleton. As soon as he figured out what that was.

❧

Penelope could bear it no longer. She had to discover what was happening. She'd spent far too much time, over the last year, sitting and waiting for doom to descend. She'd become oversensitive to the idea of events proceeding outside her knowledge, dictated by strangers. She left the estate office and made her way quietly along the corridor to the front of the house. She wouldn't intrude on Lord Whitfield's meeting, but she was determined to catch a glimpse of his visitors.

Slipping into a small parlor near the entry, she waited by the window. A few minutes later, two men walked out, settling their hats and pulling on gloves. They stood on the graveled drive, heads together, anger in the lines of their bodies. When a groom brought their horses around, they turned, and Penelope at last saw their faces.

She gripped the windowsill. She knew one of them. He'd been among her interrogators in Manchester, a cold-eyed man who'd questioned her a number of times without showing a shred of emotion. Any word she uttered he twisted. Any fact she offered he dismissed. He'd denied comforts and then doled out physical relief with contempt, as if her humanity was a sign of moral decay. He'd encouraged others to do the same. Seeing him brought back a time when she'd been alone and helpless and afraid.

Mounted, he looked at the house. Penelope pulled back behind the curtain.

What was he doing here? Had he come looking for her? She'd been cleared of any role in her brother's folly and released. But that very man had told her that an investigation was never over, that the eyes of the government would always be on her.

She dared a look. The two were riding away from Frithgerd. Why had they called on Lord Whitfield? Were they headed for her small cottage refuge now? Would she encounter them on the road as she drove home?

Penelope went back to the records room. She sat at the desk and shivered and despised herself for doing so. That man had told her that they could find her wherever she went, that they could seize her at any moment if she put a foot wrong. And as the badgering continued and no one stood by her, it had become more and more difficult to scoff at his distortions and threats. Rising, Penelope made certain the windows were latched. She closed the draperies.

She braced a chair under the doorknob. Then she sat again and fought with the memories that wanted to vanquish her.

A flurry of sound called her back. Someone was pounding on the door. The inquisitors had come. Penelope straightened, ready for battle.

"Miss Pendleton?"

It was Lord Whitfield's voice. And his house, where she'd spent so many happy hours.

"Miss Pendleton?" he called, louder.

Penelope stood, went to remove the chair, and opened the door.

Her handsome neighbor strode in. "What's happening? Why is it so dim in here?" He looked at the chair in her hands.

She put down the chair. Turning away, she went to open the draperies.

"Miss Pendleton?"

Of course she had to explain, even if the truth was humiliating. "I saw your visitors riding away, and I recognized one of them as a man who questioned me in Manchester."

"Wendell?"

"I don't know his name. He never told me. He had blond side-whiskers."

"That one? Not the other?" Whitfield looked surprised.

Penelope nodded. "Seeing him overset me, I'm afraid. He was…quite chilling." She made a slashing gesture. "How I hate feeling like this!"

"I won't let them near you."

"You won't be able to stop them. Nothing stops

them." When he would have objected, she shook her head. "What were they doing here?"

"The Foreign Office sent them to fetch my mother's notebooks."

Penelope felt a surge of relief. They hadn't been hunting her. "They want her journals?"

Whitfield nodded. "To keep them secret. They intend to lock them away in some government vault in London, along with the code key naturally."

Penelope nodded. And once they got their way, the government men wouldn't come back. A dreadful thought struck her. "Does that man know I'm here? Does he know I saw the key? He'll suspect me of... everything."

Whitfield's expression was all the answer she needed.

"I suppose I'm a spy now." Penelope didn't know whether to cry or laugh. "Do they think I'm stealing state secrets? For what? That man will want to lock me up again."

"Nonsense."

"You don't know what it's like."

"It's true I don't." He came close and took her hands. "But I will make certain it never happens to you again."

"That's kind of you to say, but you can't make such guarantees."

"It isn't kind. It's...the deepest wish of my heart. I will do whatever is necessary."

Penelope blinked back tears. He'd stood by her as friends of long standing had not, with the authorities coming for him.

"Even…" he added, and stopped.

"What?"

"I suppose if you cut all connection with Frithgerd and me, went away somewhere for a while, you would be safer from them," he said. He looked melancholy. "I must tell you that I mean to keep the notebooks for a bit. I won't be bullied. I intend to manage this matter on my own terms."

"They do bully," she replied.

"They may try, but you shouldn't be subjected to it."

"You want me to go away?" The idea was dismal.

"No! It's the last thing I want. I hate the thought." The truth of this was obvious in his face. "But your well-being is more important than my…gratification."

He was so dear to her. "I wouldn't leave you to those men. You don't know how bad they can be."

"Even though you're afraid."

She swallowed. "Yes. Some things are more important than mere fear."

"Mere fear. You really are the most amazing creature." Whitfield's hands tightened on hers. "This would all be simpler if you married me."

"What?"

"That's it." He smiled as if all had become clear to him. "We'll go up to London, get a special license, and tie the knot." He might have been talking of some simple outing—a picnic or a drive in the country perhaps. "Let those weasels see how they like facing the Viscountess Whitfield. What a marvelous one you'll make!"

Penelope stared at him, stupefied. "Of course that's

impossible." He couldn't be offering the very fantasy she'd dreamed of.

"On the contrary, it's the obvious solution."

"Obvious!"

"Utterly." His smile was tender, devastating.

"No. We can't." He didn't understand.

"Do you tell me that you don't *wish* to marry me? Because that is the only factor that would weigh with me."

Penelope tried, but she couldn't lie to him. "No, but you'd be ruined."

"So you *do* wish to marry me?"

She nearly laughed, but he was taking this too lightly. "Marriage to me would pull you into my ruin."

Whitfield shook his head. "I have a certain amount of influence. And also, I don't care a fig for society."

His hands were warm on hers. The look in his dark eyes heated her blood, and his sturdy figure felt like a bulwark. Penelope knew that she ought to continue resisting. But her dearest desire was being offered up with such generous enthusiasm. She'd vowed to take what she wanted. She found herself nodding.

Whitfield laughed. He squeezed her fingers and bent to kiss her. "Splendid. We'll leave tomorrow. In a few days we'll be man and wife, and you will never have to leave me."

If she had anything to say about it, she never would.

Sixteen

THEY'D ACTUALLY DONE IT, DANIEL THOUGHT AS HE stood beside Miss Pendleton—Penelope—before the church altar to be married. After two days of scrambling and some minor difficulties, they were ready to speak the words that would make them man and wife.

He glanced at Macklin on his other side. The earl had been invaluable to their schemes. Naturally he was acquainted with the Archbishop of Canterbury, and he had helped get the special license in record time. Daniel had expected that the older man might argue against this marriage, but he hadn't. Indeed, he'd offered them the hospitality of his town house, as well as a place to lock away the strongbox containing Daniel's mother's notebooks. Daniel patted his inner pocket. The key to the code rested there, and he would not be parted from it.

Macklin had even left his valet at Frithgerd to distract the government men until they were well away. The fellow had expressed no qualms about his ability to do so, and they'd given the Foreign Office agents the slip. They hadn't told the servants at Frithgerd where they were staying either. Daniel didn't think any of them were official informers, but gossip traveled just as fast. Macklin's town staff had been instructed to deny all knowledge of their existence. Such ruses wouldn't hold up indefinitely, but they'd last long enough.

The rector stepped forward to begin the marriage service. Miss Pendleton's young maid and Tom sat in the pews, along with a scattering of strangers who'd wandered into the church. Daniel checked Penelope's expression. Her face was hard to read just now. Happy but bewildered? Pleased but anxious? None of those?

The clergyman spoke. "Dearly beloved, we are gathered together here in the sight of God."

Daniel had heard the words many times before, but today they were for him. A thrill crackled through him, tempered by a brush of apprehension. The responses he spoke—clearly, evenly—set a course for the rest of his life. He had no regrets, but the weight of the occasion affected him. "Till death do us part" was a portentous vow.

Half an hour later, the deed was done. They had signed the register and come out into the sultry London morning, where Macklin's carriage waited to take them to his home in Berkeley Square.

"Did you see the dragon in the colored glass?" asked Kitty the maid. "St. George stuck him good." She made a clawing motion.

"It was his horse drew my eye," replied Tom. "It's all very well for a knight to be brave, but a horse who don't bolt when a giant serpent curls around his legs, that's something."

"War-horses are trained to endure the chaos of battle," said Macklin, amusement in his tone.

"The sound of cannons and all," Tom replied with a sage nod. "But not a great fire-breathing beast with teeth long as your arm. There's no training for *that*."

"Very true," said the earl, as Daniel contemplated the somewhat eccentric nature of his wedding party.

Macklin's servants had prepared a wedding break-fast, even though no guests had been invited. Their excuse was that most of high society was out of town at this time of year, and indeed, Daniel's particular friends were at house parties in the country. But they might have assembled a small group if they had not been more or less in hiding. They had sent an announcement of the marriage to the papers and left it at that. Neither of them had close family to include, after all.

His new wife—his wife!—looked dazed, Daniel thought. She had every right to be fatigued. They'd raced through the last two days like sprinters. They could rest now, however. They would stay in London a while before returning to Frithgerd. A few days, a week, he couldn't think that far ahead. His mind was full of the fact that this was his wedding day, and he and Penelope would soon be alone.

Macklin came to stand beside him. "I find I need to go out of town," he said. "There was a letter waiting here that didn't get sent on to Frithgerd."

"Ah." Daniel set aside his concern that this might disrupt their plans. "Nothing too bad I hope."

"Just a matter that requires my attention."

"We'll go when you do."

"Nonsense. You will stay, as we agreed. Please treat my house as your own."

"That's very kind." It was also a relief. Daniel didn't want to return to the worries they'd left behind.

A footman appeared in the doorway. "Mrs. Thorpe has arrived, my lord," he said to Macklin.

Daniel wondered who Mrs. Thorpe might be. Then he turned and saw Penelope looking at him and forgot all else.

The earl nodded. "Offer her refreshment, and tell her I'll be there directly. Is Tom ready?"

"Yes, my lord."

Macklin turned back to Daniel. "I'll send word to Clayton to follow me as soon as you have no more need for him."

"I believe he's done his part. You shouldn't be deprived of your valet any longer. You've been more than kind."

Acknowledging this with old-fashioned courtesy, Macklin took his leave.

❧

This place was beautiful, Penelope thought as she walked through the suite of rooms the Earl of Macklin had allotted to them. They were far from his own quarters, had he remained at home, and the combination of luxury and privacy was perfect. Their London host was a kind man after all. She'd felt no hint of the disapproval she expected from the *haut ton*. She hoped the problem that had called him away with such an intent expression was easily solved.

Movement in the corner of her eye made Penelope

turn. A large mirror hung on the wall, reflecting her from head to toe. She'd been married in one of her everyday gowns, a pale-blue muslin, and a favorite straw bonnet with blue flowers, currently sitting on the dressing table. No wardrobe of new bride clothes for her or flurry of excited friends. Gazing into the glass, she saw a solemn young woman with pale hair and wide blue eyes, utterly familiar and yet somehow new. She was married, to the husband she'd longed for, like a wish come true in a fairy tale. The figure in the mirror grinned at her. "Pleased with yourself?" asked Penelope.

The scent of roses drifted through the open window from the garden at the back of the house. Penelope went over and looked at the banks of flowers in the golden light of afternoon. A tray on a table beneath the sill held a bottle of champagne and a bowl of strawberries. The earl's staff had thought of everything.

The door opened and Whitfield—Daniel—came in. As easily as if they both occupied these rooms, together. Which they did. The thought sent a thrill through her. He held up her cashmere shawl. "Found it," he said. "It had slipped down behind the drawing room sofa."

"I could have gone myself."

"But isn't a husband meant to fetch and carry?" he answered with a smile.

"Really? I hadn't heard that." He really was her husband. She'd actually done it.

"Ah. Now I've dropped myself in the soup."

"Indeed. I'll expect all sort of services."

One corner of his mouth quirked up as he met her

eyes. A wave of heat moved from Penelope's cheeks down her whole body.

He put aside the shawl and went to the window. "Champagne. Splendid." He twisted out the cork and filled two stemmed glasses. "We must have a toast," he added, handing her one. "It's traditional."

As most things about their wedding weren't, Penelope thought.

"To a long and—"

Penelope moved. She set down her glass with a click and stepped close to him. In fairy tales, it was dangerous to predict happiness, or to ask for too much. Practically a guarantee of disaster. They mustn't press their luck. She took his glass, reached to put it by her own, and set her hands on his shoulders. He was still looking down at her with surprise when she kissed him.

Daniel was briefly startled. Then the touch of her lips, the feel of her leaning into him, set his body alight. He pulled her closer and sank into the kiss. Through a haze of desire, he thought that there was no one else like her in the world, and she was his for all his life.

They were both breathless when he picked her up and carried her to bed.

"It's not even dark yet," she murmured. "Are we to have a wedding afternoon instead of a wedding night?"

"Both," he replied. "And we will wake together tomorrow and every day after that."

They dealt with buttons and laces and hooks with soft laughter and a bit of fumbling. Eagerness on both sides made up for a lack of familiarity.

Finally, they came together skin to skin, learning each other's bodies with hands and lips. The consummation that Daniel had dreamed of for weeks was unutterably sweet, and he reveled in the sounds of excitement and satisfaction he drew from Penelope. There would be more of those, he vowed, as he discovered more about her.

Afterward, as they lay entwined, it came to him that with her, he would find the home he'd never really had.

∽

"I wonder what it would have been like if we'd met as children?" asked Penelope idly. It was their third day in London, and they were cuddled together on the sofa in their sitting room. "We might have so easily, since our mothers were friends. In fact, it's odd that we didn't."

"Mine was too immersed in her own concerns for visits," replied Daniel. "You could see that in her letters."

"We don't have them all."

"Or any reason to think the missing ones are different. And a good deal of evidence for my point." The haze of happiness in which Daniel had been basking thinned a bit.

"I can't believe my mother would have cared so much for a cold person. She wasn't the least bit foolish."

Daniel shrugged. "I can't tell. My parents always felt like strangers to me. I really didn't know either of them."

Penelope sat straighter, out of the circle of his arm.

"We could look through the notebooks. They're a record of your mother's thoughts."

Much as he regretted the loss of their cozy interlude, Daniel was curious.

"Unless you think we mustn't," she added. "Because of the secrets."

"They're mine. I'll look as much as I wish."

They fetched the metal strongbox from a locked cupboard and opened it. The pile of notebooks inside looked just as they had when they'd found them. Penelope lifted them out and put them on the table under the window. "Shall we just choose one?" she asked.

"Why not?"

"You do it."

Daniel let his hands hover over the stack. Feeling no particular connection to any, he pulled one out and set it before them. Penelope turned back the cover. "St. Petersburg, 1801," she read from the top of the page. "Russia! Do you have the key?"

Taking the folded sheet of paper from his inner coat pocket, Daniel admired the animation on her face. His wife would never be able to resist a puzzle.

"I think we need a way to make notes about the substitutions," she said. "It may be hard to keep track otherwise. We'll burn them afterward."

Daniel went to Macklin's library for paper and pen. Penelope was bent over the notebook when he came back. "Your mother listed the number of ships in the harbor and the regiments posted nearby. She used little drawings to write words when she didn't have any set code for them. See?"

He leaned closer to look at the line above her finger. The tiny pictures—birds, flowers, animals—looked like doodles rather than anything important. A stranger leafing through this journal would mistake his mother for a strange obsessive. Albeit one who could draw. Each image was distinct and identifiable. A rose, a fox, a magpie.

Penelope looked back and forth from the key to the page. She wrote out a word, and another. "Great heavens, I think this says... Yes, it says the Russian tsar was killed."

"What?"

Penelope worked through more of the code. "On March 23 in the early hours of the morning, the tsar was assassinated." She looked at Daniel.

They bent over the notebook together, but of course all he saw was gibberish.

"I think these next words must be names." Penelope jotted them down. "Bennigsen, Pahlen. They have the code for soldiers next to them. And then it says 'killers.'"

Daniel couldn't quite fathom that his parents had been present for such events, still less that they'd been observing and recording for the British government. He'd always seen them as bland and heedless, their minds devoted to trivialities.

"Do you remember such a thing? The assassination must have been mentioned in all the newspapers."

"It may have been talked of at school," Daniel replied. "I'm afraid I was more interested in cricket when I was eight years old."

Penelope nodded. "I was too young to know

anything about it." She looked down the page, consulting the code as she went. "Look at this. She's written 'Alexander' in her picture code, with question marks on either side."

"Isn't Alexander the name of the tsar now?" They stared at each other, working it out. Then Daniel spoke slowly. "Is she suggesting that he was involved in his father's murder?"

"Or wondering anyway? It seems so."

"That would be…" He hesitated to finish the sentence.

"Patricide," said Penelope. "Treason. Rebellion of a sort. Certainly, it's a question the tsar would not want raised. And hasn't Alexander had some troubles with his people? Reformers?"

"I don't know." He'd never paid much heed to politics, which his parents must have found shallow, even irresponsible, Daniel realized. Perhaps that was why they never told him anything.

"I begin to see why the government wants these notebooks under their own care," said Penelope. "This is inflammatory information."

"Indeed."

She turned the page, did some more deciphering. "They left Russia soon after that. By ship."

"Probably a good idea." Daniel looked at the date on the page. "Late March. That would have been the end of term. I suppose I went to a friend's for the school holidays. I generally did. And resented the necessity, more often than not. Though not the boys who invited me." He'd made good friends at school, Daniel thought, and those holidays had been a big part of that. Should he have been more grateful? "I suppose I must admit that the death of a world leader was more important than where I spent my off time." And yet he couldn't quite forgive his parents' long absences even so. He was glad to know they'd been dedicated and performed an important service, but he still wished they'd paid more heed to him.

"Not to a child," replied Penelope.

"True. Still, I feel a bit petty."

"If it was me, I might wonder why it had to be *my* parents who gathered information. Out of all the people who might have served the British government."

She'd hit it exactly. "And your answer would be because your mother wished to," said Daniel. "She dreamed of adventures. Not nursery duty."

"And whose dreams are more important? The parent's? Or the child's?"

Could he choose his own comfort over his mother's ambitions? Must these two things be in conflict? "I don't know. Whose?"

"I don't know either." Penelope shrugged. "But perhaps it's a question to consider before one has a child."

Daniel stiffened. He hadn't thought about being a father. Only a husband. And yet the one most often followed the other. Without much consideration, as far as he'd seen. It was expected that he would provide an heir to his title and estates. What more could he, would he, have to offer his offspring? "I understand responsibility," he said, answering his thoughts as well as her remark. "I won't be running off to Russia or elsewhere at every opportunity. Nor will you." He felt a stab of anxiety at the idea of her leaving.

"No," she said.

Daniel's worry eased without disappearing entirely. She was frowning.

"But parents who stay home have difficulties, too."

He'd seen that shadow in her eyes before. He knew what she was thinking. "Like your brother?"

"He and Papa could never agree. Not from the time Philip was very young. Yet I can't say that either was to blame. Not really. They didn't *want* to quarrel. It just kept happening. Do you think a parent has any control over how a child turns out?"

It was a daunting idea—that a family could go wrong despite good intentions. And what did he know about happy families? Did he have any chance of creating one of his own? Penelope was gazing at him as if he might produce a solution. But he didn't have one.

"Though I must say Papa wasn't very good at listening," she added. "Once he got going, he could only seem to hear himself. I've found that you can get on with most people if you listen to what they have to say. I think it must be the same with children. Don't you?"

And she was a champion listener, Daniel thought. But would he be good enough? He would learn from her. He nodded, an acknowledgment of her question and a promise to himself for the future.

"I suppose one does the best one can."

"You'll be splendid."

She looked touched by his vehemence, when she ought to have been dubious about his family history. Her faith in him was a gift. Daniel longed to give her something in return. "We should go out," he said.

"Out?"

"Tonight. You said you'd never been to a proper theater."

She blinked as if adjusting to the change of topic. "No, only amateur theatrics."

"We must remedy that. I'm sure Macklin's people can get us a box, with town so thin of company."

"I'm not sure I brought the right gown."

"Whatever you wear, you will be beautiful."

This clearly required a tender acknowledgment, and it was some time before Daniel left to make arrangements for the play.

The evening found them in gilt chairs in a box at the Theater Royal in Drury Lane. The players were presenting *Hamlet*, which Penelope had heard of, naturally, but never seen. The lower floor was full of patrons for whom society's season was an irrelevant concept. They lived in London, and partook of its amusements, at all times of the year.

Under the light of the huge chandeliers, this mass of audience members talked and ate and ogled those in the rows of boxes above. Despite the minor roar they generated, Penelope enjoyed the spectacle. "Candle wax just dripped on that man," she said, watching a burly fellow shake his fist at the chandelier and wipe the hot wax off his cheek.

"One of the drawbacks of the pit," Daniel told her.

"They call it the pit? Why?"

"Oddly enough, I know the answer to that. It's named after the old cockpit, because it was used for cockfighting years ago."

"Why do you know?" Her dear husband wasn't usually a font of obscure information.

"I had a friend who became obsessed with the theater, or with one of the opera dancers anyway." He blinked. "Er, that is… What I meant to say—"

"A friend?" Penelope asked with a sidelong look.

"Not me! Reggie Galthorpe. Known him since Eton. You'll meet him when he's back in town."

"And I can ask him all about the…theater." Penelope enjoyed teasing him.

"He certainly found out all he could about the subject, and he was only too glad to go on and on about it." Though he'd never gotten up the nerve to approach the dancer, Daniel remembered.

"There are no chairs. Do they stand for the whole play in the pit?"

"Yes. The tickets are cheaper down there."

Watching the people jostle one another, Penelope could understand why they would be. "Well, I'm glad we got a box."

"Much better," Daniel agreed.

The play began with a ghost. An actor painted in shades of gray wailed and admonished the not-so-young Hamlet, who received this visitation with great starts of surprise. As the Prince of Denmark went on to think and fret and plot, the audience in the pit freely expressed their approbation or disapproval of what was presented to them. They seemed to think nothing of shouting at the actors and criticizing their manner or appearance.

"I must say I agree with that," murmured Penelope when one of these commentators urged Hamlet to "just get on with it for the lord's sake."

"What would you have him do?" Daniel asked. "Challenge his uncle to a duel?"

"Talk to his mother?" Penelope shook her head. "His choices are unappealing. But he needn't have been so unkind to Ophelia."

"No. Though she is rather—"

"Wet." Penelope bit her lip. "In the sense of a bit spiritless, I meant."

"Rather than drowned?"

"Yes. What a stupid thing to do."

Daniel rather wished he'd chosen a comedy, particularly when they reached the pile of corpses at the end of the play. But Penelope declared herself quite satisfied with her first visit to the theater. "And one should see Shakespeare," she concluded. "It's practically obligatory."

They made their way through the crowd leaving the theater. Progress was slow, and after a bit, Penelope became aware of someone staring at her. Turning, she discovered the Pratts, neighbors in Lancashire all her life. "Oh," she said.

"What is it?"

"I know those people. They lived two miles from us."

"Shall we go and say hello?"

It would be a pleasure to have an acquaintance in London. They started toward the older couple. When it became obvious that they meant to speak, Mrs. Pratt ostentatiously turned her back, pulling her husband along with her. She pushed between two clusters of theatergoers as if a pack of foxhounds was after her.

Penelope went still. In the excitement of her first London outing, she'd forgotten that the Pratts had dropped her when Philip's crimes became known. Indeed, she'd forgotten the fact of her disgrace for a few happy days. Now humiliation and hurt came flooding back. "She gave me the cut direct," she murmured, stunned at this public rejection. "Oh, how could I have done this?"

"You haven't done anything. That woman is obviously a harridan." Daniel put his hand over hers where it rested on his arm.

"I shouldn't have allowed you to burden yourself with a disgraced wife." She felt as if everyone was staring at them, whispering about her brother's transgressions.

"You really must stop this nonsense."

"You don't understand."

"I do. You've explained it to me innumerable times. But what you can't seem to see is that I don't care a fig."

"Because you don't really *know*. The Pratts ran away as if I was poison."

He shrugged. "And who are they? Small, petty people. We need have no regard for *them*."

"They were friends of my family."

"Obviously not, or they would not have behaved so badly."

Penelope gazed up at him as the crowd thinned around them. "Why do you act this way when people I knew all my life just turned their backs on me?"

"Because I am a sterling person," he replied with a smile.

A wave of love coursed through Penelope. She wanted to throw her arms around him, to hold her happiness close. She couldn't do that here, but as soon as they reached Macklin's again, she would show him just how much she appreciated his attitude.

Seventeen

STILL, THE INCIDENT AT THE THEATER CAST A PALL
over their London idyll. While Macklin's house
remained delightful, the world outside seemed less
welcoming. They stayed in town another week,
then drove back to Frithgerd on a sultry July day
with thunder rumbling in the distance. Once again,
Daniel's mother's notebooks traveled with them in a
strongbox, returning to their place in the estate's safe.

As they pulled up before the front door, Penelope
tried to think of it as coming home. On the one
hand, she knew the place and its denizens well by
this time. On the other, she met them now in a
new role—as mistress of the house—and she had
wondered if this would cause difficulties. She found
no hesitation in their greetings, however. Even the
housekeeper seemed pleased to greet her.

Foyle, who had stayed on at Rose Cottage with
the dogs and their goat, also seemed content. He
had no desire to join the Frithgerd household. He
preferred his autonomy, at least for now. Penelope
suspected that eventually he and Mrs. Hart might

come to an understanding, and she would join him there.

Kitty was another question. She'd stayed at Frithgerd during their absence, and enjoyed the company thoroughly, as she was quick to tell Penelope. Indeed, she was full of chatter about the other servants and the routines of the place. Already, they seemed to have become more important to her than Penelope had been. "Only fancy," the girl told Penelope. "Cook learned her trade from a Frenchman who worked in the king of France's kitchens. The one whose head they chopped off!" She clove the air with one hand. "He saw the gee-o-tine come down like an outsized meat cleaver and decided then and there to get out of the country. Well, who wouldn't?"

Penelope was not yet well acquainted with Frithgerd's cook. Clearly she was worth knowing better.

"He came over on a fishing boat, not knowing a word of English and only seventeen, and got a lowly place in a pastry shop. And his con-fections were so good he was hired away by a duke. That's where Mrs. Jensen met him, when she was just a scullery maid." Kitty's pointed face was full of animation. "His name was A-tee-enn. She helped him with his English, and he showed her how to make hawt qui-sine."

Penelope wondered what else they might have taught each other. And then she wondered if Mrs. Jensen could make éclairs. "An interesting story."

"She told me while I was helping in the kitchen. And, miss, if you please, Mrs. Jensen said she'd teach me."

"To cook?"

Kitty nodded. "Particularly pastries. That's what I like best to make. Remember my Shrewsbury cakes?"

Penelope remembered the shapeless blobs all too well.

"I'd have to start out peeling vegetables and the like," Kitty went on. "But if I work hard and do well, Mrs. Jensen'll show me all she knows. She says some great houses have cooks who just do pastry. The royal palaces do." The girl's blue eyes shone.

"Have you spoken to the housekeeper?"

"Well, she knows what I'd like, but she said we must wait for you, miss. My lady, I should say." Kitty ducked her head and grinned. "Forgot. Forgot to wish you happy too, my lady."

Marveling that Kitty had found ambition, Penelope agreed with the plan. It was actually a relief. To fill her position as a viscountess, Penelope required a trained ladies' maid, which Kitty was not. She'd worried that Kitty would expect to serve her personally, but in fact, as soon as her own future was settled, she had put forward the claims of her friend Betty, who'd been learning all the necessary skills. And so the latter was appointed Penelope's attendant, Kitty plunged into the mysteries of sugar and butter and cream, and everyone seemed happy.

Henry Carson called the following morning to report significant progress on the bath project. Penelope and Daniel walked with him to inspect the small mill that had been erected on the banks of the creek behind the house. Its wheel was already turning, driving a pump that spewed water into a line of wooden pipes running off toward the house. "Quite a powerful flow," said Daniel, observing the racing liquid.

"Has to be, my lord, to get the water up to the tank in the attic," replied Carson.

They followed the line back to Frithgerd. The pipes rested first on a wood framework and then on top of the wall that circled the garden, partly to hide them and partly to maintain their elevation. Water gurgled and hissed inside.

In the bathing chamber, the walls were newly plastered and the floor tiled. More importantly, the tub had arrived. "It's as big as a horse trough," Daniel exclaimed.

"I believe it began manufacture as one, my lord," said Carson. "But it's been lined with copper and trimmed in oak."

"You could fit two people in there," said Penelope.

Daniel had been thinking the same. He caught her eye. When she flushed, he smiled. It seemed quite possible that his wife shared his imagining about their new bath. "Drains?" he asked.

"At the bottom there, my lord. We've connected it to the main one in the scullery." Carson put his hand on a sheet of metal that had replaced part of the wall behind the tub. "This tank is fitted into the kitchen fireplace. The water comes in from above and is warmed by the fire."

They rested their palms on the metal and felt the warmth.

"There's also a place to put coals underneath the tank—in the kitchen that is—to get the water hotter if need be. We'll be attaching the spigot tomorrow." He indicated a protruding stub of metal pipe, now sealed.

"And then we can try it out," said Daniel. Penelope didn't look at him this time, but she didn't need to. He could tell she had followed his train of thought. "Very well done, Carson. You've surpassed yourself."

"Thank you, my lord. It was a new sort of work, but we figured it out." The man patted the side of the tub, looking proud.

"You did indeed."

"Other local landowners might be interested in having baths," said Penelope. "If they'd like to see ours when it's done, we can arrange that."

Carson blinked, then looked intrigued at this prospect of more work. "Thank you, my lady."

How like her this was, Daniel thought. She was always thinking ahead, seeing possibilities for others. He'd provided his household with a skilled and thoughtful mistress, which was more than it had had in many years. How lucky for him that she was also a sweet and passionate wife. His heart swelled in his chest as they walked out of the bathing room through the new doorway into the blue parlor.

Penelope surveyed the trunks of papers still stored there. "We should get back to the records," she said.

"Ugh," said Daniel.

She smiled at him. "The mess hasn't gone away just because we married."

"More's the pity. Where's the fairy godmother with the magic wand? Or the elves who come in the night and finish all the work?"

Penelope laughed. "Don't they make shoes?"

"The brownies then. They clean, don't they?"

"Not the same as sorting documents, I'm afraid. I can take over the job, if you like."

Daniel was tempted. The disarray was as much hers as his now. But he realized that he liked working with her. How else was he to see that tender smile? "No, I'll help."

There was the smile. She was glad of his company. Daniel smiled back.

A footman appeared as they were about to enter the estate offices. "Callers for you, my lord."

The look on the young man's face told Daniel that these were the visitors he'd been dreading. He had left instructions about them. "I'll see who it is."

Penelope turned. "If we have visitors, I should come."

"They seem to want me."

"I want to be a good hostess to the neighborhood."

"I'll send word if you're needed."

With a nod, she went on. Daniel closed the door of the estate office behind her and turned to the footman. "Is it the two men I told you about?"

"Yes, my lord. I put them in the front parlor as you ordered."

This was the least welcoming of Frithgerd's reception rooms, right off the front door. "Good. Now you may go and tell them that no one is available to receive them. Take Joseph with you. They won't be pleased."

"I can handle them, my lord."

"I don't doubt you, Ned, but it will be better to have two large footmen ready to show them out."

"Yes, my lord."

"Their horses were left outside?"

"No one took them to the stables."

"Very good." Daniel let the footman go, then slipped upstairs to watch from a window. He kept well out of sight behind the draperies.

A few minutes later, the two Foreign Office men appeared in the drive. They were obviously annoyed, particularly the blond one with the side-whiskers, who was gesticulating angrily. His companion tried to calm him, but he turned and stared up at the house. Though he knew he was invisible in the shadows, Daniel felt an urge to step back in the face of the fellow's glare. He resisted, and after a moment, the two men mounted up and rode away.

Penelope sat at the desk in the estate office with a pile of papers before her. She was looking into space rather than at the records, however. She'd suspected the identity of the visitors from Daniel's manner and a sidelong glance. And of course she'd known they'd come. Men like her interrogator didn't give up. She felt a little guilty leaving them to Daniel, but she didn't want to see them. After all, they were here about the notebooks, not her. *Not her*, she repeated silently. It was time to put those fears behind her. Still, she couldn't concentrate until Daniel came back, after a surprisingly short time. Perhaps she was wrong about the callers, Penelope thought. "Who was it?"

"No one important."

Should she ask, or not? "I thought it might be those men from the Foreign Office."

Daniel looked at her as if he was unsure what to say.

"I prefer the truth to protection," Penelope added. The latter was an illusion. And reality was worse than ever when it was torn away.

"They called, but I didn't see them. I turned them away."

"That will only make them more determined." Such people relished breaking down resistance. They preferred a battle and acted as if every word was a stratagem. Penelope had decided, after weeks of bewilderment, that this made them feel useful.

Daniel sat down beside her. "Don't worry. I will see to this."

Appreciating the sentiment, even if she couldn't quite believe in it, Penelope smiled at him.

"What are we looking at today?" He picked up a document and ran his eyes down it.

"The top layer from trunk number two. Mostly tradesmen's bills so far."

"Good God, this one is dated 1693. Are they all so ancient?"

"These are. What is it for?" She leaned over to look. "A tester bed with carved posts and an embroidered tapestry canopy. Very grand. There are others for expensive furniture. And yards of cloth. I think one of your ancestors was redecorating."

"That sounds like the massive old bed in the east wing. Supposedly, royalty slept in it."

"Really? Which royalty?"

"I don't know."

Penelope bent over the page, her blue eyes alight with curiosity. As always, Daniel enjoyed the enthusiasm in her expression. "Let's see, who would it have been in 1693?" she asked.

Daniel ransacked his brain for school history lessons. "William and Mary? Wait, I think one of my several times great-grandmothers was a crony of Queen Anne's in her youth."

"Really? Perhaps she left letters, or even a diary."

"Well, if she was like the rest of my relations, she never threw anything out." Daniel remembered something else. "Her husband, or son, fought under Marlborough in France."

"These stories should be recorded in a family history."

"There's another job for you then," said Daniel. "I might have consigned much of this to the next Guy Fawkes bonfire."

"You wouldn't have!" Penelope looked sincerely shocked.

"Probably not," he admitted. "More likely I'd've left them where they were in the attics and shoved the piles of paper down here in with them."

"How can you not be fascinated?" Penelope asked.

"I'm interested when you tell me," he replied. "It's the hours of sifting through dusty documents I can't bear."

"I'm going to put together a history," she said. "You can tell me about the portraits in the gallery, can't you?"

"I know their names and a bit about most of them."

"And I'll find the papers they left." She looked triumphant.

"The house of Frith is very lucky to have you." Daniel enjoyed her flush of pleasure, as well as his success at distracting her from their unwelcome visitors. He had no illusion that he'd disposed of that matter, however. And indeed, later that day he received a letter from the Foreign Office agents, delivered by a neighborhood boy on a pony. Daniel took it off to the library to read in private.

The language was less insolent than the bewhiskered man had dared face-to-face, but also more formal. Daniel was required to hand over his mother's papers, they informed him, under the law of the land. As they cited no specific edicts, he didn't worry much about that pronouncement. But the veiled references they made to Penelope enraged him. The notebooks must not be "left to fall into dangerous hands." They must be kept from "those whose loyalty to the crown had been put in doubt."

Briefly Daniel enjoyed imagining the agents' reaction if they'd seen Penelope deciphering parts of the notebooks in London. Apoplexy seemed the least of it. He toyed with the idea of having her translate all of his mother's entries for her family history. But in fact, he didn't wish to cause any problems for his country. And he could see that a government records office probably was the best place for the notebooks. He simply hated the way they were going about it, and the continuing threat hanging over his wife. He knew it nagged at her. He was determined to do something about it.

Daniel wondered if Macklin had returned to London. He'd said he would be back by now, and the earl was a critical element in the plan Daniel had formulated. He'd left a letter for Macklin at his town house. It was to be hoped that the older man was even now acting on Daniel's request.

Eighteen

"You do the honors," said Daniel.

Penelope took hold of the valve handle and turned. Water streamed out of the spigot and into the big tub. Wisps of steam demonstrated its heat. "It works," she said.

"Did you think it wouldn't?"

"No, but it still seems like a miracle." She shut off the tap, then turned it on again. "Hot water at a touch. We did it."

"Mostly you," said Daniel.

"Mostly Henry Carson and his helpers. They did the actual work." Penelope stopped and started the water again, delighted.

"Of course the tub hasn't been tested as yet. In action as it were."

Their eyes met, and each saw reflected the scene they'd imagined—a figure rising, naked and glistening, from the steaming bath. "True," replied Penelope.

"We should do that."

"We?"

"Well, I don't think the very first bath should be taken alone. Who knows what might happen?"

The question filled Penelope's mind with tantalizing pictures. "Yes," she breathed.

"And although you deserve the…treat after your hard work, I find I can't wait."

Abruptly, Penelope ached with longing. What if they shed their clothes right now and leapt into the water like naiads? The vision was delicious, right up to the part where they ended up dripping with an obstacle course of corridors and servitors between them and towels. "Tonight," she said. "After the servants have gone to bed."

Daniel started to protest that he couldn't wait so long, and then realized she was right. He didn't mind the staff knowing that he was besotted with his bride, but to act out their desires publicly was outside of enough. A day of anticipation would make their adventure even sweeter.

Still, the hours dragged, and Daniel found it difficult to keep his mind on estate business. The time seemed eternal before finally, finally, they were sneaking down the stairs in their dressing gowns, whispering and laughing like errant children.

The house was silent. Shadows cast by the lit candles in their hands jumped on the walls. They saw no one as they made their way to the bathing room, and found it transformed. Two chairs had been brought in, along with a wardrobe. Opening it, Daniel found piles of towels and scented soap. Curtains covered the tiny window. A small table held a candelabra. Penelope lit those tapers from her candlestick. "I thought this would be more comfortable," she said. "I had coals put under the tank to heat the water, too."

"You don't think the servants will suspect?"

"That I might wish for a bath? Why else did we build it?"

"Indeed." As Daniel bolted the door, a thrill went through him. The combination of novel and clandestine was immensely titillating.

Penelope plugged the drain and turned on the water. The tub began to fill. Steam wafted through the air.

"I imagined you here, you know, rising like Aphrodite from the waves. Glorious."

"I imagined you doing the same. Well, from the steam."

"You didn't!"

"I did." The huskiness of her voice roused him as never before.

They laughed breathlessly. Daniel removed his dressing gown and laid it over a chair. Then he gazed at his wife, waiting.

With a teasing smile Penelope copied him and stood there in her nightdress. Candlelight shone through the thin fabric. He could see every line of her body.

Daniel pulled off his nightshirt and kicked away his slippers. She did the same, and they faced each other, naked. Penelope's blond hair was pinned up. She was as lovely as a goddess. His response was obvious. No way to hide it, and she didn't seem to wish him to. He moved closer and offered his hand. She took it, and he escorted her ceremoniously to the tub. She stepped into water and sighed. "Ah. That's wonderful."

He got in, wondering how long he could maintain control in these delirious circumstances. The water was perfectly hot on his lower legs.

They sank down to sit facing each other, water rising over their knees. Little lapping waves teased Daniel. He'd never bathed in such a state of arousal.

Penelope stretched out her arms. "So much room in a bath." She cupped her hands and ladled water over her breasts.

Daniel groaned.

"Is it too hot for you?"

"The temperature is fine. The sight of you is driving me mad." The water rose to her midriff, and higher.

Penelope giggled. "Turn off the water, or we'll have a flood."

He did so, and she slithered toward him, wrapping her arms around his neck. He drew her into a searing kiss. And another. She was soft and slippery and wildly desirable. "You're like a mermaid," he said.

"If I was a mermaid, I'd have a tail," she breathed.

"True. I was never sure how that worked."

"Worked?"

His mental faculties had abandoned him. "Er, that is…"

"My lord, whatever have you been thinking about mermaids?"

"Something like this," he answered, pushing her knees to either side of his hips. He slid his hands up her inner thighs and used all he'd learned about her body in their time together to tantalize and please her. When she cried out in release, he entered her at last, leaning back against the end of the tub to keep them from going under.

The water surged and sloshed as if a storm had hit. Some went onto the floor. Daniel didn't care. He took Penelope's lips again as ecstasy overcame him and all thought burned away.

The water in the tub calmed. Penelope rested atop him, her head on his damp shoulder. Their pulses beat, heart to heart. Their breathing gradually eased. Slowly, the world returned.

"Will I ever be able to simply wash in this bath?" she said after a while. "I'll always be thinking of…this."

Daniel laughed. It felt like the most joyous laugh that had ever come from his throat. For a timeless interval, they reclined together, nearly floating.

"The water's growing cooler," said Penelope at last. "I suppose we should get out."

"For now."

She met his eyes, promises sparkling in her gaze. And then she rose, just as he'd imagined, with water sluicing down her lovely curves amid wreaths of steam.

He followed her out, and she offered him a towel. Taking it, he applied it to her back rather than his own. She gave him a startled glance and then followed his lead. Gently, ceremoniously, they dried each other. Her hair had fallen out of its pins, and he rubbed the dripping tresses. "We should have brought a comb."

Penelope reached up and produced one from the wardrobe shelf.

"You think of everything."

"Not quite everything. I did not know a bath could be so stimulating."

"Indeed." She was delectable, adorable.

"We were so right to put it in."

"You were."

"You had the plans."

"And you had the determination. It would never have been done without you, and now you see what a boon it is."

"Boon?"

"Yes, my lady. A boon. Only think how much enjoyment we'll get out of this small chamber."

"The servants will talk."

"Let them. I believe I am allowed to sport with my wife."

Penelope laughed. "Sport?"

"Frolic, cavort, gambol, lark about, carouse."

"Carouse, my lord? Is that really proper for a respectable married couple?"

"Perfectly. At every opportunity." He ran the comb through her hair. The movement drew his eye to the small mirror on the inside of wardrobe door. There they were, half obscured by mist from the heat, naked side by side. She was all a man could want. He had to make her happy, and be sure he never lost her.

⁂

Their glorious bath was still on her mind the next day as Penelope strolled in the garden, which was at the height of its summer glory. A symphony of color and scent surrounded her as she walked. The foliage rang with birdsong. There wasn't one thing she would change about this beautiful landscape, she thought. It provided an ideal setting to enjoy the gifts of nature as well as the happiness that sang through her veins.

She noticed two men approaching from the back of the property. They wore long-tailed coats and top boots and were clearly not gardeners, which was strange. When they came closer, she recognized the blond man with the side-whiskers who had questioned her in Manchester.

"Lady Whitfield," he called.

What were they doing in the garden, uninvited? Had they been spying, watching and waiting for her to appear alone? For a tremulous moment, Penelope feared they'd come to take her away. No one would know where to look for her. She started to back away, then gathered her wits. She would *not* let them intimidate her. She'd done nothing wrong. She'd proved that over and over. She didn't have to do it again. And here, in her new home, there were people within earshot who would help her.

The men stopped several paces away.

"What do you want?" she asked.

"You are not surprised to see us?" asked the bewhiskered man, as if a normal person would have been surprised.

That was his way—to make anything one did or said seem suspicious. As the conversation continued, his tone would grow sharper, more incredulous. He would try to make Penelope doubt her own words. But she wouldn't; she'd learned her lesson about that trick. "My husband told me of your earlier visit," she said.

Her interrogator looked grave, shaking his head.

"Husband. I'd thought better of you, Miss Pendleton. Lady Whitfield, I should say. I wouldn't have said you were the sort to bring ruin on a fine old family. Because ruin follows you, doesn't it?" He nodded at his dark-haired companion to emphasize the point.

Penelope hid her reaction. "You follow me apparently," she replied.

"That you'd put the taint of treason on the viscount." The questioner shook his head and gave her his disappointed expression. She'd seen it before. She was supposed to argue now, try to convince him that she would never do that, that there had been no treason. And he would not be convinced. It was his business not to be convinced. Penelope was overcome by the terrible frustration she'd experienced under this man's badgering. He didn't care for truth; he wanted confessions. "You're trespassing," she said.

"Go and get the notebooks and bring them to us!" He used the harsh voice he'd employed in the worst of her interrogations. The bark of an officer on the battlefield, the growl of an enraged patriarch. Penelope had snapped to attention under that voice. For a long time, she'd even tried to obey. Until she learned that no justice lay behind it, and nothing she could do would appease. A stark, simple answer was best. "No."

The side-whiskered man came closer, so that he could stare right into her eyes. "Do it, or we will rain destruction on you and your unfortunate *husband*."

Penelope hid her shaking hands in her skirts. Threats were this man's specialty. He could make you imagine all sorts of disasters. And yet few of his dire predictions had ever come true, she reminded herself.

She steadied. "Leave now, or I will call someone to escort you off the property."

"You jumped-up little—"

The dark-haired man interrupted with a hand on his companion's arm, pulling him back. The latter glared at Penelope, fiercely contemptuous. "You're making a serious mistake," he said. "We will not let this go." His friend tugged again, and they turned and strode away.

When they were gone, Penelope sank onto a bench and struggled to calm down. That man was a master at destroying peace. What he said wasn't real. Deep breaths helped. "Ruin does not follow me," she murmured. But the reality was that he'd spoken her persistent fears. Her doubts began to clamor for attention.

Daniel found her there sometime later, when the late-afternoon air had grown cool. "I've been looking for you. No one knew where you'd gone." He sat beside her and took her hands. "You're cold. Come inside."

Should she tell him? Or pretend nothing had happened?

"Something's wrong. What is it, Penelope?"

She couldn't stay silent under those tender eyes. "The Foreign Office men were here."

"Today? In my garden? On my land?" Daniel was annoyed, particularly because the intrusion had obviously upset her.

Penelope nodded.

"What insolence. I'll have the gates locked."

"I brought them down on you."

"No. You didn't." He spoke sharply to shake her out of her despond. "My mother did. They'd be plaguing me for her notebooks if you had never existed."

"Oh, yes." She spoke as if she'd forgotten this detail. Her tone was distant. She'd gone to a place far from him.

Daniel suppressed his anxiety. "You see?"

"But I've made it worse. If I weren't here—"

"They would be acting just the same," Daniel repeated.

"He said I'd bring ruin on you. That they would rain destruction on us. What would that mean?"

His wife gazed at him with haunted eyes, and Daniel cursed the man who'd caused that fear. "Nothing. It's nonsense."

"And the Pratts cut me dead. They'll see that everyone does. You as well."

"The Pratts and all their ilk may go to perdition. Do you imagine I care for the opinion of petty, malicious people?" He squeezed her hands. She really was cold. "Let's go in."

"If you were cast out of society because of me, I couldn't forgive myself."

"My social position is unassailable." Daniel smiled, trying to tease her out of the dismals.

His lightness had no effect. "If you wanted me to, I would go," she added. "You could have the marriage set aside, say it was a mistake."

"It was not! And I do *not* want you to go!" He dropped her hands and pulled her close. "You vowed till death do us part."

"Yes, but Daniel—"

"No buts. You are my wife." He felt her tremble

within his arms. "And I'll take care of the blasted Foreign Office." Wondering why he hadn't yet had a reply to his letter to Macklin, and whether he would have to return to London himself, he pulled her to her feet. "Now come in and get warm."

Penelope let him lead her along the path and into the drawing room. She didn't object when he ordered a fire, though her chill was more spiritual than physical. She drank the tea he ordered for her as well. But the exuberance he so loved was not restored. Had it been a constant before the last year ground her down? The idea filled him with anger and regret. The government agents had much to answer for. "I have a plan," he said. "This situation will soon be resolved."

"You'll give up the notebooks?" It seemed the only solution.

"On my terms, not theirs."

"What terms? Men like that don't listen, Daniel."

"Let's be sure my scheme works first."

"Scheme? It's no good bargaining. They take it as an admission of guilt."

"I understand. I'll take great care. Will you trust me?"

Penelope met his earnest gaze. He was so dear to her. She wanted to trust. She could remember a time when belief in others had been automatic. But so many people had let her down since then—believed the worst, enjoyed the spectacle of her disgrace, drew back as if she was contagious. Daniel wouldn't do that. He was steadfast. But his plan might fail. She'd made plans this last year, and so many of them had collapsed.

She had to blink back tears. When she came to

Rose Cottage, she'd thought there could be nothing worse than to be dragged back into the orbit of her questioners. But there was. Seeing Daniel there, ready to throw himself against the stone wall of suspicion.

"Penelope?"

She nodded. What else could she do? That was the question, she realized. Was there anything she could do?

Nineteen

FOYLE CAME TO SEE PENELOPE THE FOLLOWING DAY, A nearly unprecedented occurrence. "Is there a problem at Rose Cottage?" she asked when he was ushered into the drawing room.

"No, miss. Lady Whitfield, that is. Well, except those daft dogs and their goat. They herd the creature into the garden to eat the veg, and when Bob tries to chase them off, they snarl at him and offer to bite."

"Bite?"

"They haven't bit him yet," Foyle said. "He thinks they will though, which is their point, isn't it? Wouldn't you think a gardener could outface a couple of hounds?"

Penelope suppressed a smile. "Jip and Jum are... eccentric dogs."

Foyle looked aggrieved. "It's my belief they're not right in the head, my lady. They wouldn't hunt, would they? What kind of foxhound refuses to hunt?"

"An odd one, apparently."

"Huh." Foyle looked as gnarled and crotchety as ever. And yet there was something different about him. "Another thing I wanted to speak to you about," he added.

"Certainly. Will you sit down?"

"I'd druther stand." He held his cloth cap crushed in one hand, and he hesitated, which was not like him. Foyle practically defined *forthright*. Finally, he cleared his throat and said, "I've asked Dora Hart to marry me."

"Ah." When he said nothing more, Penelope had to ask, "Did she accept?"

"Oh. Yes, she did." He sounded surprised as well as shyly pleased. "You may think I'm an old fool—"

"Of course I don't. I'm very glad for you. And Mrs. Hart, too."

"Thank you, mi…my lady. So we was wondering if you'd be agreeable to us staying at Rose Cottage. As tenants, like."

"Of course, Foyle. I'm happy to have you there."

He looked relieved. Had he actually been worried? Penelope was glad to have such a responsible couple occupying her property. "When will you marry?" she asked.

"The banns will be done with next Sunday."

"I hadn't heard." She had been away, but there'd been no mention of the match at the village church last week.

"Dora's chapel," Foyle said. "So they was posted over to the Methodist place."

And begun before her own wedding if they were nearly complete, Penelope noted. Foyle had been as reticent as ever. "Will you allow me to give your wedding breakfast? I should so like to do so."

"I'd have to ask Dora."

"Of course you will. Perhaps I'll pay her a visit. I haven't seen her in quite a while." Since they'd cooked together at the cottage, which felt like such a long time ago.

"That'd be right kind of you," answered her family's old servitor.

Penelope was happy to oblige. But as she prepared to leave Frithgerd the following day, she found she was worried about encountering the Foreign Office men outside the estate's walls. She sat in her bedchamber, bonnet on, carriage waiting below, and looked down at her clasped hands.

"Is anything wrong, my lady?" asked her new maid Betty. "Do you need something else? You look right smart."

The mirror told Penelope that her sprigged muslin gown and chip straw hat were perfect for a fine summer afternoon. The shawl over her arm was a lovely, filmy froth. Blond ringlets framed her face. The expression was the problem. Her features showed that the thought of going out made her apprehensive. How she hated that!

Penelope stood. She smiled at Betty and thanked her. She couldn't deny her fears, but she *would not* be ruled by them. She walked downstairs, got into the carriage, and set off. And although the sound of approaching hoofbeats on the road made her stiffen during the short journey, she didn't give in to anxiety. None of them turned out to be the agents, and she reached Mrs. Hart's small cottage without interruption.

The older woman greeted her cordially. Penelope

had sent word ahead, knowing that Mrs. Hart would like to be prepared. And she was. Two luscious cakes flanked a tea service in her parlor. And the water was boiling moments after Penelope sat down. She accepted her cup and plate gladly. "I wanted to offer you my congratulations," she said. "And our help with the wedding breakfast if you'd like it." She indicated the cakes with a gesture. "Of course you're such a splendid cook—"

"I'd dearly love to have somebody else do the cooking, my lady." Mrs. Hart smiled. "I'll be cooking every other day of my life. Ronald told me about your offer, and we'd be happy to accept."

Briefly, Penelope wondered who Ronald might be, and then she realized this must be Foyle's first name. It wasn't the least odd that he had one. And yet it made him seem such a different person.

"I'd like to have it at Rose Cottage if you're agreeable, my lady."

"Splendid."

"Supposing it's a fine day—which I hope it will be—we can put a keg in the yard near the kitchen door with tables for the food down the side. That'd save the kitchen for making tea and such."

It sounded like a village festival. "How many will be coming?"

"I've quite a few friends in the neighborhood, my lady. And at chapel, of course."

Life was going to change for Foyle, Penelope thought. She was glad for him, though she wondered if he would enjoy a throng of friends. "I can send over flowers from the Frithgerd gardens."

"That would be lovely, my lady. And I was wondering if you'd be able to take out some of the furniture at Rose Cottage. I'd like to bring my own things with me."

Mrs. Hart had always been a woman who knew her own mind. And not shy. Penelope liked that about her. "Of course." There was ample storage room at Frithgerd. "Make a list of what you'd like gone, and I'll send a wagon over to remove the things."

"Thank you, my lady. You're very kind."

"Foyle is an old friend. And you are a new one. I'm happy to help."

They agreed on various other details. Penelope ate her sumptuous cake, and they parted warmly, very much pleased with the arrangements they'd made. Foyle was a fortunate man, Penelope thought on the drive back. He'd found a congenial wife at a somewhat advanced age, and she had every hope that they would be compatible. She was so occupied thinking of them that she forgot all about the government men.

Penelope had barely taken off her hat when there was a knock on her chamber door. "Come in," she called. A piquantly pointed face looked around the panels. "Kitty, hello." The girl entered and dropped a curtsy. She looked older and more assured in the short time since they'd left Rose Cottage. It was odd. The young maid had been a constant presence in Penelope's life for weeks, and now she barely saw her except when she went to the kitchen to confer with the cook.

"My lady," she said. "I wanted to ask if I might bake the cake for Mr. Foyle's wedding."

"You've heard about that already?"

"Lots of people knew. Because of the banns. But Mr. Foyle wanted to tell you himself."

"I see." She wasn't in touch with the servants' gossip in her new household, Penelope thought. Back home in Lancashire, she would have picked up hints and drawn conclusions. That would come as she became better friends with the Frithgerd people, particularly Betty.

"I'll make him a first-rate cake."

Remembering some of Kitty's mishaps in the kitchen, Penelope doubted that. "I'll be making a plan with Cook," she said.

"She'll say I should do it."

"And she did," Penelope told Daniel that night as they lay in bed. They'd fallen into the habit of talking over their days in the glowing aftermath of passion. Each activity was as sweet as the other.

"Kitty's Shrewsbury cakes were not a success," Daniel pointed out. He toyed with a curl of Penelope's pale hair.

"They were not. I hinted as much to Cook, and was given the impression that she thought herself a much better teacher than Mrs. Hart."

"That sounds ominous. Do we have a feud?"

"More like a friendly rivalry, I think." Penelope nestled closer. "Or perhaps the pride of a professional versus an amateur. There was passing mention of the bakery prize at an agricultural fair. And it's partly because Mrs. Hart cooked for me at Rose Cottage."

"And now you are here."

"And so much grander," said Penelope teasingly.

"As your food must also be."

"Naturally." Penelope rose on one elbow to drop a kiss on his lips. He responded in a similar vein, and conversation was extinguished for a time.

"Cook wouldn't spoil the wedding?" Daniel asked a good bit later.

Penelope stretched like a cat. "On the contrary, I think it will be *lavish*. Demonstrating every skill Cook possesses. Aggressively. And she assured me that Kitty can make a creditable cake. I expect she'll see to it."

"So all's well then. The happy couple won't be disappointed."

"No. In fact, I began to wonder if Mrs. Hart knew exactly how this would unfold. And perhaps enjoyed the idea of Cook exerting herself to create a memorable wedding feast."

"You think the future Mrs. Foyle is so devious?"

"Mrs. Foyle," Penelope repeated. "How odd that sounds. For all my life Foyle has been—"

"The resident gargoyle?"

She hit his shoulder playfully. "A steady, *solitary* presence. I never felt he wanted any family other than ours, which is vastly selfish of me, I know."

Daniel shrugged, his shoulder moving against the side of Penelope's face. "I don't know him well enough to say. But perhaps he feels his work is done."

"What do you mean?"

"You're the last of the family, and you're settled here. With me." Smug satisfaction tinged his voice. His arm drew her closer.

"Huh." Penelope contemplated this new idea.

"Or perhaps he simply met the right woman at

last," Daniel added. "A man can have no interest at all in marriage, and then suddenly, between one week and the next, be determined to wed."

Penelope smiled. "Indeed, my lord?"

"Oh, yes. There's no warning. You know nothing until the blow falls, like a thunderbolt from the blue."

"Thunderbolts knock things to pieces and set fires."

"Precisely."

She ran her fingertips over his chest. "Are you calling me incendiary?"

"Utterly. Unprecedented, revolutionary, the dawn of a new epoch."

"Epoch? How will I live up to such a grandiose label?" She let her hand drift to his ribs, and started tickling.

"Hey!" He retaliated, and their discussion dissolved into an orgy of giggles.

❧

His cook had certainly outdone herself, Daniel thought a week later as he walked along the row of tables that held the wedding viands. She and her assistants had produced a spread to rival one of the Prince Regent's banquets. There were terrines and jellies and timbales and other delicacies he couldn't even name. Piles of tartlets and special breads and macaroons. Roasted meats punctuated the offerings. And at the end, young Kitty stood beside the cake, a tall fantasy of frosting, receiving compliments as if to the manor born. She appeared to find Mrs. Hart's—Mrs. Foyle's—astonishment especially gratifying.

Shoals of villagers and Frithgerd servants marveled

and ate and chatted and ate some more. Many he knew, but there were others who looked only vaguely familiar. The bride seemed to be acquainted with everybody in the neighborhood—at least well enough to feed them. She looked warmly matronly in a dark-blue gown and satin bonnet. Foyle, standing at her side receiving congratulations, seemed a bit dazed. His craggy face was occasionally split by a smile, but mostly he was glassy-eyed.

"It's strange to be back here in such a different way," said Penelope, coming up to join him.

Daniel turned to look at her. He never tired of doing that. Each time he saw her, he seemed to notice a new facet to her beauty.

"I was just making sure the dogs are all right in the barn," she said.

"With their goat."

Her smile was wry. "With Jemma."

"She has a name now?"

"Foyle gave in on that score."

"So he's become resigned to her presence?"

"Actually I think he's grown fond of her." Her expression grew pensive as she surveyed the wedding guests. "When I first arrived, I thought I'd live here for the rest of my life. Or as far as I could see ahead, at least. Once, I imagined Kitty and me as a pair of gnarled old women, still tending Rose Cottage after fifty years."

"What a terrible waste!" Daniel exclaimed.

She raised her eyebrows. "Is that what you think of solitary women?"

"Kitty would never have become a baker. We'd

have none of those teacakes she sent up on Tuesday. Or the macaroons. No, it doesn't bear thinking of."

She laughed.

The champagne was opened, and toasts began. The newly married pair approached the cake, and Dora Foyle picked up a knife. For a moment, it seemed that Kitty would stand in defense of her creation. But then she stepped back with an openhanded gesture, though she did wince at the first cut.

"Delicious," said Daniel with his first bite. "I suppose Kitty really does make her confections? It's not some elaborate plot with Cook to pay us back for mocking her Shrewsbury cakes?"

But Penelope didn't seem to be listening. She held her cake plate as if she'd forgotten it and stared over his shoulder as if she'd see a ghost. Daniel turned.

The two Foreign Office agents sat on their horses on the road in front of the house, watching the festivities. They made no move to dismount, no gesture to acknowledge Daniel's gaze. They merely sat, solemn and stern, making their presence felt.

"All this jollity is just a skim of illusion over a far different reality," said Penelope.

Daniel was furious at the agents. Could there be two more irritating people in the world?

"Disaster can strike at any moment," she added.

He started to argue, then changed his mind. "That's true. Look at my parents, sailing home from another of their adventures, with one of those notebooks full of secrets, I suppose. Swamped by a storm at sea between one instant and the next." He took her hand. "But, Penelope, that doesn't mean the rest is illusion."

She turned to look at him, her blue eyes wide and apprehensive.

"Foyle's slightly nonplussed happiness, and this mouth-watering cake, and your comical dogs are just as real."

"They can be swept away, just as the waves did that ship."

Daniel shrugged. "Possibly. Probably not, but it might happen. And then we would pick ourselves up and work on a remedy."

Penelope blinked, then spoke slowly. "The last year was horrible, but I got through it."

"Like a champion," he replied. "And then you met me." He squeezed her fingers and tried a smile.

She gazed up at him. "If Philip hadn't brought everything down, I never would have met you. Or perhaps I might have, during the season in London."

"But would my sterling qualities have been so evident, dancing at a stuffy ball or trotting sedately through the park?"

Her expression eased. "Possibly not. And you might not have appreciated mine. I'd have been just another deb."

"Sylphlike," said Daniel.

"What?"

"I never pursued acquaintance with the wispy, sylphlike girls. Can't abide their simpering."

"I'm *not* wispy! And I have never simpered in my life."

"I know that. But I wouldn't have from across a drawing room." It was perfectly true. He'd have turned away. And that certainty made Daniel's blood run cold. "I never would have found my mother's notebooks either, hidden like that. Or the letters she wrote your mother. Wouldn't have known anything about them." And he would have gone on thinking that his parents were simply selfish, shallow people.

"You might have come upon the letters."

Daniel shook his head. "With so many other papers to sort through? No. And I was on the point of giving up on those. I'd have lived like my forebears, half-buried in fusty records, making a mad search for the right document when a need arose."

"You would have gotten a new agent," she said, as if to defend him.

"Yes. But he wouldn't have noticed the trunk linings or looked through my mother's personal correspondence. Too much else to do."

Penelope nodded. "I suppose I would have accepted an offer from some acquaintance of the Pratts."

"The Pratts?"

"Mrs. Pratt was to sponsor me for my first season," she replied.

"That sour old biddy?" He was newly outraged. "You didn't mention that at the theater."

"It was no longer relevant." Penelope grimaced. "She used to be much kinder. But I would have met the gentlemen she presented to me."

"I certainly would not have been one of them," said Daniel.

They stared at each other. Another future opened out before them, like a chasm yawning at their feet in an earthquake, revealing dark depths. Daniel wanted to clutch her to him. The people around them seemed to recede, as if they stood alone together.

"The dreadful things that happen make you what you are," said Penelope.

"Like tempered steel. Or porcelain that has passed through the fire."

"How poetic!"

"You don't know everything about me yet."

"But I have years to learn."

"All the years I'm allotted, and all that I possess. Which is more than any silly fellow presented to you by the Pratts."

Penelope knew he didn't mean his title or fortune. Adversity had given him depths, as it had her, perhaps. "We'll make a life together, even with disasters." She looked again and discovered that the agents were gone.

"Not alone," he answered. "Precisely."

She had felt so alone, and now she didn't. "I love you so much."

"And I love you with all my heart."

Penelope felt a qualm. "I'm still worried that you're giving up—"

"Nothing that I value. And I've gained far more."

She took him at his word, but even in the midst of her happiness, she was left with a niggling fear that one day he would find social position more important than he did in this moment.

"Health to the bride and groom," called a booming voice on the other side of the yard. "And on top of that, our sympathies to the poor man, who'll soon find he's living under the cat's foot."

"Don't be a fool, Jem Fallon," said Dora Foyle. "Any more than you can help, that is. You never could hold your drink."

"See there?" answered Mr. Fallon, raising his glass higher and winking.

Daniel and Penelope joined the general laughter.

Epilogue

LORD MACKLIN ARRIVED AT FRITHGERD FOUR DAYS
later with his valet but not Tom. "I've brought a
confidant of Castlereagh's with me," he said when
Daniel and Penelope greeted him. "He thought it
best to stay at the inn until we'd spoken and he could
dismiss those two agents who made such a mull of
things." The earl's blue eyes glinted. "I understand
they've been given a new posting at the very back of
beyond. You won't be seeing *them* again." He turned
to Daniel. "He's also come to take charge of your
mother's notebooks."

"On my terms?" Daniel asked.

"Yes. I'm sorry about the delay. It took some time
to get in to see Castlereagh. He's a busy man."

"I appreciate your efforts in the matter," Daniel
said.

"What efforts?" asked Penelope. "What terms? Is
this the plan you mentioned?"

Daniel nodded as Macklin turned to her. The earl
held out a square of paper. Penelope looked at Daniel,
who shrugged his ignorance. Taking the card, she

scanned it and gasped. At Daniel's inquiring look, she said, "This is an invitation to a ball in my honor. At the Castlereaghs'."

"A token," Macklin said. "Proof, if you require more than Castlereagh's personal word and his promise as Foreign Secretary."

"Those are certainly good enough," Daniel said. "Though it's good to have something tangible as well."

Penelope stared at the bit of paper. Lady Castlereagh was a leader of the *haut ton*. Her stamp of approval guaranteed social success. Seeing her own name in such a context seemed like a dream to Penelope. "I don't understand."

"In exchange for me freely giving up the notebooks to the Foreign Office, I asked that the Castlereaghs…repair your social standing. With invitations to parties and a show of friendship and acceptance. Lady Castlereagh is perfectly suited to ease your way into society."

Penelope stared at him, then at Macklin.

"I reviewed your circumstances with Castlereagh," said the latter. "He was shocked at the way you'd been treated. He doesn't always agree with Sidmouth, you know, though they are both in the government."

"This was your doing?" Penelope said, still trying to take it in.

The older man shook his head. "I merely carried out your husband's request. The idea was all his."

She turned to Daniel.

"You worried so about society," he said simply.

"You said you didn't care."

"But you did. And that Pratt creature made me mad

as fire when she snubbed you. I hope she sees every moment of your success. From the outside."

"I never expected anything like this," murmured Penelope. She knew it was a silly comment, but she was feeling overwhelmed.

"The government rather owed you something after the way you were treated," said Macklin.

She gazed at the older man. "I'm not sure you always thought so."

"Once I got to know you, I saw that you were the just the woman to make Daniel happy."

"Hear, hear," said Daniel.

Penelope turned to him. Her eyes blazed with love, and she saw it reflected back with equal strength from her husband's gaze.

With his customary tact, Lord Macklin slipped out of the room.

About the Author

Jane Ashford discovered Georgette Heyer in junior high school and was captivated by the glittering world and witty language of Regency England. That delight was part of what led her to study English literature and travel widely in Britain and Europe. Her books have been published all over Europe as well as in the United States. Jane has been nominated for a Career Achievement Award by *RT Book Reviews*. Born in Ohio, she is now somewhat nomadic. Find her on the web at janeashford.com and on Facebook at facebook.com/JaneAshfordWriter, where you can sign up for her monthly newsletter.

Brave New Earl

The Way to a Lord's Heart
First in a brand-new Regency romance series from
bestselling author Jane Ashford

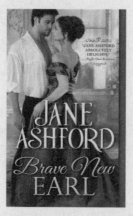

Widower Benjamin Romilly, Earl of Furness, has given up
hope of finding happiness. His wife died in childbirth five
years ago, leaving him with a broken heart and a child who
only reminds him of his loss.

Miss Jean Saunders doted on Benjamin's late countess,
and can't bear it when she hears rumors that the earl is too
bereaved to care for his young son. She arrives on the scene,
questioning his abilities. She simultaneously infuriates and
invigorates him, and she might be the only person who can
breathe life into his neglected home—and his aching heart…

"Filled with wit and charm."
—Fresh Fiction for *Nothing Like a Duke*

For more info about Sourcebooks's books and authors, visit:
sourcebooks.com

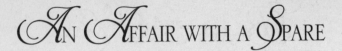

An Affair with a Spare

The Survivors
Regency romance full of flair and fun from
award-winning author Shana Galen

Rafe Beaumont, fifth son of an earl, uses his irresistible charm
with the ladies to glean dangerous war secrets. Now he's
putting those skills to the ultimate test: capturing an elusive
assassin by seducing his daughter. The problem? She's entirely
immune to Rafe's flattery.

Never before has Collette Fortier met a man as attractive as
Rafe. But her father's life is at stake, and succumbing to Rafe
would be disastrous. When Rafe turns the tables on her, offering
support and friendship instead of a fleeting affair, Collette finds
herself tempted in ways she never could have imagined…

"A passionate, page-turning tale."
**—Lorraine Heath, *New York Times* bestselling
author, for *Third Son's a Charm***

For more info about Sourcebooks's books and authors, visit:
sourcebooks.com

Earl to the Rescue

Gwendeline Gregory doesn't know what to think when she encounters the dashing Alex St. Audley, Earl of Merryn. She's in over her head in London Society, trying to fend off a scoundrel who will stop at nothing to ruin her. Just when she most needs him, the earl arrives on the scene. But are his motivations trustworthy? And can he avert ruin for both of them?

"Jane Ashford absolutely delights."
—*Night Owl Reviews*

Scandalous Ever After

Does love really heal all wounds?

After being widowed by a steeplechase accident, Lady Kate Whelan abandons the turf. But eventually her late husband's debts drive her to seek help in Newmarket amidst the whirl of a race meet. There, she encounters Evan Rhys, her late husband's roguish friend—whom she hasn't seen since the day of his lordship's mysterious death. Now that fate has reunited them, Evan seizes the chance to win over the woman he's always loved. But soon, long-held secrets come to light that shake up everything Kate and Evan thought they knew about each other.

"Romaine's elegant prose, inventive plotting, brilliantly nuanced characters, and refreshingly different setting make her latest superbly written romance de rigueur for Regency romance fans."

—***Booklist*, Starred Review**